A TEST OF CHARACTER

A TEST OF CHARACTER
WITCH OF THE FEDERATION™ BOOK 06

MICHAEL ANDERLE

LMBPN Publishing
PMB 196, 2540 South Maryland Pkwy
Las Vegas, NV 89109

Version 1.00, December 2021
Previously Published as part of the megabook *Witch Of The Federation II*
ebook ISBN: 979-8-88541-038-0
Print ISBN: 979-8-88541-039-7

To Family, Friends and
Those Who Love
To Read.
May We All Enjoy Grace
To Live The Life We Are
Called.

THE A TEST OF CHARACTER TEAM

Thanks to our Beta Team

Crystal Wren, Daniel Weigert, James Caplan, John Ashmore,
Larry Omans, Mary Morris, Nicole Emens, and Robert Brooks

Thanks to our JIT Readers

Angel LaVey
Daniel Weigert
Dave Hicks
Diane L. Smith
Dorothy Lloyd
Jeff Eaton
Jeff Goode
John Ashmore
Larry Omans
Misty Roa

If We've missed anyone, please let us know!

Editor
The Skyhunter Editing Team

CHAPTER ONE

Unmerciful flights of consciousness gripped Stephanie in a twisted battle of thaumaturgic power. She fast-forwarded through a confused realm of dreams in which she caught only a glimpse of one before she jerked into the next.

Some were calm and comforting and others violent and distressing, but none lasted long enough for her to break her body's self-imposed hibernation. Her magic tanks were empty, and her body snatched at the MU floating around her in an instinctual effort to pull it in. She lay unmoving, her hands folded, her breathing steady, and her eyes closed.

On the outside, she looked peaceful and at rest, but on the inside, she traveled. Through dimensions? Maybe. Through time and space? Possibly. Only the magic knew, but until the world around her stopped its kaleidoscopic wandering, Stephanie had no idea.

Days passed as she lay in silence, the faint beeping of the monitors the only sign of life. Her nurses, guards, and allies came and went, stared sadly at her, and wondered when she would open her eyes.

Conversations were held at her bedside, and Lars talked to

her every day. Around her, the doctors and nurses spoke of her heroism as they tended her body and checked her vitals before moving on to other duties.

Somewhere during her travels, she began to hear her own voice—the one she used when she tried to calm herself. Her dream self was breathless from being shuffled through so many different realities, and she walked a very fine line between sane and crazy.

Concentrate, Morgana. You have to stop moving. Control it. Control it.

It took her a few more moments before she could force herself to an abrupt stop. She kept her eyes closed, focused, and felt her pulse slow and the sick sense of fear subside.

A sense of weightless suffused her. Her arms floated out to the sides, her head rested unsupported, and the exhaustion drained from her body—the one in her dreams, at least.

Slowly, she opened her eyes before she blinked and looked around. At first, she could see nothing but blackness. It wasn't dark because she could see herself perfectly. The weightlessness reminded her of space, but there wasn't a star or a ship in sight.

As she registered that, her body shifted so she stood upright. Her feet touched a hard surface the same color as the rest of her surroundings.

Her weight returned to normal and she could feel the slight static of her magic waver at the tips of her fingers. All around her, the strange darkness remained.

"It only stays strange if you want it that way." A woman's voice echoed through the blackness, startling her where she stood and she tried to make sense of this strange development.

She glanced around. "Hello?"

As if to answer her call, a woman descended in front of her. She landed lightly, straightened, and quickly smoothed the pleated skirt of her knee-length gray dress.

Stephanie took a moment to study her and noted the thin black belt that cinched the dress at the waist and the gray, short-sleeved jacket that covered the woman's arms. Her hair was pulled back in a simple but elegant pompadour style. Whoever this was, she wasn't flashy or done up—and her eyes gave her away.

She took a step forward, tilting her head to the side. "Morgana."

The newcomer smiled and returned her gaze. "As are you."

The older woman looked around and put her hands on her hips. "This is quite the space...but you'll probably be more comfortable with...this!"

She snapped her fingers and a flash of purple sparked from them. Suddenly, the unmistakable ambiance of Meligorn surrounded them. Stephanie gazed at the lush field with purple flowers teased lovingly by the breeze and felt herself relax. "Thank you."

Her companion studied the scene and her eyes widened slightly at the sight of it, then she shrugged. "Well, each to their own, I guess. You must *really* like purple."

As though the sight of Meligorn was an everyday occurrence, the woman walked forward and scrutinized the girl with a critical eye. Stephanie watched her approach, suddenly self-conscious of the hospital gown she wore. "Are you hurt?"

She frowned, then nodded. "I think so. I used all my magic to save people."

The other Morgana pursed her lips, her expression a little regretful. "That will do it. The world always was a scary place. Especially where I am, now. I did what you did, once—and I spoke to the Morgana who came before me." She sighed. "Well, I guess it's my turn, and I don't have a lot of time."

"Your turn for what?"

"To tell you the things you might not know. Listen carefully, because I'll only be able to tell you once. The Allies have a break at the moment, but we'll close in on Hitler's SS soon, and I'll have to go. Are you ready?"

Hitler's SS? It took her a moment to connect the term with a distantly remembered history class, but she nodded anyway, and her companion began her explanation.

"I will assume you are aware that there are four types of energy."

"Four?"

Her puzzlement must have shown because the woman stopped and sighed with obvious impatience. "Yes, four. The first…" She floated a translucent orb with small sparks of light flashing inside. Enlarging it, she continued, "The first is Creation Energy. This is the energy repurposed by our world and its life." She looked around at the world of Meligorn and added, "And, most likely by other worlds, too."

Thinking back, Stephanie realized this Morgana would never have seen another world and probably thought the likelihood of humans ever reaching one was pure fiction.

Until now. She looked at the orb. "I call that gMU, and the variants that repurpose it eMU and MU."

The older Morgana smiled and brought a rainbowed orb down to eye-level. "This would be your eMU and MU, then. I call it Variant because its form varies on each planet dependent upon the flora, fauna, and life forces there."

She returned the woman's smile and reached out tentatively to touch the orb. The different color magics wavered at her touch. Her predecessor set the two orbs aside and brought a third orb into being. The magic it held was like pale-green fire and spun wildly inside.

Her gaze grew distant and she stared into the orb as if she recalled fond memories. "This is Neutral Energy. It absorbs gMU and the planetary variants. It is an interesting type of energy— almost completely in tune with those who possess the power to wield it."

When she set the Neutral Energy globe aside, she brought the last forward and grimaced with distaste as she handled the orb. The black energy inside pulsated and actually emitted a small growling noise like the muted roar of an approaching tornado. "The is Nihilistic Energy. It is the opposite of Creation Energy and expands when the matter housing Creation Energy is killed or destroyed. When those vessels crack or are damaged, it does not expand because only destroying the form releases the other energies for it to consume. For instance, a cracked or broken vase would not let Nihilist Energy expand, but one powdered to dust would."

Stephanie reached up to see how the magic would react to the proximity of her hand, but the older Morgana quickly collapsed the orb. "I wouldn't stick your finger too close to Nihilistic Energy. Such actions have...regrettable consequences."

She nodded and clasped her hands in front of her. "Right. Do you do any work with Nihilistic Energy?"

Her companion took in a deep breath and put one hand on her stomach. "Those working for Hitler study Nihilistic Energy and are in contact with others from somewhere not of Earth. These others are teaching the Nazi's more about Nihilistic Energy, including the use of death ceremonies to provide the wielder with advanced abilities."

She paused and raised an eyebrow as she stepped closer. "That is all I have for you, now, but there is one thing I need you to tell me."

Stephanie waited, not sure what her ancestress could possibly need to know from a future she knew nothing about or a descendant she'd only just met. "What?"

Anxiety clouded the Morgana's features. "Do we win?"

Stephanie took a breath to reply, but the woman held her hand up. "No details. I only... I need to know if it's all worth it, or if...if we lose anyway and are merely wasting our time...and the lives—" She paused. "Was he stopped?"

She held her breath and studied the woman's face as she tried to decide on her reply. How much could she say without saying too much? In the end, she could think of only one safe answer. "Yes. He was stopped."

If the older Morgana was anything like her, she knew that answer would be enough. When she faced her darkest moment, that was the knowledge that would get her through

Her companion sighed with relief and nodded. "Good. That is all I need to know—that we *are* doing something right."

Stephanie smiled and gazed at the face in front of her, amazed that so much about her seemed familiar. "Yes, you are."

The woman returned her gaze and her smile and shook her head. "I'm not sure how many greats I would need to put in front of granddaughter to be accurate, but you are the spitting image of my mother. Are you all well?"

She nodded. "I suppose. I don't know a lot about the Morgana side of the family, only what my mother has shown me through a journal passed down to her. My father..." She sighed. "I don't know where he went, but I did read about you and your time on Earth."

Morgana laid a gentle hand on her shoulder. "Whatever you don't know will eventually come to light. Wherever your father is, I'm sure there is a good reason for it. Morganas—both the men and the women—are bred with a sense of responsibility and loyalty. Either way, it is good to see your face. I have sensed you for a while and attempted to project myself here, but it took you a while to reach this point."

Stephanie laid her hand over her companion's and simply stood in silence to soak in the sense of closeness to her.

The older woman looked around at the scenery and sighed. "This has been good for my soul—to know we still exist and yet I am sad, knowing a Morgana is still needed. I must once more put my Morgana mask on for the sake of all sentients."

She removed her hand and turned as though to leave, but

paused. "Stay true to your bloodline, and may you be the Morgana your people need."

Her form began to fade but wavered when she asked, "Will I see you again?"

The other Morgana gave her a sad smile and shrugged. "Who knows? Perhaps one day, we will meet again. Be at peace and trust your instincts. They are the only things that will always be with you."

Stephanie watched as the woman winked out of existence and the Meligornian field along with her. She thought about the words "your people need" and wondered what she'd meant.

Who *were* her people? The Meligornians? Humans? And what about the Dreth? Or any other species of beings she might meet later?

If she was the only Morgana, would *everyone* be considered her people? Maybe it was a personal choice. She could choose any or all of them to be her people.

No one could force her to accept everyone, but who did that leave her? Only the people she liked? She shook her head. No. It had to be more than that.

"Those who need my protection," she said, "and only those who deserve it."

Because there was no way in all the worlds that she would protect those who weren't worthy.

She peered cautiously into the blackness her ancestress had left behind. It didn't seem quite as overwhelming as before, even if she still didn't know where to go. It surprised her when she heard a voice, one that knew her name.

"Stephanie," it called. "Stephanie..."

Intrigued, she stopped and listened for it to call again. When it did, the sound came from behind her. As she pivoted quickly, she discovered her surroundings had changed.

In the distance, a pinprick of light glimmered and grew steadily brighter and she felt a small pulse of energy.

This she recognized. MU, and it was exactly what her body needed.

Without a second's hesitation, she surged toward the life force that called to her and seemed to draw her into a welcome reunion.

The hospital on the Meligorn side of the space station, on a normal day, was very quiet. Ambassador V'ritan arrived with Brilgus in tow and his robes flapped wildly behind him. His footsteps echoed down the corridor and his face held worry and anger. Those who saw him paused in what they were doing to watch him stride out of sight.

He swept through the doors leading into Stephanie's ward and pushed them both open. The nurses looked up from behind their station and recognized him immediately. "Ambassador."

Before they could stop him, he had already passed them. They glanced at each other, unsure of what to do.

The ambassador raised a hand dismissively as some vague form of acknowledgment. He'd meant to stop and ask where Stephanie was, but he spotted Marcus and Frog outside a room down the hall. That was more than enough for him.

He ignored the panicked scramble in his wake and focused only on the men ahead. Brilgus, however, moved to intercept the staff before they could intervene. "I wouldn't do that. He is extremely worried about a friend."

They exchanged nervous glances, then looked at the bodyguard. Being only half-Meligornian, he was much larger than they were. Two of them backed away but the head nurse stood firm.

She came around the desk and stood in front of him. "He might be the ambassador, but he should have let us know he was coming. Fortunately, we think she can handle *one* visitor, or I'd be fired for hauling him out of there. Next time, though..."

"Yes. I will make sure you are notified," he reassured her, not at all sure he would given how the press would react if the news were to reach them.

He fixed her with a stern look, and she stared defiantly in return with no apparent concern for either his size or the ambassador's not inconsiderable power, political and otherwise. Brilgus considered that a good sign. It meant she cared enough for the patients to do what was best for them regardless of who might be in the way or the consequences. It meant Stephanie was in good hands.

Frog stifled a yawn as he turned and glanced down the hall. His eyes widened and he nudged Marcus with his elbow and directed his attention down the hall.

The other man took one look at the ambassador and nodded. "I will speak to him."

As the visitor neared the door, he intercepted him, stepped in his way, and blocked his path to the door. His teammate stood in front of the door and watched them both as he used the team's comms to call Lars.

Being the Meligornian side of the station, they'd had to source the local equivalent of Earth tech to use for comms. Those had taken a few days to source but now, they had enough for four of them to be on the floor, armed and in contact with each other at all times.

Ambassador V'ritan stopped and regarded the two guards calmly, but before he could speak, Marcus extended his hand. He ignored every protocol of Meligornian greeting he'd ever been taught.

The visitor, used to Earth's customs, didn't hesitate but reached out and shook his hand. "Marcus. I need to see her."

The guard stood firm but he didn't disagree. "Of course, sir, but I must warn you, she's in a coma. She's unconscious but here, as far as we can tell. We're not sure if she can hear you when you talk to her, but Lars speaks to her every day."

Behind him, Frog spoke softly into his comms. He stopped and listened for a moment before he tapped his partner on the shoulder. "The Ambassador can go in now."

Marcus gave the V'ritan a brief smile. "I'm sure she'll recognize your voice, sir," he said as he and Frog returned to their positions on either side of the door.

"Thank you." The Meligornian slipped past him swiftly and into the room, not worried when the door closed immediately behind him.

Down the corridor, Brilgus watched as the head nurse set her assistants tasks that took them down another corridor. Once they were gone, he looked at her.

She was unfazed. "I take it you don't want to call the hospital and give that warning."

He shook his head. "The lines are not secure."

"Call me, then. That way, if it leaks, you only have one person to blame. I'll let you know if she needs isolation or can be seen. Agreed?"

"Agreed," he said and took her private number before he trundled down the corridor to Stephanie's room and greeted the guys as he arrived. "Marcus, Frog, good to see you."

He indicated the door. "Is he in there?"

"He and Lars are with her," Marcus told him, knowing the information he needed.

He watched as the bodyguard took a quick look in the room to check and waited until the large man had closed the door again and turned to him. "What happened?"

Frog looked up and down the corridor but relaxed when he saw it was empty. "You've seen the news, right?"

Brilgus nodded. "And read the official reports. What I want to know is how Stephanie got hurt."

Marcus picked up the story. "The pirates took the ship. There were two boarding parties. One went for Engineering and the other went for the Bridge. When the team on the Bridge demanded the ambassador or they'd blow the ship, Stephanie stepped in."

"And you let her?"

He laughed and shook his head. "You know Stephanie. When her mind is made up, there is no stopping her. We went along to try to keep her safe." His face sobered. "We didn't do so well, obviously."

The bodyguard looked sympathetic. "She's still here, isn't she?"

Marcus sighed, and Brilgus added. "Tell me how it went down."

He explained how Stephanie had used her magic to disguise herself as the ambassador and then hide them from the cameras so they could reach the Bridge undetected. The other man stopped him when he got to the fight.

"There was a Meligornian?"

"Yes. It turned out they were Resistance and not pirates. Their captain made the 'ambassador' hand over his MU and then attacked. We eliminated the pirates and saved the crew, while she dealt with him. Then, Steph insisted on taking care of the bomb."

Brilgus rolled his eyes. "Of course she did."

Marcus continued. "We fought them out of the corridors and all the way down to the atrium. You've seen it?"

When his companion nodded, he went on. "They'd planted the bomb on the third floor, so we killed the invaders and Steph cut the floor out from under it and floated it down to the main entry."

The man whistled. "That is very powerful work."

He shook his head. "She had help. There were two Meligornians on board who helped her, and they're the only reason she made it as far as she did. We'd have been in a lot of trouble if they hadn't been along."

"Worlds of hurt," Frog confirmed.

Marcus ignored him and kept going. "We got the bomb onto the pirate ship and Steph pointed the vessel away and set it to move at top speed. She also got us back on board the liner, but things weren't over."

Brilgus raised his eyebrows.

"The pirates had planted a worm and it cycled the engines to drain the batteries until they became too depleted to operate the engines before the ship's tech team could clear it. With the controls back online, Steph powered the engines. In fact, I think she almost overpowered them, then she transitioned us right out of there."

He paused at the memory, and his face clouded with concern. "If the Meligornians hadn't been there, we'd have lost her, but they gave her some power crystals and healing, and she's still here."

"And Johnny," Frog added. "Crystal gave him enough to stop the bleeding or he'd be gone."

"She didn't heal him completely?" Brilgus was unimpressed.

"We were still fighting the Resistance at that point. I think she was conserving her power...and we're glad she did."

The bodyguard glanced at the door. "Yes, we are. And Johnny?"

"He's over on the human side. They say he'll be fine."

Before any of them could say any more, they heard the bell at the nurses' station being rung incessantly at the other end of the hall. The three of them looked up to see what was going on.

Beside Brilgus, the two guards became instantly alert. Frog

backed up and spoke into his comms, and Marcus moved to put himself between the station and his partner.

Seconds later, Frog reported back. "They're on their way."

They all glanced at the nurses' station and focused on the Meligornian dinging the bell at the counter and the four guards arrayed around him. Two of them had noticed the group outside the room and moved to block their line of sight—and fire—to the bell ringer.

Marcus glanced up at Brilgus. "Is that anyone you know?"

At the nurses' station, the king tapped his foot and rang the bell again. He was not impressed when the nurse behind the counter reached over and slid the bell out from under his hand. She didn't even look up but kept her eyes glued to the screen in front of her, while she used her other hand to jot notes down on the tablet in front of her

"Leave the bell alone. You'll wear it out."

The king cleared his throat, but she didn't look up.

"I'll be with you in a moment. In this hospital, the patients come first, no matter *who* thinks they need to see them."

"The ambassador?" the king drawled, and Temerl—the closest guard and Head of Royal Security—glanced at him. He met the man's eyes just as the nurse replied.

"Anyone who is impatient," she snapped. "You can't simply barge in when a patient needs quiet to recover and I won't allow it. Now, if you'll give me a few more seconds, I'll be right with you."

The guard smirked, and the king raised his eyebrow as he wondered what his head of security found so amusing. The smirk vanished and the man shrugged.

They waited for another few moments, which meant a necessity to stand there and deflect the wide-eyed glances from the few people who walked past. Quite understandably, most of them stared in disbelief when they saw the king of Meligorn standing at the nurses' station like anyone else.

When the nurse continued to ignore them, he cleared his throat and leaned forward. "I understand the ambassador was a little impatient, but if you make *me* wait much longer, I'll make his impatience seem as if it was mere impertinence."

The nurse's hands paused. "Well, who do you think you are? The king?"

She looked up and her disapproval was instantly swept aside by an expression of horror. "Oh, I'm so sorry, my king—"

Her mouth stopped moving and she froze for a moment. He suppressed an amused smile and watched as she shut her mouth and stood hastily. She moved so fast that she almost knocked her stool over. "Oh, I'm so sorry, my king. We get so many people in every day and—"

The king held his hand up. "Which way?"

She swallowed hard and pointed down the corridor with her stylus. "Down that way and the eighth door on your left. There should be people outside."

He looked down the hall and noticed Brilgus with two human guards stationed at the door in question. Farther up the corridor, he saw another two humans fast-stepping to join them. All were heavily armed. Again, he glanced at his security chief.

The man looked past him and studied the scene. "Brilgus is there. He will explain."

With one last look at the stunned nurse, the king stepped away from the counter. "I see. Carry on."

He turned and moved with his guards toward Stephanie's room, leaving the nurse standing behind the desk, her mouth once again hanging open.

Temerl walked with the King. Usually, he'd have stayed at the palace, but this was too good an opportunity to miss—an impromptu visit, and two of the biggest threats to their cause in one place. He narrowed his eyes and brushed his hand lightly over the blaster at his hip

Ahead of him, Stephanie's team saw the gesture, tensed, and relaxed only when he moved his hand away from the weapon. There were more guards than he had originally accounted for, but they'd remain outside the room and shouldn't be in any position to stop him. Either way, he wouldn't allow the witch and the ambassador to get in the way of his faction's plans to work with the coming alien force.

The king might not see it but working with the newcomers rather than against them was Meligorn's best hope for surviving the coming war—and V'ritan would only stand in the way. Besides, V'ritan was a useless piece of royal history who needed to be finished.

He needed to be removed before he became the King's Warrior once again. If that happened, it would upset the invaders' plans for Meligorn. Plans that were already underway.

As the king approached, Marcus, Frog, Brenden, and Avery prepared for action. Judging by his guards, the newcomer had to be important, but he was nothing compared to the task of keeping Stephanie and the ambassador safe. The simple truth was that important didn't always mean safe.

They watched Brilgus and noticed that the bodyguard-advisor was tense but not alarmed. He kept his eyes on the approaching entourage and answered Marcus's question, his voice soft with shock. "It's the king."

Frog began a muttered conversation into his comms again, and Marcus swore.

The large man snorted softly. "Yes."

The most important-looking of the royal escort took a step forward and placed himself in front of the king. A second guard followed the movement, and the first guard moved swiftly ahead as if he intended to walk through the door.

Temerl appeared to ignore the team and strode at a steady pace, much like he didn't care who they were or what they were doing. He only stopped when one stepped in his way and put his hand out, holding his palm up inches from his chest.

Marcus held the guard's gaze and curled his lip. "Exactly where do you think *you're* going?"

The security head looked down his nose at the man, glanced at Brilgus, and stepped around the warning hand. This time, when he stopped, it was because the two guards had jammed their blasters into his belly.

He held his temper in check and made a show of looking down at the blasters and then into their eyes. A small smirk moved across his lips and he arched an eyebrow.

Marcus wasn't impressed. He gritted his teeth and shoved his blaster a little harder against his stomach. "I'll fill you so full of lead, you will shit metal for a week. You don't pass without permission."

Frog held his weapon firm and leaned into his teammate. "Uh, I don't think they shit, Sherlock. And besides, that's a blaster you're holding. It doesn't have slugs."

The other man didn't budge. He kept his eyes locked on the leader, who hadn't moved, but remained aware of the other four Meligornians at the rear. Avery and Brenden moved up alongside him, and Brilgus leaned his shoulder against the door.

The king knew a volatile situation when he saw one, even if he didn't understand why Temerl appeared to be trying to provoke a fight.

He laid his hand on his security chief's shoulder, aware that two of the humans had moved to cover him and that another of his guards had stepped into their line of fire. With quick glances at the two security teams, he spoke quietly. "Temerl, these men are doing their jobs. Perhaps we should simply *ask* them if we may pass."

The guard's lip twitched, and he eased back slightly. "For your protection, sire."

He felt the king move back to give him more room, and he took another step away from Frog and Marcus, careful to keep his hand away from his weapon. His expression was one of sour disapproval when he spoke. "The king of Meligorn should not have to ask permission to go anywhere on his own world."

The human leader paled a little at the challenge, which brought a small stab of satisfaction. They might not hesitate to stop him from entering, but they were unlikely to prevent the king from doing so. He was counting on that, but the man still did not back down. He *did* swallow nervously and flick the king an uncertain glance, though. Temerl stared back, watched the truth sink in, and decided to give the humans some credit.

Faced with possibly committing one of the biggest gaffs possible, they still refused to give way. The king, however, was puzzled at his guard's previous statement. "Protect me from what?"

This time, the guard glanced at him and gestured toward Stephanie's door, mild reproof in his tone. "We still do not know if it is safe for you to be near this human, sire."

He raised his eyebrows. "You said nothing of this when we left —or on any occasion when we planned the ceremony. Why now? And how does antagonizing her guards help?"

Temerl rolled his shoulders and returned his focus to Marcus. "The concern was less before she showed her powers. Now, I am not so sure if you should be near a..." He hesitated, as though searching for the right word.

Frog snorted. "Human witch. It's okay, we know what she is."

Marcus smirked. "And I'm telling you not to go in because it won't be healthy for you to do that. It's very simple, and if you don't understand it, we'll be more than happy to discuss it with the king."

His adversary glared at him. "So, even when you know who he is, you continue to stand in the way."

"He is not *my* King," he pointed out. "He is the king of Meligorn and we are not sure whether or not *he* is a threat to Stephanie. Diplomatic incidents aside, we're not willing to risk it."

"You *insolent*—" Temerl growled and the king cleared his throat.

"Enough," he ordered and looked at Brilgus. "I take it my ambassador is with her now?"

The bodyguard nodded and straightened, easing his weight off the door.

"And *he* is perfectly safe?"

The reply was solemn. "Yes, Your Majesty or I would not be out here asking her guards what happened."

But the head of royal security had apparently not finished. He glared at Brilgus. "These men might not be your subjects, but *he* is, and subjects or not, we are all standing in your territory. It may be above the surface of your planet, but we are in a hospital you commissioned, and they have the gall—"

The king laid a heavy hand on his shoulder. "Enough, Temerl. This is not what we do. Now, if it is safe for V'ritan, it is safe for me. These gentlemen will certainly not deny me entry when Brilgus can vouch for me."

He used his grip on his security chief's shoulder to move Temerl to one side and stepped forward. His movement almost brought him into contact with the barrel of Marcus's blaster, but the guard lowered his weapon hastily and his partner took a step back.

As far as Frog was concerned, the royal visitor wasn't his to deal with. The uppity security guard, on the other hand... He kept his weapon aimed at Temerl as Marcus gave the king the traditional Meligorn Royal greeting.

Surprised, he returned it hastily, then studied the human who had bothered to learn the custom well enough to give it without error. The guard, however, was still not ready to let him pass. As he straightened, he said, "You have to understand, your Majesty, the hospital insists that only one visitor is allowed at a time. That could be circumvented and it's not our real concern here. More importantly, I must remind you that the human we protect could be the most important being in the Federation. No disrespect intended."

"None taken," he told the man. "And there are at least two other people who consider her the same. So, I agree she must be protected, but I need to see her for myself."

He waited expectantly as Marcus shifted his gaze to Brilgus. The ambassador's advisor nodded and stepped aside to let him pass. When Temerl went to follow, Marcus intervened. "Only the king. We'll stand guard out here."

The man snarled and tensed, and his hand dropped to his blaster.

"Temerl," the king murmured, and a warning laced his tones. "If it is safe for the ambassador, it is safe for me. You and the guard will wait here."

"Sire..." he began, but the royal was firm.

"Those are my orders." He inclined his head toward Marcus and the team and stepped past Brilgus into the room. As he did so, a startled shout behind him made him pause a split second before he was shoved away from the door and into Brilgus's arms.

***

Stephanie pursued the energy through the blackness. It held steady, a beacon that drew her unwaveringly back to where she belonged. Once she reached it, her senses slowed, and she became aware of her body.

She flexed her hands slowly and slid her fingers across the sheets beneath her. They were softer than any she'd slept in on Earth, which meant she was either on the ship or on Meligorn.

Well, there's only one way to find out.

Someone moved beside the bed. They shifted restlessly as though leaning forward. She opened her eyes cautiously and blinked at the bright lights above her.

Two faces appeared above her—the ambassador's and Lars's. When he saw she was awake, V'ritan smiled. "*There* you are. It is good to finally see you wake up."

From the way he said it, she had the impression that hadn't been guaranteed. She tried for a reassuring smile. "I couldn't leave you hanging."

Someone snorted in the background, and her smile widened. "Or you, Lars. I can't keep you out of trouble otherwise."

She was shocked at how weak her voice sounded and how frail the rest of her felt. When she recalled the warm glow that had drawn her back, she focused on the ambassador. "You gave me energy."

He smiled again. "I hoped it would make a difference."

Stephanie's smile faded. "It did." They were both silent for a moment, then she asked, "Am I on Meligorn?"

"Close," he told her and opened the viewscreen to reveal a spectacular view of one of the moons outside. "You are on the Meligorn side of Alerus, the joint human-Meligorn space station. You've been out for quite a while. How do you feel?"

She pressed her lips together and tried to push herself upright. Lars came over and worked with the ambassador to help her sit, and they both tucked the blankets in around her.

"Here," Lars said and handed her a glass of water. V'ritan found the bed controls and raised it to support her back.

Suddenly aware of the dryness at the back of her throat, she took small, steady sips. Her body welcomed the hydration, her fogginess eased, and she became aware of the abundance of energy around her.

Seeing it was enough and she immediately began to draw it in, filling her tanks until she felt revitalized enough to speak. After a few more minutes, she was able to reposition herself without help.

The ambassador took the glass from her hand and set it down on the cabinet beside the bed. "It's like the only time we see each other is when you're hurt."

She opened her mouth to protest but realized he was mostly right. She shrugged. "True, but at least this time, they missed you."

"Yes, I am curious about that," he told her. "How exactly *did* you come to be me?"

Stephanie was almost ready to show him, but Lars intervened.

"Use your words, Steph. Don't make me come over there."

"Like you're not already?" She smirked and he gave an exasperated sigh from beside the bed.

"Do you see what I have to put up with?"

The Meligornian chuckled. "Words would be best. I don't want to wait another two weeks for you to wake up."

Stephanie had just taken a breath to explain when the door opened and Marcus shouted in alarm. Both her companions pivoted, and Lars drew his blaster. The ambassador's hands arced with magic.

CHAPTER TWO

Temerl did not hesitate. He drew his blaster with one hand and used his magic with the other to sweep the king and Brilgus from his path. Ignoring the King's startled cry, he released the magic in a wave at the guards who stumbled back from the force of it.

With the path to the door clear, he leapt forward and raised his blaster in readiness. Behind him, one of the guards shouted a warning.

"Incoming!"

Inside the room, Stephanie had already responded. She focused on the door as she continued to pull the magical energy in, stored the MU, and pushed any gMU into an internal vortex to concentrate it.

The first thing she saw at the entrance was the muzzle of the intruder's blaster. He turned as he saw them and aimed at the ambassador. She and Lars reacted at the same moment.

He fired three quick shots, and she used one hand to direct MU toward the ambassador and push him to one side. With the other, she hurled an assault at the intruder with such force that he was flung back through the door and into the wall opposite.

The sound of bone cracking echoed, and the assassin uttered a short, sharp cry of pain. But before she could ready another attack, someone else was shoved through the door. Breathing hard, she gathered more magic but let it dissipate when two of her guards bolted in after the newcomer and kicked the door closed behind them.

One of them reached out to the man who'd been pushed through in front of them.

"Your Majesty," Avery said as he helped the newcomer regain his feet and virtually dragged him to one side of the door. "I must apologize."

***

Marcus had stepped aside as Temerl was thrown past them out of the room and he now turned to kick the blaster from the guard's hand while Brilgus shoved the king inside. The ambassador's advisor joined Marcus, seized the assailant, and hurled him to the floor.

He held him down and secured the royal guard's hands and feet, then helped Marcus and Frog search him. They found the two extra weapons he had hung on a utility belt hidden beneath his robes.

"The man came prepared," Frog said as he removed a grenade from a small pouch strapped to the outside of Temerl's thigh.

When he saw it, Marcus let out a low whistle. "He wasn't coming out alive from that."

"No one was, but that is a wish we can grant—for him at least," Brilgus told him, his face somber.

"You don't understand," the man protested. "They must both die. Their survival will cost millions of lives. Let me finish—"

The ambassador's man didn't let him finish and simply punched him hard in the face.

As their prisoner slumped, unconscious, he let him drop to the floor. "I'll search him again," he said. "Just to be sure."

When he was done, he stood and stared at the Meligornian's limp body. He noticed the purple blood staining Temerl's robes and the faint swirl of energy that seeped from his fingers and swore. "A dead traitor tells us nothing."

Raising his head, he bellowed, "Nurse!"

He was about to call again when an argument erupted inside Stephanie's room. The door was flung open and the ambassador stormed out, his eyes aflame with anger.

Marcus and Frog guessed his intent and moved to intercept him, but he swept them aside with a swipe of his hand. The magical push sprawled them several feet away.

Brilgus stepped into his path and put his hand sternly on the Meligornian's shoulder. "I know your anger is deep and your need for revenge is wide, but this is the highest-level insurrectionist we've located. Don't kill him…*yet*."

The anger in V'ritan's eyes softened slightly and he looked at his loyal advisor. He laid his hand over his companion's and nodded to acknowledge the point.

They moved to the side as staff barreled down the hallway and a stretcher followed in their wake. The head nurse glared at all of them as she approached.

She was definitely not happy with them, but she couldn't exactly tell them to leave—especially not with the king and ambassador in attendance.

Instead, she turned to V'ritan for instruction as her staff began to triage Temerl's injuries.

"This is the head of the Royal Guard," she began. "What happened? Is the king okay?"

The ambassador glared at her. "The king is fine, and this is no longer the head of the Royal Guard, but a traitor and assassin. Make sure he doesn't die. As for his comfort? Don't waste any time on it."

The woman froze and her face revealed that she'd understood the information. She stared at him for a moment and then at Temerl, now surrounded by her nurses who worked hard to save his life.

Meligornians were known for their kind hearts and giving nature, but when it came to those who went against the people, they could be ruthless. She understood this.

It didn't make her happy, but she could deal with it.

Inside Stephanie's room, Lars studied the royal visitor.

"Are you all right, Your Majesty?" Avery asked and examined him nervously. "I apologize for the rough handling, but your men couldn't reach you in time and we wanted to get you to safety."

The king shook his head. "I am fine and I understand. You have yet again come to the aid of Meligorn, and I thank you."

He turned to speak to Stephanie and stared when he caught sight of her.

She sat on the edge of the bed. Sparks of energy flashed around her, her lips pressed firmly together and a far-away look in her pitch-black eyes. Lars caught the king's gaze and followed it back to his charge.

"Well, damn," he murmured when he realized that she was on the edge of going full Morgana on them. "What the hell's the safe word… Todd!" he shouted and ran across the room. "Todd."

He knelt in front of her and placed one hand on her shoulder. Positioned carefully so he could block her view of the doorway, he lifted her chin with the curled forefinger of his other hand so she would look at him and not toward the door.

"Hey, Steph, look at me. Just look," he urged. "It's okay. We are *all* okay. The ambassador is fine. You got the assassin." He glanced toward the door. "You got him and Brilgus disarmed him. They're taking him away now. Everything's okay. Come back, Steph. Brilgus will see to him."

He went silent and studied her face while he waited for his words to take effect. Lars had almost given up when she blinked her eyes slowly and the black faded to blue.

They both exhaled at the same time, and Stephanie teetered on the edge of the bed. He stood quickly, slid his arm around her shoulders, and helped back onto the bed.

As he settled her beneath the covers, Avery took the bed controls and lowered it so she could rest. He watched as the team leader pulled the blankets up to her shoulders and moved a strand of silver hair gently from her face.

She sighed and twisted her hand over the edge of the blanket. Her gaze shifted to meet his. "Can't a girl get any rest without some asshats trying to kill her friends?"

Lars chuckled, glad to see she could try humor after what had happened. It had been the first time she'd woken since she'd collapsed on the ship, and for this to have happened...even the thought made him angry

He smiled when she yawned and covered her mouth, turned onto her side, and mumbled, "I'm so tired. The magic takes me down every time."

"Go to sleep then." He patted her shoulder through the blanket. "We're all here and no one will go anywhere. You will be safe."

Stephanie frowned as her eyes closed. "But will you?"

With an even bigger smile, he stood, tucked the blankets in, and walked over to the king, who stared at her in wonder. "Has she done that before?"

Lars nodded. She curled up and drifted into a dreamless sleep as if Morgana had only been a figment of his imagination. "Yes.

It's what saves people. But she hasn't fully learned to control it. When someone she loves is in danger, she has no power over it. Protecting them is all she can think of."

Hours later, Stephanie slid her feet under the sheets and consciousness brought the sense of other people in her room. Not yet ready to face the world, she kept her eyes closed until she was fully awake.

V'ritan's voice sounded close to her bed. He spoke softly, his familiar tones comforting. The female voice that responded, however, caused her to tense. Its guttural tone and depth denoted only one race.

A Dreth?

She forced herself to relax and simply listened.

"I had no idea that my head guard had any connections," a third voice replied, and this time, she detected a Meligornian accent in its slightly familiar tones. She listened harder as it continued. "I would never have allowed it. You know that. I'd have had him put down in the killing fields before anyone was hurt."

"Luckily," the ambassador responded, "he was the only one hurt, but how many times will we be in that situation before she is no longer here to save us?"

It seemed obvious that the discussion was about the would-be assassin, but it was only when the third voice referred to the man as the head of the Royal Guard that she realized who it was.

The King!

Now she knew where she'd heard that voice before. Its deep but prominent tones had been clear in Strike's impossible scenario where they'd been tested on their knowledge of royal protocol and had to fend off a surprise attack by hidden forces.

Stephanie recalled hearing it, too, after she'd woken up and the sound of it brought back memories from before she'd fallen asleep. She remembered catching a brief glimpse of the crest on his robes and seeing the thin, twisted vine of magic resting lightly on his flowing silver hair. *Shit!*

That was not how she was supposed to meet the king of Meligorn for the first time. And meeting him like this wasn't much better.

To her horror, she realized she was in bed and wore hospital scrubs, that her hair needed a good wash and brush, and that she probably looked like she'd taken on a nest of vampires and lost. This was so very much *not* how she was supposed to meet the king.

When she'd met him in her imagination, she'd been dressed in her best, worn flawless makeup and her prettiest smile, and looked exactly like a hero of the Federation should look. She hadn't been stuck in a bed with royalty standing at her bedside not two feet from the nearest bedpan.

Shock and embarrassment flooded through her, and she'd almost decided to keep her eyes closed until they left when the Dreth spoke again. "We would never think that of you, King Grilfir. You were a noble and confident leader long before the humans were discovered, and so you are today. Whatever his motive was, Temerl targeted the girl and the ambassador, but he pushed you out of the way. He had every chance to kill you and he didn't."

Now that she thought about it, Stephanie recognized the voice of the Dreth. She'd heard it on television and in history reports. This was the Dreth ambassador, the one who'd spoken in every Dreth attempt to make peace with the humans.

Now she truly *did* want to pretend she was asleep until they left because this was *definitely not* the way she'd wanted to look when she finally met the Dreth ambassador.

Unfortunately, she also knew she had no choice. They were in her room and they didn't look like leaving anytime soon. And speaking of bedpans...

With her eyes still closed, she decided to let them know she was no longer asleep.

"Can someone," she began and swallowed against the dryness of her throat while she kept her eyes tightly closed. "Can someone *please* tell me why the three most important people on this space station are *all* in my hospital room?"

The voices ceased and a hand settled on her shoulder. She assumed it was supposed to be comforting and hoped it belonged to either V'ritan or Lars. The alternatives were not to be considered.

As the silence lengthened to one of real discomfort, she forced herself to open her eyes and grasped her blanket firmly as she struggled into a sitting position. V'ritan sat beside the bed.

The ambassador located the bed controls and raised it to support her as she stared at the other occupants of the room. The king returned her gaze and smiled. "Your eyes are not black anymore. That's a pleasant change."

"Thank you." Stephanie chuckled and blushed. "Although I've never actually looked in a mirror when it happens. I can only imagine that I look quite terrifying."

V'ritan smirked. "Never too terrifying. You are still Stephanie the young and kind human. Even when the magic takes you over and you become the Federation's witch."

The Dreth ambassador stepped forward, tilting her head to the side, and studied her. Despite her awkwardness, she gave her a smile and received a solemn look in return. She wasn't surprised by this since the Dreth were known for being blunt and straight to the point—even rude and arrogant in their dealings— and concealing their thoughts and feelings from all but their closest friends.

"I am Jaleck," the Dreth told her, "and to answer your question, we are using your recovery and heroism as a way to speak about the traitor you defeated earlier without it looking like we are having a secret meeting."

Stephanie blinked. "Excuse me?"

Ambassador V'ritan took a deep breath and rose to turn to the Dreth. "I'll handle this one. Thank you, Ambassador."

Jaleck nodded and moved to lean on the wall beside the King. Stephanie studied her furtively and noticed that the female Dreth looked very different than all the male Dreth she had seen.

While her skin was slightly scaly and her teeth still fanglike, her long tentacle-like dreadlocks were pushed back over her head to create a slightly voluminous effect instead of hanging free. She had pouty red lips and silver and blue eyes and was also tall. However, instead of being heavily muscled, her body was slim and curvaceous and similar to a human female's.

She realized that she hadn't studied very much Dreth anatomy and that it might help her in combat if she did. Knowing where to strike would be a great advantage.

Hoping those thoughts didn't show on her face, she pulled herself straighter as V'ritan moved to sit on the end of the bed and patted her leg.

Looking from Jaleck to Stephanie, he explained. "The man who attacked us was the head of the king's Royal Guard. Right now, trust is at a minimum."

She glanced at King Grilfir, who spoke softly to Jaleck, a look of sadness on his face. "Okay, but why here?"

He glanced at the door. "You have a very good team that cares immensely about you. Currently, they do not allow anyone but me, King Grilfir, and Ambassador Jaleck into the room. And, because the king is in here, his security won't let your security team enter."

At this, she glanced around for Lars and realized he was missing. V'ritan noticed the worry on her face and spoke hastily. "At first, your men did not like it, but they wanted to keep the peace, so they are all out in the hall. That means only we—and you—are privy to our discussions about a problem we have tried to understand for decades."

Stephanie raised an eyebrow. "And it's okay for me to be here why?"

The Dreth ambassador snorted and drew everyone's attention. She glanced at the two Meligornian men. "You said she was plain-speaking. Now I see why."

Her English was accented by her native Dreth and reminded the girl of a man who had delivered newspapers in the Gov-Subs. He'd been from the last remaining islands before they'd been covered by the sea to create a city beneath the waves.

His skin had been darkly kissed by the hot sun and his eyes had sparkled with the joy of life. He had a thick accent, and Stephanie had loved listening to him as a child. Jaleck's wasn't as thick, but it was still oddly comforting.

As she remembered the newspaper man, the Dreth ambassador approached. She walked over to the bed and reached out with slender, scaled claws. Her eyes swirled silver and blue as she touched Stephanie's cheek gently and she smiled.

"You are young, powerful, and a human. Not usually the best of traits."

"Normally, true," King Grilfir agreed and raised his voice slightly but with a trace of humor to it. "However, with her saving V'ritan from assassination on Earth, citizens from all Federation worlds on the liner from pirates, and then both V'ritan and myself from a traitor to the crown when she had barely recovered. I think I can safely assume she isn't working for the enemy."

He settled his focus on her. "In fact, I would say you have done more for Meligorn than you have for your own planet, and I have a mind to claim you for Meligorn."

The three visitors laughed and V'ritan stood and gave her a wink. She didn't see what was funny, but she didn't have a problem with it either. "Grant me dual citizenship if that would make everyone happy. Then I can represent all of you when I'm out."

They all stared at her, now, but she continued. "That way, I won't have to wonder who I need to help when I get there. I feel connected to all of you anyway. And although the Dreth have encountered my vengeance more than the others, I have a feeling that won't always be the case. Not after seeing who was inside the Dreth Resistance ship."

"Are you sure they were rebels?" the king asked. "We'd heard that might be the case, but..."

Stephanie nodded. "Oh yeah. They were rebels, big time, and there were members of the Resistance from all over the Universe. There can't be only one enemy in our midst—which, I suppose, would make it a lot harder to know who to trust. But I trust my men and the ambassador, and hopefully, I can trust you two, as well."

She paused and tried to think if there was anyone she'd missed before she added, "Besides that and a couple of people currently on Earth, I don't see the need to spread my trust much further."

They nodded in agreement, and Jaleck gave her a look of approval.

"Dual citizenship," the Dreth murmured.

At her words, they all glanced at each other, and the king looked at V'ritan. "What about the Royal Award of Decarth? And possibly our Congressional Talon of the Families?"

Jaleck turned to study the viewscreen that revealed the vast emptiness of space beyond. "That would be an appropriate medal."

"And both of those," the king added, "can only be provided to those who are citizens. It makes it very simple to knock out two...two...oh, what is that Earth saying? Two cats with one can?"

His ambassador frowned, clearly trying to think of it as well.

"No, more something like two cows with one bell? There was something about a cowbell." She pressed her lips together in an effort not to laugh. The Dreth did the same and shook her head as the men began to work through the animals of Earth.

When they got to elephants, Jaleck raised a clawed hand in protest. "Shhhh, you are giving me a headache. The saying is, to kill two *birds* with one stone, not two elephants with one villager. Good grief."

Stephanie allowed herself a giggle as the king and V'ritan's eyes lit up. "That's the one, right there. The Dreth save the day again."

A loud knock on the door interrupted the moment and everyone looked toward it as Brilgus stuck his head in. "Sorry to interrupt, but uh… We have a nurse out here willing to push her way through a group of men with guns to see her patient—and she is not playing around. She threatened to beat one of the guards with a krifton if they don't let her through."

Her visitors all grimaced, while she didn't have a clue. "Okay, someone tell me what a krifton is."

V'ritan flipped through his phone and held a picture up. She blinked and looked at them in disbelief. "But that's…it's a hamster. Why are you afraid of a hamster?"

Jaleck shook her head, glanced at Brilgus, and lowered her voice. "No, not a hamster. That is a krifton. I've heard of this hamster and the two creatures are on entirely different spectrums. The krifton…well, it's better to leave those alone. They are dangerous."

Stephanie looked at the phone and then at the Dreth, shocked that something so furry and cute with its little pink nose could have both Dreth and Meligornians sounding a warning. "Where are they from?"

The Dreth pointed both of her thumbs, one at the ambassador and one at the king. "The lovely planet of Meligorn. Someone brought a couple of them to Dreth too and now, the place is crawling with the furry menaces. I blame you people with the pointed ears."

Brilgus cleared his throat. "If you please, the nurse is most insistent."

V'ritan looked at him and replied in Stephanie's voice. "Oh, yes. Give me two seconds and then let her through."

She stared in astonishment, but before she could say anything, her three visitors crowded close together as the ambassador waved his hand. The quick gesture released a layer of magic like a soft floating blanket. As it fell over them, they vanished. "Whoa."

When the door opened shortly after, she tried to look like nothing had happened. The nurse glanced around the room as she came in.

Seeing nothing out of place, she shook her head. "What's so important that there needs to be a million people out there? I'll take your readings now, okay?"

She paused and smiled at her. "Good morning, by the way. You slept for a long time. We're glad to see your eyes open at last."

Stephanie smiled in return and let the nurse scan her body using her tablet, take her pulse, and then her temperature.

When she was done, the woman patted her on the knee. "You'll be fine. I am not ready to give you a clean bill of health yet, so we'll keep you here a little while longer. You're okay to start walking around whenever you feel up to it. The reporters are starting to hang around outside, though, so don't leave your room."

She nodded. "Thank you."

The nurse gave her another kind smile. "That is what we do. We take care of you. I've finally realized who you are, so you stay here until you feel good enough to deal with those people. Then, we'll let the ambassador know so he can organize secure transport for you."

She took a couple of steps toward the door and the stopped.

"Oh, and I know that horrible Royal Guard has already been taken to jail, so don't worry about him coming in again. I think it's wonderful the ambassador was here to deal with him. You have been through enough lately. It's high time someone looked out for you."

Stephanie gave her a large smile and her gaze drifted to where her visitors had disappeared. "Thank you for doing that," she managed while she fought an urge to laugh.

With a cheerful wave, the nurse opened the door and stepped out.

She could hear her giving the teams a hard time as the door closed behind her. "I'll be back in two hours and you'd better let me past or I won't be happy."

After a few moments in case the woman returned, she giggled and cleared her throat. "All right, you can come out now."

The magic dissipated from the top down to reveal the three VIPs, all on their tablets like bored teenagers. She couldn't believe how alike they were, and not only the three of them but humans, too.

It took V'ritan a moment to realize the magic had gone. He elbowed the king, who looked up and tapped Jaleck on the shoulder. She swatted irritably at his hand as she finished what she was doing and tucked her tablet away.

Stephanie gave V'ritan a confused look. "Are you apprehending the assassins, now?"

He chuckled and shook his head. "Of course not, but it is much easier to say I did it than try to explain that you did. There are people who would think you tried to hit the king and missed. We will let them know the truth soon enough."

She shrugged. "That's fine. I don't really like the spotlight. I simply want people to know I'm on their side and to trust that."

"Most of them already do," the king replied, "but there are still a few..." He shrugged

Jaleck agreed. "It is harder for my people because the ones

doing most of the killing are Dreth, but those who stand behind the Federation already love you."

Stephanie blushed and tried to suppress a smile. "That's so nice. I think I should start a fan club. Brilgus can be the president."

The King and Jaleck chuckled, but V'ritan seemed to be somewhere else. His lips were pursed as if he were deep in thought. She waited as he considered whatever was on his mind. When he had finally pieced whatever it was together well enough, he spoke. "I want Stephanie tested for inclusion into the Mysteries."

King Grilfir turned to him, resignation on his face. "I wondered when you'd come to that."

Beside him, Jaleck's eyebrows raised and her mouth dropped open.

She closed it abruptly and hid her feelings like before. Stephanie was also surprised, having heard about the Mysteries as more of a story—a rumor filled with secrecy and magical wonder.

Her first impulse was to ask more about it but before she could, Grilfir turned to her and looked very concerned. "If I am to allow the Royal Award, then I have no reason to prevent her from trying for the Mysteries," he said and returned his gaze to V'ritan. "But are you sure? They won't go easy on her because she's human. It will, in fact, be quite the opposite."

Stephanie lay back and attempted to take in everything they said. She felt suddenly drained as if her body were saying she'd done enough.

Using every ounce of energy she had, she tried to keep her eyes open but it was no use. Sleep overcame her and she slipped into slumber and to a place where dreams seemed to find her exactly when she needed them to.

Hours passed as she whirled around Meligorn, danced with Todd in the streets of her youth, and hugged her mother and father in their Gov-Sub flat. When she finally woke, the king and both ambassadors were gone.

Only Brilgus and Lars lounged in chairs in her room and snored loudly as if it were a competition. The sight of them and the sound made her smile. It was probably the best way she could have woken.

CHAPTER THREE

"Be...prepared..." Stephanie was sure she heard the voice as she opened her eyes once more. She was still in the hospital, the lights dimmed and the halls quiet, with neither Lars nor Brilgus and their snores to keep her company.

She sat up in bed, rubbed her face, and smoothed her hands up and through her hair. A little more awake, she cracked her neck and paused to assess how she felt.

Tentatively, she turned, put her feet on the floor, and stood slowly. Surprisingly, she seemed fine and no longer felt weak or tired. She felt good. In fact, she felt right for the first time since she'd woken up on the station.

Relieved, she looked around and noticed a set of clothes laid neatly over the back of one of the chairs. Thankfully, it seemed Lars had brought in some of the clothes from her luggage.

She could imagine the condition of what she'd worn when she'd arrived. With a grimace at the thought, she picked up a t-shirt and pulled it over her head. As she reached for the yoga pants, she glanced in the mirror and startled. Almost all her hair had turned silver.

The sight made her pause. It was strange to see it that way but it reminded her of the small streaks of silver in her Morgana ancestor's hair.

With a smile, she waved her hand over her hair and tidied it into a similar style to what the old Morgana had worn, only without the updo. She was plainer than that and she liked it.

When she was fully dressed and satisfied with her appearance, she cracked the door. Brenden, Frog, Lars, and Marcus stood in the hallway.

"You'da thought the nurses would have been hotter this side of space," Frog grumbled, and Marcus rolled his eyes.

"And *you*'da thought we had more important things to do than ogle the staff."

"Maybe you should talk to Johnny, then," Frog snarked smartly, and Brendan snickered.

"Nope. You really shouldn't. That man is prone to exaggeration."

"Pssst," Stephanie hissed as the team leader sighed, and they all turned toward the door in surprise.

With a grin, she moved to one side, pulled the door wider, and gestured for them to come in. Lars looked at her with concern. "Should you be out of bed? Are you feeling all right?"

She smiled. "I actually feel great. And I'm ready to break out of this joint."

"Technically, you won't be breaking out," Frog pointed out cheerfully. "The docs said they'd discharge you today if you showed signs of improvement." He gestured to where she stood. "That's some impressive improvement, right there."

"Are you saying I can't go yet?"

"Nope," Lars told her. "We're saying you have to wait until the doctors show up on their rounds."

"Fine." She pouted but quickly turned her attention to the main problem they faced. "No matter. Okay, talk to me about the reporters. You've probably already noticed them, right? Do they have us boxed in?"

"Basically, yes," Marcus replied. "And we don't have a back way from here to Johnny, so we'll have to run the gauntlet from the Meligorn side to the human side of the station. There *are* back halls we can take there but getting to them might be a problem."

Stephanie pursed her lips as she thought about it, and the guys were silent as they did the same. The mischievous grin that suddenly lit her face was almost as worrying as the reporters outside, but she was already speaking before they could protest. "All right, *this* is what we'll do."

A short while later, a short, stout man with a flushed face raced down the corridor outside Stephanie's room. His face was flushed, and he pushed a very pregnant woman in a wheelchair as fast as he could go.

"Watch out!" he shouted, reached the press pack in the foyer, and made no effort to slow down. "Coming through! Pregnant woman here. Came to the wrong side. Watch out. *Watch out!*"

The mob parted like magic. Several people looking horrified, and others moved quickly to avoid being run down. The woman in the chair huffed and puffed, held her belly, and groaned as she hunched over another contraction. They were accompanied by four older people—two women and two men, clearly the grandparents in this whole debacle.

The women were dressed in floral dresses but wore running shoes, and the men sported brown pants, suspenders, and bow ties. All of them flapped at the press as they passed.

"Watch out, now. She's gonna blow," earned one older gentleman a sharp slap from his partner. "What? Well, she is!"

The group bounded through the hospital corridors and to the elevators and traveled up and across to the human side of the station. When they exited, they found more reporters.

These seemed excited about something, but they stepped out of the way as smartly as their colleagues on the Meligorn side had. The wheelchair hurtled past them, the woman holding her belly, and the chair tipped on two wheels as the group took the corner and out of sight.

The reporters were so focused on news of the witch's pending release that they didn't notice the lack of nurses in attendance. The witch's guard was also being released, and there was sure to be a reunion.

Well away from the foyer and its press pack, Johnny sat on the edge of his bed, dressed and ready to go. He rubbed his leg and wondered if he'd ever regain full use of it.

The magic Crystal had used had been enough to keep him from bleeding out, but he'd still needed surgery when they'd brought him in and was on a program of rehab that was enough to make his teammates wince.

Despite his worry, though, he was grateful the doctors were letting him go. He'd had enough drama and more than enough of hospitals.

Suddenly, the door burst open and a short, fat guy wheeling a pregnant woman barreled in. Two old couples followed and shut the door behind them. They all lined up in front of the bed and stared at him as though he was in the wrong place.

Johnny returned the stares, wide-eyed. After a moment, he cleared his throat, and said, "I think you may have the wrong room. She needs to be in maternity."

The woman stopped holding her huge belly and pushed herself awkwardly out of the chair. While he tried to decide if he could get out of the room without punching anyone, she waddled up to him, doubled over, and clutched her belly as she arrived.

"Seriously," she complained and glared at the fat, bald man when she straightened again. "You could have made it fake. I'm in real labor here."

The group laughed as the bald man waved his hand and their

bodies morphed while Johnny gaped in growing consternation. The bald guy turned into Stephanie, and the four older people became Marcus, Lars, Brenden, and Avery.

The pregnant woman in front of Johnny slowly transformed into Frog, and he wailed with laughter. "Did you see that one reporter's face downstairs? He was terrified he was going to catch it or something."

"I was waiting for Frog's water to break," Marcus bellowed.

Johnny sat there, stared at the team, and shook his head. "You guys need help. Seriously. *Real* help."

Stephanie pouted, hurried over, and hugged him tightly. "How do you feel? Are you ready to get the hell out of here?"

"Uh *yeah*," he said. "I sent you guys a message, like, twenty minutes ago."

"Sorry." Avery chuckled. "Frog was struggling to stand up straight. That belly really did him in."

Frog plopped down in the chair. "Mad respect for the ladies, bro. *Mad* respect."

Together, the team followed the back corridors out of the hospital. Using Frog's hacked schematics, they ducked into side doors and scuttled down staff-only passages until they reached the station's civilian accommodations.

While Steph and Johnny had been in hospital, the team had snagged a private suite in one of the mid-range hotels for when she was released.

It was nothing special, merely four rooms off a small common area consisting of a lounge and kitchenette. The bedrooms were functional with two beds apiece, drab-colored linens, and a phone. She was the only one who didn't have to share.

She sat on her bed and sighed. "Ahhh, quiet. At least for a day or so."

No sooner were the words out of her mouth than the phone rang in the common room. She gasped, rushed to the door, and reached it as Lars picked it up. "This is Lars… Yes, ma'am, she has been… Yes, he has too."

Stephanie raised her eyebrow and wondered who could have worked out where they were so soon. He nodded and cracked a smile. "Perfect. We'll be down at the bay in five minutes."

He hung up and looked at Stephanie. "Are you ready to take a royal shuttle down and get your feet on Meligorn?"

Her eyes lit up and she jumped up and down before she rushed over to hug him tightly. "I've been ready for that since I was a little girl."

She took two steps toward the door before he shouted to the team. "Grab your gear, guys. We're transferring planetside for a few days."

"Really?" she squeaked and ran to her room to pack.

As soon as the team had their bags, they headed down to the shuttle bay. It was a relief to find the hotel had remained true to its word and kept their location a secret. Lars told them to keep the booking as it was and paid them extra for their discretion.

The manager grinned. "I never did like the press. Anything to get one over on them," he said but was glad to accept the extra payment too.

The team took a circuitous route to the shuttle bays and entered the VIP passenger lounge shortly afterward. They were quickly surrounded by a team of waiting Meligornians, all dressed in robes of teal and gold.

They loaded the team's luggage into one of the waiting shuttles, showed them to their seats in its plush interior, and made sure they had snacks and drinks for the short ride down to the surface.

She was far too excited to care about any of that, however. Instead, she sat at the window as the shuttle lifted and navigated clear of the station and watched in wonder as they descended to Meligorn's surface.

When they landed, Stephanie stared longingly at the purple fields beyond the tarmac. She sighed when the shuttle taxied into a large hangar and blocked the fields from view. A young Meligornian woman wearing the same teal and gold of those who had greeted them on the station waited for them.

"Hello, my name is Ilbis and I will escort you to your quarters. If there is anything you need, feel free to ask me."

"I'm only glad there are no media," Frog muttered.

"Oh no," Ilbis replied. "Not here. These are the royal hangars. The media isn't allowed anywhere near them. Now, if you would follow me."

She turned and the team followed her through the doors at the back of the hangar. They entered the hallways beyond into a world of opulence and wealth.

The ceilings seemed to reach to the sky and color swirled wildly through them until it was like staring at a storm-rent sky. The décor reeked of age and history, and Stephanie was sure she caught the gleam of magic sliding across its surface.

The people in the pictures appeared to greet her as she walked past, and the statues moved. Some even danced in place. The Meligornians they passed all wore the teal and gold of the royal household and all smiled a welcome for the visitors.

They went from one hallway to another until they reached a large wooden door. Here, Ilbis stopped and turned to them. "These are your quarters. Inside, your rooms each open onto a large common area. We thought you would all want to be close."

"Thank you," Lars replied.

She opened the doors and led them in. The guys all oohed and aahed at the grandeur of the place. Stephanie, though, stayed silent. She walked through, her hand tucked against her chest, completely taken aback.

It was absolutely beautiful. To her right was a room with her name etched into the door. She walked into it and raised one hand to her cheek.

It was like the illusion of the castle bedroom the ambassador had created for her so long ago. Every detail was perfect—a huge four poster bed, lavish linens, hand-carved furniture, and large windows that gave her a clear view of Meligorn itself.

"Let us know if you need anything," Ilbis told them. "I won't be far."

After she had left, Lars hurried over to her and tapped her on the shoulder. He put his finger to his lips and mouthed the word "security." She rolled her eyes but nodded. With a sigh, she worked her magic and dispatched several globes of energy to search the rooms for any listening devices or hidden cameras. Together, the team watched as they ranged throughout the suite and moved from floor to ceiling as they went.

They gathered around her and listened closely until they heard a succession of popping noises. Stephanie jumped, then narrowed her eyes in annoyance. "I can't go anywhere."

"Now you can." Lars chuckled as all but Marcus dispersed to see what had made the sound. "You blew those things up."

She closed her eyes and began to pull energy in without ceasing, merely absorbing wave after wave of MU into her chest. "The energy is so free here. I could spend the entire trip punch drunk on MU. Then, I could easily ignore the haters."

Marcus stood in the doorway of her bedroom and watched her draw the magic into herself. "You know, drunk people don't usually have a high kill rate...unless they have an accident. Usually, they simply end up heading home in a cab and sleeping it off. But, if *you* get drunk, it'll be worse than any drunk behind the wheel because you might actually blow up an entire city."

Stephanie opened her eyes, sighed, and swayed slightly as purple mist wisped in through her nose. "Okay, that stopped being funny. Whoa."

He walked forward and grabbed her under the arm to stabilize her. "Will you explode with this much energy?"

She shook the dizziness out of her head. "No. I have it on good authority that Meligorn energy is only a subset of another type. It's not that strong. I simply have to learn a way to put it in my larger storage tank…wherever that is."

The Meligornian pirate sprang to mind and she frowned. "I don't want a repeat of what happened on the ship where someone pulls my energy and leaves me short. I want to leave enough MU in my system for it to seem like a large amount…for a human."

They were interrupted by a knock on the doorframe and turned to find Avery peeking around the corner. "Oh, that explains it."

He retreated and she began to pull energy again, this time a little slower. She was interrupted by another knock and Avery once again darted his head around the corner. "You might want to stop the purple light show. The ambassador is on his way with what looks like a couple of annoyed people in robes."

Stephanie lowered her arms and released a disgruntled groan as she followed the guys out to the common area.

"Troublemaker," Lars whispered and smirked at her discomfort as he led her over to sit in the lounge. Avery, Johnny, and Frog brought a pack of cards and sat down with them.

Before she could reply, there was a knock at the two main doors, and Ilbis stepped inside. "I'm sorry to bother you, but Meligorn's ambassador to Earth and the Lords Ashti and Crimpor would like to see you."

She didn't wait for their agreement but opened the doors wider and stepped aside to let the visitors through. Lars rose from his seat and Stephanie stood as well as Ambassador V'ritan sauntered in the room. He glanced at them and gestured for them to sit.

"Don't trouble yourselves," he told them as the two nobles

followed him in and immediately broke away, clearly searching the room. He turned to her, smirked, and added, "Where did it happen?"

She raised an eyebrow as she sat and picked up the hand of cards someone had dealt her. "Where did what happen?"

The two nobles looked at her. "The magical explosion. Where did it happen?"

Startled, she allowed a small frown to crease her forehead. "I have no idea what you're talking about."

The Meligornians glared at her and returned to their search.

From their seats, the team watched the lords move around the room, not surprised in the least when they stopped momentarily where each of the small explosions had occurred.

They didn't linger, though, but continued to work their way through every room as if the source of a magical explosion was easy to hide. Finally, looking more disgruntled than ever, the robed Meligorns headed out and Iblis closed the doors behind them.

As soon as they were gone, V'ritan narrowed his eyes and opened his mouth to speak. He remained silent when she held her hand up.

Frog and Marcus left the table silently and followed the path the nobles had taken through the rooms. It wasn't long before they hurried up with several slightly singed items in their hands and several more identical, untarnished items. These, they passed to their visitor.

The ambassador shook his head and looked slightly amused as the items disappeared into glittering light. "Amateurs. You probably blew someone's ears out when you exploded the first lot." He sighed. "I wondered what they were bitching about. I thought something else had happened security-wise and was ready to throw magic and save *you* for once."

Stephanie smiled. "Hopefully, you never have to do that. It wouldn't be fun for anyone. But thank you, nonetheless." She scowled. "I didn't know they could have listening devices in here."

He chuckled and looked around the room. "They can if you don't get rid of them. Those two, though, are part of the group responsible for keeping the building safe. They can be trusted not to share anything embarrassing but they do get most annoyed when their devices are destroyed."

"*They* get annoyed?" Stephanie snorted. "How about the person who is desperately trying to have a little privacy? Those pops almost gave me a damn heart attack. Will I have to keep doing that? Checking every five seconds for new ones?"

V'ritan shook his head. "No. They can't put them here without physically doing it themselves, so they used me to get in." He gave Lars a stern look. "Don't let them come back."

"Not a hope in all the universe," Lars told him solemnly.

She giggled and shuffled over as V'ritan sat on the couch beside her. "So, how are you doing? I haven't been able to ask."

He chuckled. "I'm doing well. Better now that you are here under the king's and my protection."

"And your wife?" Stephanie asked. "Whom I have not gotten to meet yet."

The ambassador laughed. "Elza? She is doing wonderfully, and she is very much looking forward to meeting you. She has talked about it non-stop for the last few days, asking me when you will be released and when you will be here. The king is the king, of course, but the queen and my wife talk about little else. It's entertaining to watch."

She shook her head. It felt strange that so many important people wanted to meet her. "Has everyone been busy with the assassin? Has he given you any new information?"

V'ritan puffed his cheeks out. "He gave us some, and the king and queen are busy flushing out the traitors inside the government and palace. It doesn't matter how much they claim to act for the good of Meligorn and the universe, the royals won't have it. They will find and remove them, one at a time."

Her face fell and she tapped her hands against her knees. "I'm sorry."

His face scrunched and he squeezed her hand gently. "What for?"

She shrugged. "I don't know. I guess I feel really bad for causing so much trouble. Had I not been here—"

"Had you not been here, the traitor would still be head of the Royal Guard, privy to the king's personal security and our world's plans for the future," he replied. "Do not apologize for that. You did not mean for any of this to happen. You're a destiny-changer, Stephanie. You can't change that about yourself. It's merely what you are."

"Am I?" she asked. "Or am I simply a girl with some cool powers who tries her best to use them for good? I don't know."

The Ambassador smiled. "I have never met a human like you. You are so powerful, you could have all the worlds at your feet. Yet here you are, questioning your own relevance and asking others how they are when you're the one who just got out of the hospital and had her privacy violated."

"I don't understand what you're trying to say," she told him. "If you have something that could be used to help everyone, wouldn't you share it?" She paused, then added, "My mother taught me that when I was little."

"She is a smart woman," V'ritan told her. "And to answer your question, yes, I believe you are a destiny-changer. I believe you hold the knowledge and the power to change our world and many others, to make a better universe, a better planet, and a better life for all. And I know that sounds like a lot—"

Stephanie scoffed playfully. "Too much? No way. Merely changing everything from bad to good in the whole galaxy and everywhere beyond. No big deal. I can knock that out on my lunch break."

The ambassador tilted his head back and laughed. "You know what? Give it a couple of years and I bet you'll be able to. It will be no sweat for you at all."

She laughed and shook her head. "Yeah right. So, tell me about the Mysteries. Unless it's a mystery up until it's *not a mystery*."

He looked thoughtful. "Well, there are three Mysteries you will need to complete in order to pass. Whether you pass or fail is not only dependent on the tester. There are parameters you have to work within and goals you have to meet, even if the tester has the final say—so don't give them too much sass when you roll in."

"Me? Sass? Yeah right," she told him. "I know how to be serious. I've practiced that my entire life."

"Good, because once you're in it, you will probably go right back to that mode," he replied. "If you pass all three, you will be set up as an honored Meligorn Mage. If you fail, you will have a chance to try again in ten years."

"Ten years—that's a long time for a retest," she replied.

He shook his head. "You have to survive to wait for it. Don't fail. I can promise you it won't be in your best interest."

Stephanie went serious when she heard the concern in his tone. She realized right then and there that she was heading into something she really didn't understand but had to trust him enough to follow the process. That was a lot to ask of anyone, including her.

Lars finally spoke from his seat beside them. "What are the three tests?"

They both looked at him, and she wanted to tease him until she caught the worry on his face and saw it was reflected in the expressions of the rest of the team.

V'ritan could see it too, and he clearly shared that worry. "The first concerns the illusion of magic. The second concerns its extent. And the third is the presupposition of the power of magic.

All three tests are meant to see if a student is ready to wield magic in a wise and gentle way or if they will seek to…"

He thought about it for a moment and snapped his fingers. "I think the humans say, when you have a hammer, everything looks like a nail. We seek to make sure that those who wield great power do not treat everything like a nail."

"So it's not only a physical thing, it's a spiritual thing as well," Brenden said and looked up from his cards.

The ambassador nodded at him. "Yes, very much so. A Meligornian—or any magical person—must be in touch with themselves. They must be connected to their inner souls and not only the surface view of what magic can be used for. The full extent of that needs to be shown. Once one passes the crucible, they are allowed to see the inner Mysteries and ponder them for the future, contemplating where greater power comes from."

Stephanie puffed out a breath. "This is far deeper than I expected. I assume these are not easy tasks—that there is some danger involved."

"Of course," V'ritan replied but didn't elaborate. "Although the specific scenario for each test is usually different, I have seen my fair share to know my way around them. I am, however, forbidden to speak to you about specifics before your time. They will know if you have been told."

She nodded. "Are the examiners Mages?"

He thought about it for a second. "I believe so, yes. Of course, they are part of the mysteries. We merely call them Teachers. There are currently three—two women, and one man. You have exactly two days to prepare, and I will meet you here on the third day to take you to the first master. I may escort you to the test and back, but for the test itself, you are very much on your own. Something I know you can cope with."

"I sure hope so," she told him, but the pressure of it weighed heavily.

Stephanie wasn't the only one under pressure. A galaxy away, Todd looked at the group of guys he would train with. It was a lot smaller than any of the groups he'd been with before. They'd been told they'd move into the more real-world scenarios and that part of that was to split into smaller teams since operations seldom involved forty guys.

Most missions would require a small group, and that team would become like a family. Each member would have a specific task, and everyone would work together to get the job done. To start the process, their intake had been broken into small groups.

The guys he was with were like him—near the top of their course with one particular skill they excelled at. If he thought about it, he was with a fairly good team.

This time, the pod scenario had taken him to a dark hollow between two hills, where the team leader slapped him on the shoulder and introduced him to the rest. "All right, Todd here has made a strong showing in small arms and defensive tactics, as do Caplan, Fieroza, and Dreigus. They'll be responsible for making sure the rest of us get in and out with the target. Edgeworth, Zoreck, and Teifler, your primary role is to secure the target and bring him out. Once we get in there, however, I expect you to flex with the situation, because you all know what happens to plans, right?"

The guys chuckled and he continued. "We're responsible for retrieving a captured Federation Navy sailor, one Melena Alvarez, from the building behind us. We need to get in and get out without being seen, and we need to do it fast. Once we're out, the overwatch will call in an air strike to level the place, so don't leave anyone behind."

The team set up and headed down to the building. They moved through the shadows, cautious and quiet.

Getting into the building was easy, and they made it to the

room without being discovered. Petty Officer Alvarez was badly beaten but she could walk so they tucked her in the center of the team and headed out. Todd brought up the rear.

The trip out proved far more difficult. They had to stop several times to avoid more people as they crept through the building. It was only once they'd begun to cross the last hall that they were discovered, and all hell broke loose.

Bullets and las-bolts erupted as the enemy soldier shouted the alarm. Todd and Fieroza covered their tails while their team-mates hustled Melena to the exit.

Zoreck moved to cover Edgeworth and Teifler but the enemy caught the sailor before he could find cover. He took a bullet to the shoulder and fell, so Todd hauled him up and over his shoulder. Fieroza maintained fire as they bolted to the door.

As soon as they were out, the team on overwatch gave the green light for the strike and the first missile howled in.

The team kept moving at a steady pace. Todd carried Zoreck and Edgeworth now carried Melena. By the time they reached the pick-up point, they were exhausted but happy.

The scenario ended and they emerged from their pods to find the chief waiting.

"I suppose you misbegotten sons think you did a *great* job," he began as they formed up in front of him. "Well, you're lucky *any* of you got your sorry asses out of there alive, let alone the sailor you were sent to rescue. You!" He rounded on the team leader and dressed him down for what he'd forgotten before he moved onto Edgeworth and then down the line.

Todd was left until last, and by the end, he had no doubts about exactly what he'd done wrong...but also a vague idea of what he'd done right.

"Dismissed!"

Never had that word sounded sweeter, and it was followed by, "You're off duty until oh-five-hundred. Make it a team night out."

"Hooyah."

As soon as the chief had left, Zobeck turned to Todd and shoved him in the shoulder. "Thanks for getting me out of there."

"You better be thankful," Caplan told him. "I'da left your sorry ass behind to slow them down."

Zobeck laid his hand over his heart and replied in mock shock. "I'm hurt, Cappy. Really hurt." He made a show of rubbing his butt cheeks. "I'll have you know this ass deserves your utmost respect."

"Just for that, your ass is buying the first round," the team leader snapped and jerked a hand toward the door. "Let's get out of there before the chief comes back and changes his mind."

The team laughed and headed over to the bar for well-deserved beers. Once they arrived, the team leader stood on his chair and raised his glass. "Tomorrow is our last test, then we are done. So make this beer your last for the night. I can tell you right now, I'll be as lucky as hell to get to serve with any one of you bastards."

They all cheered, drank their beer, and reluctantly switched to soda as they scarfed their meals. While they'd rather have gotten rolling drunk, not a single one of them was willing to mess up their chance to get the hell out of Dodge.

CHAPTER FOUR

Stephanie sat in the back of the shuttle and jiggled her feet, her hands pressed together in front of her. She was nervous knowing she still had a lot to learn.

For the first time since the ambassador had suggested it, she was afraid she couldn't possibly pass the test. She leaned back, pressed the back of her head against the wall, and closed her eyes. *If you can't possibly pass, then why be so nervous? Go into it calm and do what you can.*

This shuttle was smaller and moved much more swiftly than the one that had brought them down from the station. V'ritan had explained the technology but she still didn't get it.

It had something to do with the crystalline transfer of MU into the power circuits and blah blah blah. She looked out the window as they flew low over a small village, and she looked out in awe. The place was absolutely enchanting.

The village consisted of thatched-roof homes with small painted doors and wildly colorful gardens surrounding a small town center. It looked like it had jumped out of a fairy tale, and she loved it.

They left the village behind and the shuttle descended and

skimmed its way along a narrow dirt track to a small cottage set well away from the main thoroughfare.

It was only a short flight, but it would have taken someone the best part of two hours to reach it from the village. Stephanie checked her safety straps as the shuttle slowed and pivoted to land carefully in a stone-lined circle outside.

Once they landed, V'ritan moved to the back where Lars and the team sat anxiously.

"This is where she leaves you," he said to them. "I will be with her and we will be back soon."

"Not happening," Lars told him and stood. Marcus and Frog stepped alongside him. "Our job is to protect her. We can't do that if we're not there."

The ambassador looked at him, then surveyed the rest of the team. When he saw the determination on their faces, he sighed.

"One," he agreed finally. "I think I can have the Master forgive that, but the rest of you will have to stay with the shuttle. We'll bring her back."

Lars looked at Stephanie and frowned. He studied V'ritan's face and saw his own determination reflected there. With a soft growl of protest, he nodded.

"Very well. Marcus, you're in charge of keeping Frog out of trouble. The rest of you do what Marcus tells you to. If we're not back by nightfall, you know what to do."

The team nodded and slapped hands with her as she walked out. Lars immediately moved ahead to ensure the area was clear. She put on a brave face for the guys but on the inside, her magic swirled restlessly, and her feelings were in chaos.

As V'ritan followed her, she reached the landing pad and looked around in awe. "It's beautiful here."

He smiled and kept a watchful eye on Lars. "It is. The village is there to support the Master and those who wish to see her. Almost everyone travels by foot."

"I see you brought a friend," a voice called from ahead of

them. "It's a good thing I understand the human protocol, V'ritan."

Lars moved back to Stephanie and they looked up as a tall Meligornian woman approached. Realizing it must be the first Teacher, Stephanie watched as she reached out, took the ambassador's arm, and bent low.

She couldn't help but notice how elegant the Teacher made the movement seem, although she was surprised when they embraced. When the woman turned to greet her, she kept her hands in and greeted her like she should address a Mage of her rank.

The woman nodded in appreciation but, although she acknowledged Lars's presence, she did not greet him and merely fell in step beside the ambassador and led them into her home. "You look good, V'ritan. Old but good."

V'ritan laughed and glanced at Stephanie. "Melistar and I are distant relatives. She has had to put up with me all three hundred and twenty-three years of her life."

The Mage leaned toward Stephanie. "Which requires more patience than I care to admit."

She laughed quietly and nervously. The woman was younger than she'd expected, and her face gave her the idea that they might be close in age...although how that could be possible, she didn't know.

Melistar studied her for a moment. "You must be worried about the fact that you're human. So, let me put your mind at rest. I am not here to test your species, merely your understanding of the Mysteries here."

Stephanie relaxed a little and Melistar beckoned. "Come. Let us begin."

Leaving V'ritan and Lars in the first room, Stephanie followed Melistar through to a room where there was no furniture and no windows or door. It was empty save for a slick white marble floor and a roof that was open to the sky.

The Mage brought her to a halt in the center of the room and raised her hands. "Close your eyes and relax. You will begin when you open your eyes. Take your time. Think about it and trust your instincts."

With a nod, she shut her eyes. Melistar pressed her fingers to her temples and whispered. "To the gates she storms, bring her to the beginning of three."

She felt a rush of air as if she moved really fast. When it stilled, she opened her eyes and looked around. She was inside a small cottage. A little girl hummed as she skipped past and played with a shuttle similar to the one they'd arrived in.

Her gut told her to follow the girl, so she did. The child did not react to her presence but continued to move uninhibited, skipped out of the room and along a corridor, and out the back door.

When Stephanie emerged, she heard the child crying and saw she had fallen. She raced to her and found she had skinned her knee.

Her first instinct was to bring her hands up to heal her, but she remembered a time when she had fallen and skinned her knee on the sidewalk. Her mother had picked her up and taken her inside to clean and cover the minor scrape. The pain had soon faded, and the graze had healed in only a couple of days.

She frowned. It seemed such a little thing and one easily fixed on its own. It would be far too easy to use magic on it, and for what? To heal something that posed no threat to the child's life? To spare herself a few tears, which would soon dry?

The easy solution made her immediately suspicious, and she paused. Instead of using her energy, she leaned down and scooped the girl up, took her inside, and set her on the counter exactly like her mother had done. She looked around the tidy kitchen and soon located a first aid kit high up on a shelf, but when she turned, the little girl was gone.

Slightly confused, she looked around until the room shifted

like a pod session finishing in the Virtual World, only much more violently. The kitchen blurred and she felt like she was falling.

She jolted to a stop in what looked like someone's front yard. It was late at night and when she saw no one, she assumed they were all asleep.

There seemed to be no obvious reason for her to be there, and she wondered what the point was when she heard voices. They were hushed, as though their owners didn't want to be heard, so she walked carefully down the side of the house to peek around the back.

There, at one of the ground-floor windows, were two men. Both were dressed in black and one held a crowbar. "Break the window," the other urged. "The girl's upstairs. Snatch her and we can get the hell out of here."

Stephanie felt a swirl of anger. She wanted to fireball the pair so badly it hurt, but she knew this was a test. Rather than follow her first instinct, she studied her surroundings. She found a discarded baseball bat near an abandoned glove and ball. There was also a jump rope tossed over a bush nearby.

Slow and silent, she snuck over to retrieve what she needed and devised a plan. Half of it was simple enough to do without magic, while the other half needed only a small amount to ensure complete success.

As she gathered the bat and rope, the kidnappers broke the window and muffled the sound using one of their jackets. She crouched in the shadow of a bush as they cleared the glass, folded the jacket over the windowsill, and climbed inside.

When they'd disappeared, she hurried over and followed them. She entered quietly as they started up a set of stairs inside. A trace of magic muted the sound of her movements as she crept up the stairs behind them, looped the rope around their ankles, and yanked it tight.

A quick tug toppled them heavily on the stairs and the sound echoed through the house, but she ignored the noise. She released the magic and used the baseball bat to keep them down and knock them out before she tied them up.

A Meligornian male appeared at an upstairs doorway.

"What the— Who are you?"

"You need to call the authorities. These men were planning to kidnap your daughter."

One of the would-be kidnappers groaned, and she swung the bat, connected with his head, and knocked him out.

"Hurry," she urged when the man simply gaped at her. "I can't keep hitting them like this."

He disappeared into the room, and the scene faded.

This time, she didn't fall. Instead, she somehow flew into the sunrise that reflected in a lake below her. The sound of children's laughter reached her, and she smiled as the scene shifted and placed her on a hill overlooking what was clearly a local swimming spot.

Three children swam in the lake, two close to the dock and one farther out toward the lake's center. Moving a little closer, she recognized the child furthest away as the little girl from the first test.

Stephanie walked down to the edge and watched them, wondering what could possibly happen out there worse than what she'd already prevented. That was when she saw it.

The ripples in the water started slowly and approached from the far shore. They formed a 'V' and grew in size as whatever beast created them moved toward the girl. She fumbled instinctively to remove her shoes, but it soon became clear that she was too far away and wouldn't reach the child in time.

A shadow in the lake water showed her clearly that the beast had almost reached the little one. She shook her head, released her shoes, and straightened as she called the magic inside her.

Her gaze fixed on the child, she saw when the monster, its jaws wide, leapt from the water, ready to devour the screaming girl. She thrust her hands out and launched two huge bolts of magic at the creature.

One struck hard and drove it back while the other wound around it to hold it in one place so it couldn't attack a second time.

"Help me," the little girl screamed, and her arms flailed as she tried to swim and keep an eye on her attacker at the same time.

She was panicked and her uncoordinated movements did little to keep her afloat. If someone didn't reach her soon, she'd drown. Stephanie pulled more energy into herself and raced down the hill to the lake.

Buoyed by her magic and her momentum, she skipped across the water. When she reached the child, she pulled the little one into her arms and carried her to the shore. As soon as her feet touched the grassy bank, she slowed and sat and enveloped the girl in her arms to comfort her.

After a moment, the child vanished, and she stood. The world appeared to fold in on itself and a dark blotch grew larger and seemed to move directly toward her. She closed her eyes and flinched, unsure of what to expect.

A tap on her nose brought her out of it, and she opened her eyes to see the ambassador and the Teacher looking at her. Lars was behind them, peering through the door, but he didn't interfere. Melistar spoke first. "Tell me what your thought process was."

Stephanie shook the tension from her shoulders. "The first test would have been easy to fix with magic—a quick healing and all done. But I remembered that simply because you can, does not mean you should. All children get scraped knees. It's part of being a child, so I looked for a first aid kit."

The woman nodded and gestured for her to continue, so she did. "For the second one, I used only enough magic to keep myself from being noticed until I could deal with the kidnappers without using magic. It was a little risky, but I didn't need to use magic to stop them, so I didn't. Those two needed to face justice and be questioned, and it was better for the father to call the authorities than for me to kill them on the spot. "

Again, Melistar nodded. "Go on."

She took a deep breath and continued. "For the third test, I used magic when it was obvious I had no alternative. If I hadn't, I couldn't have stopped the child from being eaten or reached her before she drowned in panic. My guess is that the test was to be able to recognize when magic is the most practical answer and to only use it if I had to. In that instance, I had to if I was to stop the beast and save the child from drowning, but I could use a towel to dry her."

She looked up and saw they were both nodding but she pressed on. "So, I guess the thing is to know when we need to use magic and when there are better ways and to trust our instincts to be able to tell the difference."

Melistar laid a hand on her shoulder. "Very good. You have passed. I will give you a gift—some wisdom that might be of use in your next test."

Stephanie couldn't help but grin. The woman pressed her finger to her forehead, but as soon as she made contact, the Teacher gasped and collapsed.

CHAPTER FIVE

Stephanie and V'ritan knelt beside Melistar. After her collapse in the testing room, they had carried her to the old flowered couch in the Teacher's small living room. Together, they had waited for her to wake.

Her stillness had them incredibly worried until a Meligornian bird landed on the windowsill and chirped at her, its song accompanied by a fresh breeze. At the sound, she opened her purple eyes, blinked the purple haze away, and immediately focused on Stephanie.

"Your memories...the final wisdom I wanted to give you... It was too much." She smiled. "From what little I shared, I believe it is safe to say you understand the mystery of the illusion of magic without further knowledge from me. Go. You have my blessing."

As she spoke, she grasped the girl's right wrist. After a brief flash of purple light, Melistar released her.

A hasty glance at her wrist revealed a sigil of a flower with thorns that appeared to be burned into her skin. She looked from the mark to Melistar. "Can we get you anything?"

The Teacher shook her head. "Oh, no. I'm okay. I think I'll

take a nap right here in the breeze. I'm glad to know you have come. There is hope, now."

They said goodbye and returned to the ship. Lars trailed in their wake. The team was very excited and wanted to go out and celebrate, but she shook her head. "We can celebrate when the other two are done. I need a clear head until then."

Frog pouted and the guys groaned, but none of them argued. V'ritan suppressed a smile as they rolled their eyes and muttered a reluctant but unanimous, "Fine." None of them argued when the pilot set a course for the palace, and she decided they should eat in so she could get some rest.

At first, Stephanie thought she would have trouble getting to sleep, but that wasn't the case. She drifted off thinking of the stars and spent her night floating among them, listening to the sound of the voices of loved ones past.

Normally, that would have made her sad, but when she woke, she felt renewed. The presence of the Meligornian who had befriended her on the liner stayed with her, warming her spirit as she rose to face the day.

After a quiet breakfast, she met V'ritan and led the team out to the shuttle. This time, their destination lay almost a full half day away. The ambassador reminded her that day's test was for the illusion of the extent of magic.

He looked at her as the pilot brought the shuttle in to land. "The next one will test how far magic can be wielded. And that doesn't necessarily mean distance...so be aware."

She nodded. "Right." She glanced at the team as the pilot released the hatch. "I'll be back, guys."

The Meligornian shook his head. "On this one, you get to take your team with you. This test is more about emotions, feelings, and how you can't make someone love someone they do not."

Stephanie nodded again and hoped the test wouldn't try to force individual team members to fall in love with each other. Firstly, because it wasn't something she wanted to do, and then because, if she tried it and succeeded, they'd be pissed at her forever.

V'ritan led them to the door of another small cottage and gestured for her to knock. She was answered shortly after by an older Teacher with silver hair, a wrinkled face, and lively blue eyes.

The woman walked with a slight hunch but still moved easily and swiftly in spite of it. She stepped out of the house and walked them to the back yard, where she gestured toward the trees beyond.

V'ritan knew her as Ashgren, but she didn't introduce herself to Stephanie when she addressed her. "You, human, are to take your team into the forest and use magic to find two creatures that regard themselves as alphas in the world and which hate each other. You must then use your magic to create a way for them to love each other."

She went on to explain. "There are at least two beasts in these woods that cannot stand each other. You will see them sooner or later. The ambassador and I will wait for you here. You are to bring the creatures here once you have succeeded."

Stephanie nodded and bowed to the ambassador before she turned and led her team into the woods.

He watched her go with a slight scowl on his face before he glanced at Ashgren. "I have always found this test barbaric."

"Then you have missed the purpose of it," she replied. "Its purpose is to teach the student not to mess with nature and that sometimes, there are things stronger than any magic. Hate can be one of them. Most, if they survive it, come out changed—both physically from injuries as well as emotionally and intellectually."

"Well, that sounds *wonderful*," he replied and stared morosely after the team as they entered the woods and merged into the shadows beneath the trees.

Stephanie dispatched two magic orbs and asked each one to look for a creature that would fit the Teacher's criteria. While she waited, she retrieved her tablet and searched for references to forest predators known on Meligorn.

It didn't take her long to pinpoint two which met what the Teacher had asked for. She called the orbs back and sent them out once more. They moved forward as first one, then the other, signaled a new direction to follow.

They searched through the forest for hours and finally arrived at a clearing in the woods. The orbs had done their task. They had located and drawn two alphas of the rival species to the same place.

The team could hear them long before they could see them. Low rumbled growls became a series of drawn-out yowls that reached the scale of threat and vengeance. Stephanie hurried forward and the team kept pace. They burst through the foliage at one edge of the clearing, completely ignored by the two Meligornian cats standing opposite each other.

One was white with black stripes and had six legs, whilst the other was black with yellow stripes and had four legs, four eyes, and horns. Their tails twitched stiffly with irritation, and their fur stood on end as they showed their fangs in an angry challenge.

Both were a little gaunt and glanced constantly at the large hairy carcass that lay in the middle of the clearing. The blaster burns in its side showed its death wasn't natural and that it had lived long enough to escape the initial hunter, even though hunter had caused the injury that had killed it.

Stephanie crouched in the brush to study the furred adversaries and the team gathered around her. "Humans call the one on the left a Zee Cat, and the one on the right is a Yellow Jacket—apparently it has a sting in its tail like the wasps on Earth. They usually stick to separate territories, but when they *do* meet, they're always enemies. Both are predators, and these two will be the alpha males of the region, the most dominant of their kind in the area."

Lars shook his head. "From the looks of that kill in the middle, food must be scarce."

She studied both cats and kill and agreed. "Then they're perfect."

Before he could stop her, she stood and stepped into the clearing. She slapped her hands together and pulled up an orb of sparkling purple and pink light which caught the attention of both cats. They growled and sank low to the ground but didn't retreat.

From his position at the clearing's edge, Lars watched as her expression altered and she pulled the orb back into her. She studied both cats and sighed. "There is no way they will love each other—ever—and there is no point in trying to force them to."

The guys remained where they were but readied themselves to defend her against both animals if they attacked. "You can't give up."

Stephanie shook her head. "I'm not giving up. I'm trying something different."

She gestured with her hand in a circular motion to create a large tub of meat beside her.

The first thing she did was to magically toss a piece of meat to each feline. From the way both beasts fell on it, Lars' assessment of the food scarcity seemed correct. The next two landed closer to her—not by much, but enough to require the cats to step closer to each other and her.

With each piece she threw, she called out a one-word command coupled with their name. "Zeekat, come!" "Bumblebee, come!"

The two beasts eyed each other and her before they stepped forward to claim the food. She repeated the process until they moved toward her after she'd called the command but before she threw the meat.

From the sidelines, it looked like they were obeying her commands and then being rewarded. She kept it up until reaching their morsel would bring them within striking distance of each other. As if they realized this, both cats glared at each other and gave a low, moaning growl that set her teeth on edge.

The attack, when it came, was lightning-fast, but Stephanie was faster. As the felines launched into their attacks, their claws extended, she thrust her hands out to encapsulate each of them in a field of magic.

"No!" she shouted and lowered them to the ground. They stared at her in astonishment and she released the black-and-white one. "Zeekat, come!"

Instead of obeying, the cat lunged toward its enemy and was stopped in mid-jump by another magical bubble. This time, she set it down farther from the meat. She turned to the yellow jacket. "Bumblebee, come!"

The animal ignored her and tried to attack its rival. Again, she stopped it and set it down farther from the meat but closer to its rival. Both cats hissed.

Stephanie lifted the meat and put it back in the barrel. They stared at her, clearly shocked that their food had been taken away. This time, when she lifted a piece of meat, she walked over to the black-and-white cat and waved the bait in front of its face.

It hissed at her, and she tapped it on the nose. "No."

The feline glared, and she offered it a small piece on her palm. After a moment's hesitation, the cat scooped it up with its tongue. "Good, Zeekat," she told him and scratched him along the jawline.

Magic shielded her hand before his teeth could close, and she wagged a finger at him. "No."

She turned to the other cat and repeated the process, then alternated between them until they both accepted the food and caresses without any attempt to bite her. Both made small sounds of complaint when she returned to her position beside the meat bucket, and she smiled. "Good, cats."

Both felines watched intently, and she turned to the yellow jacket. "Bumblebee, come," she commanded and released the magic that secured it.

This time, although it looked toward its rival, the cat didn't attack him. It moved toward Stephanie instead and was rewarded. "Good cat."

Zeekat proved he wasn't a slow learner and obeyed her immediately, and Bumblebee simply watched suspiciously. Slowly, she brought the cats closer again and this time, she only had to separate them once before she repeated the process to bring them back to the same point.

When she had them standing side by side as they accepted the food from her hands and allowed her to pet them, she glanced at the team.

"Okay, boys, this is your cue. Someone, come up and try to attack me."

Lars exhaled a deep breath and shook his head, but he didn't hesitate. If he did, he'd think about what he was about to do and he'd never do what she needed. He ran toward her with a yell, caught hold of her, and hauled a fist back as though to strike.

The bucket of meat vanished, and the cats reacted. With twin roars of outrage, they attacked and lashed out at him until he released her, then pursued him across the clearing.

What they would have done if she hadn't called out was frighteningly clear, but her cry of "Bumblebee! Zeekat! Come!" and the reappearance of the bucket of meat effectively ended their pursuit and they bounded back to her.

Lars turned and trotted toward her once again, only to be greeted by two snarling cats who spun to meet him. It took her some time to get them to accept him as a friend, but it had been worth it. Once she had them at a point where Lars could feed them, she introduced them to the rest of the team.

From there, she began to test the creatures. She asked the guys to attack her and had some of them to help the cats defend her. After each attempt, she brought everyone together to feed the cats before a different group attacked.

It took the felines a few attempts to understand that this was some kind of a game, but they were as intelligent as the research indicated and soon, they didn't need to accept the attackers as friends after each bout. Instead, they watched as she divided the team and cocked their heads almost in anticipation as the enemy team moved away.

At one point, Zeekat forgot Bumblebee was on his side and took a swipe at him, but both teams attacked Stephanie to force the cats to work together to protect her. At the end of that round, they regarded each other warily until she petted them both. "Play nice, boys."

She divided the team and had them attack her—again and again—until the animals worked together to drive their adversaries back before they raced back for her approval. "One last time," Stephanie said. "This time, it's all of you against them and me."

The felines waited as the guys jogged to the edge of the clearing, then tensed as they prepared to attack. This time, they both roared loudly to warn the guys and paced around one another. Every few feet, they bumped each other and rubbed their heads together. Her mouth fell open and she began to laugh. "That's it. They understood it. They know we're all fighters and that everyone here is working for me. They're bonding."

"So...uh, we can stop, now?" Frog asked, his voice almost pleading, and she laughed out loud.

"Oh, hell, no. Bring it on, boys! No holds barred."

Lars led the charge, then dropped back and let his teammates confront the animals while he worked his way around the battlefield in an effort to sneak up on her from behind.

When he reached her, she murmured, "I can see you, you know."

"Yeah, and?" he asked as he lunged into a bone-jarring tackle.

He'd thought he'd won...right up until a black-and-yellow streak barreled into him from the side and bowled him away. Bumblebee kept going as the momentum of his strike carried him over the man and away. Before the team leader could move, a large black-and-white form landed on his chest and a loud rumble engulfed him.

Stephanie laughed so hard she couldn't call the cats away until Zeekat had settled himself on Lars's chest and begun to groom him. When she did, both animals bounded over to her and wound themselves around her legs, purring loudly.

The guys stood there and watched them. When she overbalanced and fell, giggling, the two big creatures rubbed their large furry faces against hers.

Lars raised an eyebrow and Frog came up to put his elbow on the man's shoulder. "Well, she *is* a witch, and witches love cats soooo..."

He turned his head slowly and fixed Frog with a horrified look. "No. We are not keeping those cats. They are far too big to be house pets. Besides, how would we even get them home? How do you think they'll manage on board a ship? They might eat the entire crew and the passengers too." He shook his head. "Nope, not happening"

She rolled free of her furred friends and stood. "All right, let's do a couple more fights, these ones all out." She turned to the cats and pointed a finger at them. "But don't eat my guys."

"I don't like the sound of this," Frog said and swallowed hard.

They went through several fights, during which they used the clearing and the trees around it. The felines leapt at them as she used magic to block their blows. The team came up with different routes to follow. Sometimes, they would move behind them and sometimes, from the side. During the final battle, though, they might have been a little overzealous.

Three of the guys attacked from the front and blocked blows from the animals while the others rappelled from the trees, landed behind them, and yelled a battle cry. The cats appeared to turn berserk, backed up in front of her, and leaned their heads back. They roared so loudly, it set birds to flight for miles around. Frog froze, visibly shaking as the creatures advanced toward him.

"Bumblebee! Zeekat!" Stephanie called, but they ignored her. His gaze fixed on his adversaries, his mouth worked soundlessly as his legs kept him frozen in place.

She tried again. "Bumblebee! Zeekat! Come!" she yelled, but they acted as if she wasn't even there. They had locked onto Frog to the exclusion of everyone else. She tried one last time and waited until they pounced.

As soon as they left the ground, she wrapped Frog in a shielded cocoon. The cats pounded into the shield and rolled it around as Frog found his voice inside.

She paused to watch them for a moment, her hands on her hips and her eyes narrowed. The felines both licked the cocoon and clawed at the magic until it began to fray beneath their paws. She remained motionless but watched, ready to intervene, as it unraveled.

As soon as it had disintegrated, they both leaned down and licked Frog from chin to forehead until he started to sputter with laughter. The others joined him and chuckled as he tried to push the two large beasts off him.

They hadn't intended to kill him. she laughed with relief. "They were teasing. Oh, man, this is golden."

"It was the first attack from the inside in many years," V'ritan told Ashgren as they discussed recent events while they waited.

She shook her head in disgust and was about to reply when something caught her attention at the edge of the woods. The ambassador raised his head to follow her gaze and anxiety creased his face.

He frowned as the team emerged from the woods. They moved slowly and appeared battered and bruised. Beside him, the Teacher caught his eye and smirked. "Well, some of them survived."

V'ritan narrowed his eyes and turned back in time to see two large cats trot from beneath the trees. They pawed at each other and tumbled together in the grass.

Finally, Stephanie stepped out of the shadows and looked surprisingly unscathed. V'ritan looked at the Teacher and smirked at her in return.

The felines ceased their rough and tumble play, ran to her, and rubbed their heads against her legs. They hung back and followed her, showing their respect for her.

Both the ambassador and the Teacher were shocked and lost for words. Finally, Ashgren found her voice. "She is the first to ever fully complete this specific test."

He smiled. "I knew she could do it."

The Teacher waved her over and Stephanie jogged up but directed the cats to the side with the guys. The woman scrutinized her carefully and sighed. "How did you do it? I *must* know."

Stephanie chuckled, slightly out of breath. "The answer is in the Illusion of Magic."

Her team all looked down to hide their grins. They wouldn't admit a single thing. All they'd done was support her, even if they'd earned a hefty share of scratches for their trouble.

Stephanie shot the ambassador a glance and focused on the Teacher. "I think the point of this exercise is to show that there are some things that cannot be changed by magic. You see, those two will never love each other."

She held her hand up as the Teacher went to protest that the cats seemed to do exactly that. "Technically, these guys aren't in love, but I did manage to convince them that they were part of the same team and on the same side, which was, perhaps, the point. Now, while I used magic to make it happen, the magic didn't change their natures. Nothing can do that."

As she spoke, Ashgren nodded her head. "Yes. You understood the problem exactly. Well done. You may proceed to the final test."

The Teacher turned, took V'ritan's arm, and let him escort her inside. The team returned to the shuttle and Stephanie stopped as she reached the edge of the stone circle. She dropped to one knee in front of the cats and caressed them both. "You can come with me, or you can return to the forest. It's your choice."

As if they understood her and each other, the felines exchanged glances, looked back at the woods, and then to where the team boarded the shuttle. Finally, Zeekat rose onto his hind legs and put his front paws on her shoulders so he could lick her face.

It was no more than a swift dab on the nose before he dropped again, and Bumblebee repeated the process and licked her face. The two trotted unhesitatingly toward the craft.

When they reached it, they dodged around Lars. He tried to protest and was thoroughly ignored. "But...ah, man."

Frog grabbed his belly and laughed loudly. "Bwahahaha. Look who won."

Ashgren shook her head. "Shocking. They understand her intent, if not her words. If I had not seen this with my own eyes, V'ritan, I would have said you were lying. Now, I shall go to my grave wondering exactly how she accomplished this great feat."

The ambassador scratched his chin, his brow tight in a frown. "Me, too."

He said goodbye to Ashgren and so did Stephanie, who walked back from the launch pad once the cats had made it into the shuttle with the team.

"Thank you," she told the Teacher. "I learned a lot, today."

"You are very welcome, child. Please come again. I'd like to hear how you succeeded."

"As soon as I can," she told her and hurried to the shuttle.

V'ritan followed her and glanced over his shoulder from the shuttle's entry hatch to where Ashgren stood at the circle's edge. "Wish me good health."

She nodded and waved, and he closed the door. As the shuttle lifted, she stepped back, folded her arms, and chuckled for the first time in a very long time. "Good health to you, my friend. You may need it before your shuttle lands."

CHAPTER SIX

The next morning, the team were back on board the shuttle. This time, Stephanie had managed to sneak a canteen of coffee aboard.

As they traveled into the morning light, Frog laughed loudly, looked up from his tablet, and shook his head. "I'm watching the feed we set up in the common area. The cats are basically running the world, right now. The two Meligornians who clean the rooms are plastered against the wall, absolutely terrified."

"They are an unexpected turn of events but hey, I have two giant cats now." She chuckled.

Lars smirked. "Oh, boy."

She laughed and patted him on the shoulder as she walked past to sit up front with V'ritan. "So, this is the third and final test," she said as she settled into the seat. "What should I expect?"

He didn't look as carefree as he had the day before. "This one is for the presupposition of the power of magic, but I must warn you. The Teacher, Tethis, is much, much older than either of the other two. I wish I could tell you how it will go, but this Teacher is difficult to read, and he's been more and more ornery with each person who is brought to him for testing."

His heavy sigh wasn't at all encouraging. "Sometimes, I think he deliberately makes things too hard. Honestly, we probably should have pushed for his retirement a while ago, but at that time, I never expected you to go through the Mysteries and so didn't think his prejudices would be a problem."

Stephanie shook her head. "I'm not worried about him. What are the rules?"

V'ritan shook his head. "Unfortunately, I can't divulge that. The rules of each test are for the Teacher to explain, and the Teacher alone. Part of their duties is to come up with their own parameters for these things."

He thought about that for a moment before he added, "I *will* say that from what I have seen in the past, this test usually involves a spell which pulls a lot of energy to accomplish. In theory, this should be a simple test for you. You have considerable experience in that."

She rubbed her face to ease a little of the tension that had crept in. "I have considerable experience running myself almost to death."

The ambassador shook his head. "No, what you've done is learn what you can and cannot do in these situations. You've found your weak spot—your Kryptonite."

Stephanie looked up, surprised. "Superman? You don't know Earth sayings but you know Kryptonite?"

V'ritan smirked. "Superheroes were the first thing I learned about Western culture when I came to Earth. They were secretive about it, but all the bigwigs have these huge collections of superhero memorabilia."

She gasped. "They told us they burned all of them. Those belong to the people. Wonder Woman, Batman, the whole DC universe. And don't get me started on Marvel with Thor, Iron Man, the Fantastic Four, Daredevil—oh, the pain this brings me."

He patted her leg. "I'm sorry. I should have kept that to myself. But know that somewhere out there, someone is reading a superhero story, even if it's only a politician, and they are thinking of you."

Her nostrils flared. "So, this test will probably suck ass, won't it?"

"Probably," he agreed, "but that *does* seem to be your special gift."

Stephanie blinked and looked slowly at him. He shook his head and stumbled over his next words. "I did not mean your special gift was…*actually* sucking…uh…"

She sliced her hand through the air. "Enough said. We shall never speak of this again."

Frog popped around the edge of the seat and put his head on her shoulder. "So, I hear you have some seriously kinky special gift going on. Who knew your witch powers took that particular bent?"

Stephanie, with a straight face, shoved his head away and shook hers furiously as she buried her face in her hands. "You did this."

The shuttle touched down and V'ritan winced. "My apologies. Truly. We don't have… It didn't cross my mind because—"

She shook her head. "Let's go get this over with."

"Yep," he replied quietly.

They stood and approached the hatch, climbed out of the craft, and waved to the guys as the door shut slowly behind them. She looked back and frowned. "No, Lars?"

"No, I... convinced him you'd be better off if you were the *only* human to appear and that I could keep you safe."

He said that so quickly that she gave him a suspicious look. "You can't guarantee that, can you?"

The ambassador blushed and bowed his head. "I can only hope it doesn't come to that."

"It's okay," she told him. "I've got this."

She looked around, puzzled. "Uh, where is this Tethis guy?"

He pointed ahead at what looked like the entrance to an old

cave. However, as she squinted for a better look, a front door came into focus. It looked more like a run-down Hobbit hole than a cave and it was all the more creepy for it.

As she moved toward it, the door creaked open. The Teacher, Tethis, emerged to greet them, his robes faded with age.

His long silver hair had become snow-white and hung in a tangled mass down his back. He held a twisted staff in one hand and used it to steady his walk as he moved away from the house.

The closer he came, the nimbler he grew, although he was still obviously very old. Stephanie was in awe. She'd never met an old Meligorn before and she walked up and moved into a traditional greeting. He simply turned away to acknowledge V'ritan instead.

She was slightly hurt, but the ambassador *had* warned her, so she was able to shake it off. Instead, she used the moment of their conversation to study the Teacher a little more. His skin was mottled with age and wrinkled by time.

With his greeting finished, V'ritan attempted to introduce her but Tethis ignored that as well. She began to wonder if being here had been a mistake—if allowing her, a mere human, to undertake the Mysteries was some colossal error. Apparently, Tethis felt the same. "I don't like seeing you go to all this trouble for a *human*, Ambassador."

The other man held his temper and tried to explain. "This human is a witch, Teacher, and the most powerful one I have ever seen. She has saved my life, the king's life, and the lives of thousands on board a luxury starliner. She has more than earned my respect."

At this, the Teacher turned to study her intently with his dark, beady eyes. "Yes, well, I don't know her and her tricks. I'll be straightforward, Ambassador, I have no interest in testing a human, nor do I have any interest in allowing one into the Mysteries. It is a sacred calling and it is meant *only* for the magical. It is not for those only able to dabble in tricks."

"This test has been ordered by the king," V'ritan replied, handing over an official-looking envelope.

The old Master waved it away and almost snarled in fury. "It could be ordered by my mother and I would *still* be appalled." He snorted. "Besides which, what will he do if I refuse? Sentence me to death? It's about time. Put me in jail for the rest of my life? That will be a very short sentence. This is not something that was *ever* meant to take place. Period."

As she listened, Stephanie's anger began to rise. Sure, V'ritan had warned her that the old Teacher had some very...*traditional* views, but this was ridiculous—and far too much like the prejudice directed at people from the Subs for her to tolerate.

Finally, she'd had enough. She fought to maintain her tight control over her temper as she stepped forward to interrupt their conversation. "You gentlemen *do* understand that I am a sentient being and that I am *right* here? I can hear every word you are saying, and I don't appreciate it."

The Teacher shook his staff at her. "Oh, you can hear us, can you? Well, good for you, young lady, but that doesn't change the fact you come from a species not yet out of diapers."

He made a show of another disdainful scrutiny—literally from head to toe—and curled his lip in disgust. "And *you*—why you're barely old enough to be out of diapers, let alone change one, much less be acknowledged as a Mage. When I was your age, I was playing outside in the mud and finding treasures in each nostril. I had no idea of what a grown-up was, let alone how to be one."

He waved his hand in frustration. "This...this is ludicrous!"

The ambassador tried to cut in, but she held up her hand and fixed her gaze on the Master, even though he refused to return it.

"Oh yeah?" she challenged. "Can't little babies teach the wise but old Teachers something new? Or is being taught something new by a young species merely the proof that the Teacher needs to retire? Perhaps that's it since he isn't grown-up enough to acknowledge that even babies become adults, given time—and that some are more grown-up than he could ever be."

At these words, he finally raised his gaze to meet hers and his eyes burned with fury. He straightened his back and, through clenched teeth, snapped, "Impertinent, aren't you?"

V'ritan rolled his eyes and groaned, but Stephanie wasn't there to fight. She was there to pass her test and move forward. Her focus on what was important, she didn't give him a chance to intervene. "What is the task? Or has your prejudice blocked your ability to carry out your role as a teacher?"

"Ridiculous," Tethis sputtered and seemed almost too angry to speak.

She shook her head, disgusted by his attitude. "Humans have played with the energies of the cosmos for hundreds of generations, regardless of whether you're capable of acknowledging it or not."

The Teacher pivoted between them, glared at her, then fixed the ambassador with such a fearsome look that V'ritan took a step back.

As if the man's retreat was some kind of signal, the Master called magic to his fingertips and released a whole universe of small dots to float around their heads. "What do you know of power? Have you held the glory of the cosmos in your body? Have you felt the sun melt you from the inside? Can you handle the pain of being burnt by a planet's fiery core as you focus your will?"

Stephanie pursed her lips, hating the idea that she had to prove herself to someone like this. Of course, he took her silence as a no. He also decided to prove his point by going forward with the testing.

"This will be over quickly, and both of you—" He eyed Stephanie and settled his gaze on V'ritan as he continued. "Both of you will agree that I will never accept another human for the testing for as long as I live…whether the king grants it or not."

He looked happy with that idea, then added, "And rest assured that I will live another hundred years simply to spite the hell out of the both of you."

The Mage whipped around and walked to a wide, open space to one side of the cave door. She followed him and stopped when he did and watched him use his staff to raise a battle stage from the depths of the earth.

The long stone platform had Meligornian etchings down the side, but Tethis ignored it. He pointed the staff from her to the platform to indicate that she should go up.

She remained silent and simply complied, but he launched a silent magical shot before she'd reached the second step. Nonchalantly, she waved it away and it chipped small pieces of stone off the edge of the platform as it struck.

At this, she did look at the Teacher, and their eyes met grimly as he continued the attack and hurled magical bullets, arrows, orbs, and darts at her.

Stephanie continued to climb onto the platform and fended off the missiles as they came. Tethis followed, walked carefully up the steps behind her, and continued his barrage until she worked so rapidly to block them that her hand moved in a blur. Finally, after she'd successfully defended herself against a hailstorm of spiked energy orbs, he lowered his hand.

In the brief moment of respite, she drew a deep breath and waited for the next part of the test. The Teacher held his hand up and scowled. "You will allow me to test your ability to contain power."

He pointed at a rock in front of her. "Hold it until I give you the signal. You cannot leave the circle I place around you."

Stephanie acknowledged his instruction with a brief dip of her chin and watched as he used the staff he wielded to generate a rigid line of magic and carve a tight ring around her. "If you cannot accomplish something, you must say, 'I submit!' Now, prepare yourself."

Without any more notice than that, he raised his hands and began to thrust power into her. She stood there and he observed her with a smirk as he expected to easily overcome her ability to hold the magic.

She had no doubt that, in his mind, there was no human alive or dead who could hold the kind of power a Meligornian could, much less a Master and Teacher of the Mysteries.

Rather than try to resist it, she braced herself, opened the wells inside her, and accepted every ounce of MU he poured into her.

While she had never heard of a being who could hold its own magic as well as the magic of a Master at the same time, she hadn't heard of anyone who could trade MU for gMU either. She was also sure that Tethis didn't have a clue about what she could do.

He certainly didn't know that she replaced the MU he delivered with the less concentrated gMU. As she absorbed wave after wave of the energy, the Teacher's face began to fall into doubt.

He stared as she grew stronger and more accepting. Finally, when he was almost out of power, he cut the flow and watched as she raised her head, a smile on her lips. With a frown, he continued to stare as she began to draw even more power from her surroundings.

The Master snarled with anger when she stood, spread her arms wide, and tilted her head back. He seemed mesmerized when she began to move her feet from side to side. Her body rippled like water and her arms swayed over her head as she coalesced and tightened the magic inside her.

While Tethis could not see that part of the process, he *could* see when her body began to glow and shimmers of bright light erupted from her eyes and mouth.

He banged his staff angrily on the boulder beside him. "Release it into the rock. Now!"

The large stone acted as a grounding rod to accept magic

from any magical being and release it into the ground below. Stephanie looked at the stone and focused on it.

Once she was sure she could control the power surging within, she pushed it out. The energy arced, a wild orgy of power that reached high into the air before it pounded into the stone. She continued to direct power outwards, aware of the shocked expression on the Teacher's face.

On the outside, she looked like a stern-faced mage, but inside, she was smiling. Little did Tethis know that she still held half as much again in the form of gMU.

The grounding stone glowed so brightly, it was hard to look at as the energy flowed into it, then over it to disappear into the soil beneath. As Stephanie steadily discharged her energy, the ground, too, began to glow until the grass smoked and the pebbles popped and hissed into nothing.

After several minutes—longer than it had taken to fill her— she finally let the last trace of MU trickle from her palms into the now glowing stone. She breathed in, exhaled the breath, and twisted her neck slowly from side to side. She felt almost a hundred pounds lighter, although magic was the kind of weight she didn't mind in the least.

The Teacher swung his arm out to the side and pointed at V'ritan. "You. Release all your energy as well. I won't have you tempted to interfere."

V'ritan chuckled quietly, not at all surprised at the old man's lack of trust. He made no protest and simply did as he was asked, walked over, and touched the stone.

He had yet to use any of the day's energy, but the flow didn't last as long as hers. Nor was it as bright.

When the ambassador had discharged his energy, he raised his hands to show he was done. Tethis motioned for him to step back and straightened to focus on Stephanie, sure that she was empty and without power. "Let's see what you have now."

The mage began to throw small rocks and propel them

toward her with magic. She dodged some and used minute amounts of energy to veer the others off their trajectory.

He guided one right, then left, and caught her across the cheek. She hissed and held one hand to the cut. Blood flowed between her fingers. Anger flared in her eyes, but she controlled it.

There was no way she would allow him to make her lose her temper.

At the shuttle, the team had emerged and lined up to watch the proceedings. When the rock struck Stephanie, they moved restlessly, and Lars laid a hand on Marcus's shoulder to stop him moving to intervene.

"Why does it look like he's trying to kill her?" Frog asked.

The team leader tried for nonchalant, but fury edged his answer. "He'll have to do a lot more than that."

As they watched, their expressions smoldering, Tethis continued to lift rocks and hurl them at Stephanie. He directed the magic with one hand, while he stretched the other out to pull more energy into himself.

In the circle, Stephanie shifted, and he slammed his staff down. "You are forbidden to pull even an ounce more energy."

Her lip twitched into what might have been a smirk, and the Teacher let the rocks he'd gathered drop to the ground. He glanced around him and finally stared at a massive rock three feet away.

"Uh oh," Lars muttered as the Mage gave a soft laugh and gestured with his hands to guide the massive rock into the air.

Lines of purple MU wreathed it as he moved it quickly into position some twenty feet above Stephanie's head.

She looked at it, then back at him, but displayed no fear. "So, your idea of testing me is to drain me of power and drop a rock so that I yell out and you win? How is that a test?"

His laughter echoed around them. "You stupid human. Do you really think I care whether it's *fair* or not? I'm fed up with this sham of a trial. It makes a mockery of all that is sacred. *Fair* doesn't even come close. The only fair thing to happen today will be that humans are seen as the unworthy, weak specimens they truly are."

This time, Lars had to grasp both Frog and Marcus. "Let Stephanie handle it," he ordered and kept his voice low as V'ritan protested.

"That isn't part of this—" the ambassador began, but Stephanie tapped her leg with her index finger and stared at him in a mute command for silence.

Before he could respond, she looked at Tethis and smiled. "Fair?" she asked, and Lars groaned. "Here it comes."

"All right, then. Let's *make* this fair."

He rolled his eyes and jerked his hand downward in a short crisp slice to command the boulder to descend as he released the magic holding it. He was about to turn away when the world skated around him and he slid into the circle with Stephanie.

The Mage gasped, raised his hands, and unleashed magic up and into the plummeting boulder, vaguely aware of shouts of alarm from the direction of the shuttle and the ambassador. Sweat beaded on his forehead as he brought the huge rock to a halt and held it suspended it over their heads.

A hasty glance at the girl revealed that she had her arms folded and a very satisfied grin on her face. It infuriated him beyond endurance. "How dare you? I will have your head, human."

He might have said more but the boulder shifted inside the magic and reminded him he had more important things to focus on. With a flick of his wrist, he attempted to hurl it out of the circle and away, but it didn't move.

He tried again and struggled to control it when it impacted an invisible boundary and bounced back. "Seluthor's ass!"

With a sharp upward gesture, he gave it more height and tried again to flick it aside, only to have it rebound once more. "Fornication of the Gold!"

That was clearly a reference to royalty, and Stephanie giggled. He snapped an angry glare in her direction, but she remained unfazed.

"Here's the thing," she told him, shimmered out of existence in front of him, and reappeared on his right, smiling slightly. "Since you chose to allow unfair testing, I'm testing you. As you have finally deduced, you can't push the rock outside the boundaries of the circle *you* set."

Her smile broadened. "So, here's how it will go. "We'll stay inside the circle as agreed, and I'll wait until you say that *you* submit."

She put her hands out to each side and rose into the air. Tethis watched her but found no suitable words and simply gaped in frustration and disbelief.

Her smile took on a wicked twist as she continued her airborne ascent. "See, you said nothing about me staying on the ground where I could be crushed."

Stephanie tutted reprovingly and finally touched the rock. "You really should be more thorough with your explanations, but by the looks of this boulder, there might not be a next time. Of course, that would be a shame since I'm sure you wonder where *my* power comes from considering you had me discharge all my MU."

At the feel of the rock above her, she flipped upside down, set her feet on its surface, and spun it so she now stood on top. Tethis grunted as the boulder shifted and her weight made it more difficult to hold aloft. He could feel his power waning, but she remained unperturbed. "Since you don't seem to be aware of what being a Teacher of the Mysteries means, I'm not sure I can show you how I do this. You know, since I'm from an immature species and all."

She moved and the boulder tilted again. The Mage dropped to

one knee as he struggled to control it. Frustration was followed by alarm and finally, defeat when he realized he either had to admit she was worthy or die proving she wasn't.

Stephanie looked over the edge at him and tapped her chin. "So, I'm up here. I need no more power to pass this test. I'm very aware of how much power you have left, and I have more than enough to keep you inside the circle. What will it be? Are you willing to die for your prejudice? Unable to see the future how it transpires? Either way, you will no longer be a Teacher of the Mysteries as witnessed by the king's right-hand advisor. Of course..." She grinned. "I could always start pushing from up here."

The ambassador covered his mouth and fought to hide a smile as Tethis gritted his teeth, not yet willing to give in.

She tilted her head to the side and flicked her finger down to direct a tiny ball of energy into the rock. A loud crack echoed, and the Mage shouted with alarm as it plummeted toward him.

He thrust his hands up and launched a massive surge of magic into the falling boulder to stop it from crushing him. When he had it mostly under control, he narrowed his eyes, turned his head, and glanced over his shoulder. "I hardly call that proof." He sneered, although it seemed strained.

Stephanie peered over the stone once more, her face twisted with frustrated anger. "The problem with old prejudicial idiots is they can't see when someone might hold the power of the cosmos to save thousands of lives."

She created multiple orbs of magic, large and small, and swirled them around the rock to emulate the universe. "When one feels the pain of a thousand suns, your useless ass seems inconsequential to the future good of the Mysteries. It might be time for you to suffer from your own idiocy."

The boulder pressed downwards, and Tethis shook with the effort. Suddenly, he dropped to his knees and cried, *"I submit!"*

His hands thumped onto the stone platform in front of his

knees and he fell forward, his eyes shut tightly against the expected blow. It didn't come.

Instead, he still knelt within the circle, very much alive and unscathed. He opened one eye and glanced upward to where the boulder hovered above him. As if it felt the weight of his gaze, the gigantic rock spun slowly until Stephanie, defying all the laws of physics, hung upside down, her feet planted firmly on its surface.

She didn't address him directly but turned to V'ritan. "Is this official?"

He nodded, his arms folded and an amused look on his face. "It is."

After a moment, she pushed off the boulder, executed a casual half-flip, and landed gracefully on her feet. She extended her hands to curl streams of magic around Tethis, lift him up, and carry him from the circle.

Once she had set him safely on his feet, she gestured with one hand and allowed the boulder to fall. Both she and the Teacher winced when it crashed behind them.

The mage retrieved his staff and used it for support as he pushed to his feet. Sweat poured down his forehead and soaked the front of his robes. He turned to V'ritan, his expression frustrated and weary. "Would you have allowed that to happen?"

The man smirked. "What was I supposed to do? You had me release my power, remember?"

Tethis stared at him in shock when he realized the ambassador had been so certain Stephanie could pass the test that he really *had* surrendered his stores of MU.

The other man had truly been unable to help him and would be able to say as much if he was later questioned. He rebuked himself mentally for not realizing that the ambassador had given in far too easily to his demand and walked toward his home, his head bowed and shoulders hunched.

"On your head, V'ritan," he conceded, his tone almost a growl.

"She has passed the last of the tests and my time of teaching is over."

Stephanie approached V'ritan, put her arm on his shoulder, and watched the old man shuffle toward the cave. She shook her head. "He needs to know."

He frowned. "Know what?"

She walked after the Teacher and called to him. "Master Tethis."

At first, he ignored her, but she tried again.

"Master Tethis."

He stopped and stood perfectly still before he turned to look at the girl who had vanquished him. She clasped her hands in front of her as she addressed him. "Please. Pay attention and learn."

To his astonishment, she gave him a soft, sad smile and her eyes turned pitch black as she began to move her hands to produce ribbons of purple and blue energy. They twisted and spiraled to create a curtain of colors and bounding energy.

With a happier smile, she leaned into the magic and moved her entire body in a dance that reflected the universe. Her eyes remained a pure, fathomless black and her magic flickered and sparkled.

"Welcome to the cosmos," she said, her voice pitched low although it echoed around them.

She swayed rhythmically, raised one hand, and drew downwards to pull wisps of pure black energy from the sky and weave it through the purple and blue. When the three colors mingled, she wound it around the boulder Tethis had threatened to crush her with and tossed it high.

The guys' jaws dropped as it soared through Meligorn's purple skies and out into space. V'ritan and Tethis gasped in astonishment when it vanished from sight. They exchanged glances and looked at Stephanie.

The ambassador's eyes were as big as saucers, and Tethis

gaped like a beached fish but she ignored them. She had long since come to the conclusion that no matter what she did, people would be shocked.

V'ritan looked at the sky and snorted. "I hope there weren't any ships in the way."

The Mage searched the sky for the rock's return but finally concluded that it was gone. He stared at her. "You could have stopped it at any time."

She met his eyes and nodded. "Yes."

He continued to use his staff for support as he edged toward her. "You sought to make me admit my prejudices and insisted on teaching me what I didn't want to see."

"Yes." She nodded again.

The old man fell silent and his hand stroked his long white hair while he looked at the ground. He stayed like that for several minutes before he slowly lifted his gaze and studied her face.

Tethis met her eyes without flinching and noted that they had transformed to their normal blue. "Thank you, Master Morgana."

With a bow of his head, he turned away and took a few more steps toward his front door before he looked over his shoulder. "Please, come again some time. We shall speak of the Mysteries." He focused on V'ritan and curled his lip. "But leave him behind. He can be a pain in the ass."

She covered her mouth to hide a smile and the ambassador shrugged and made no effort to hide his grin. He waved goodbye to the Mage, but the old man merely flapped a hand in dismissal and turned away.

Tethis vanished into his house without looking back, and Stephanie and V'ritan returned to the shuttle pad. The team boarded ahead of them and Lars waited at the door as she stepped inside.

As she reached the top step, her knees went weak and she staggered slightly. The Meligornian caught her by the arm and helped her to regain her footing.

"Sorry," she murmured as he guided her to the seat at the front. "Who knew throwing a rock into space required so much energy?"

He chuckled but she slumped in her seat, pulled the safety harness over her shoulders, and snapped it in place. As the pilot warmed the engines, she looked out at Tethis' door.

Foreboding washed over her in a chill wave, and she shivered. She wrapped her arms around herself as she stared at her companion. "Something is coming, and we will need all our peoples to fight it. There is no reason to ignore the old because I'm pissed at them."

"Yes, Master Morgana," he replied and smirked when she rolled her eyes at him. "Get used to it. It is your new title here on Meligorn. Besides, it could be much worse. I *am* aware of some of the nicknames given on Earth over the centuries."

Stephanie smiled. "Like what?"

V'ritan stared out the window as the ship lifted into the air and turned for the return journey. As they accelerated, he wrinkled his nose in thought. "Some girl was called Snookie generations ago. And I think there was a Woogie too, but they didn't know each other. Snookie lived in New Jersey and Woogie liked a woman named Mary. It is all very strange."

"No. Snookie only *visited* New Jersey," Frog interrupted from behind the seat. "She *lived* in New York. You have to get these things right or you'll upset someone."

She caught the startled look on the ambassador's face and all she could do was laugh.

CHAPTER SEVEN

A network of corridors, cells, and chambers existed deep beneath the royal palace. Unknown to the public, they were lit by magical flame and seen by very few.

Temerl's screams echoed along them and reverberated from the stone. In a small chamber, held in place by chains, he stopped and leaned his head back against the wall. He breathed heavily and winced with every movement.

Four guards stood before him and watched as the Truth Bringer dropped his hands and stumbled back. Skilled in mental magic, the Truth Bringer's task was to find information from another's mind—regardless of their target's wishes.

The interrogator leaned against a small wooden table and watched as the once-head of the Royal Guards let his chin drop to his chest and dangled awkwardly in the chains. Sweat rivered down his bare chest. The Truth Bringer turned away, poured himself a glass of water, and used a nearby towel to mop the sweat from his own face.

When he set both towel and glass down and turned back, Temerl shook his head. "No more."

He lifted his lip in a snarl and glared at the prisoner. "Then tell us."

The guard shook his head and straightened in the chains. He curled his hands into fists, raised his head, and squared his chin. "No."

The Truth Bringer sighed and walked over to the wall. "Making me find the answers is not fun for anyone involved. You'll have your mind broken apart and I—" He swallowed and pursed his lips. "I have to tear apart the head of someone I've known and respected all my life."

He stopped in front of the traitor and took a deep breath, then raised his hands. "But…have it your way."

His expression regretful, he pushed his sleeves up, stepped forward to press a hand on each side of Temerl's head, and rested his thumbs on the guard's forehead. He exhaled slowly, closed his eyes, and eased into the would-be assassin's mind. It was a simple matter to return to the fortified point he'd discovered earlier, and he probed further while Temerl fought him and screamed in agony as the barrier began to shatter.

The Truth Bringer groaned as the guard attempted to block him, then attacked in return. The defense caught him off-guard and slashed at his mind and he roared in pain and drew back.

When he opened his eyes, the guard's lips had curled in satisfaction, even though his breath came in pained gasps. The interrogator glared at him. "This would be a lot easier on both of us if you would tell us without making us do this."

When the prisoner made no response, he continued. "This isn't good for either of us, but since I'm not the one who tried to kill someone against the king's wishes, I'll worry less about your pain than mine."

He took another deep breath, returned to his gruesome task, and pressed his fingertips to the guard's head. This time, the barrier broke, and he found what he was looking for. "There are connections galaxy-wide," he murmured, and shock etched his tones. "Nobles on Meligorn, but Darian Vaucluse is an Earth name and Brageth is Dreth, Senmele of the House Merilon, Thomas McGuire of Epsilon Enterprises... Karath mor—"

He flinched and his words cut into a sudden scream. His fingers dropped from Temerl's forehead and his body crumpled.

At the same time, the traitor shuddered briefly in his chains and released a long, rasped breath before he went limp. Blood glistened as it trickled from his nose and ears.

Two of the guards nearby scrambled toward the interrogator, who shook violently before he fell unconscious. Another ran for the internal comms and requested a healer.

The fourth crouched beside the Truth Bringer and rested his fingers lightly on the Mage's forehead. After a moment's silence, he looked up in fear. "His mind was still connected when Temerl died. He is alive but lost inside his own soul."

As a medical team raced to aid the Truth Bringer and Temerl's body was prepared for cremation, Stephanie and her team celebrated. Inside their quarters, food had been brought and laid out in a buffet.

With three days until the awards ceremony, the team celebrated her recognition as a Mage and advancement to Master within the Mage hierarchy, but it prepared for the ceremony, as well. The palace had offered its assistance to ensure they were ready, and it hadn't taken no for an answer.

Earth champagne had been brought from the Space Station Alerus, and the cats were on their best behavior. The palace had sent its tailors to measure the entire team for "clothes fit for the ceremony" and they worked amidst the cheerful chaos.

The guys stood on small pedestals as Meligornians measured, pinned, and altered. They roamed the suite in tracksuits and dressing gowns and responded willingly when they were called.

Frog held a chicken wing in his hand and ate while three tailors worked on his trouser legs. "This is seriously awesome. I am here, getting fat, while people dress me. This must be what being a king is like."

Lars snorted. "Oh yeah. That and the responsibility of ruling an entire planet, but hey, simply getting to eat chicken on a pedestal is the highlight of his day."

The other man shrugged. "It would be mine."

He yelped and almost fell off his perch. One of the tailors helped to rebalance him and apologized profusely for mishandling the pin.

Stephanie walked out of her room and looked at the uniforms hung on separate stands beside each team member. She whistled when she traced her hand over the fabric and noted the details.

Each uniform had two additional stripes to signify their membership of a special group associated with both the Meligornians and the Dreth. As Johnny dragged his shirt over his head, he ran his finger over the sigil on the outside. "What's this for?"

The tailors all shook their heads to indicate their ignorance and continued to focus on their work. He glanced at his teammates, who simply shrugged.

A couple of days later, on the morning of the awards ceremony, Marcus stood with his chest out and uniform on and admired himself in the mirror. "This probably means Order of the Ballbusters."

Johnny blinked and looked unimpressed. "Right, maybe if those giving us medals were fraternity brothers."

Everyone laughed and finished getting dressed. They inspected each other to make sure they looked perfect but paused when there was a knock at the door. Lars and Marcus answered it as the others formed up around Stephanie.

"Time to go, guys," Lars told them and gestured with his head to a squad of Royal Guard waiting outside. They were led to the throne room, surrounded by guards dressed in formal uniforms.

Their path took them through halls where the castle servants wore silken robes and fresh flowers. As they walked in, they were struck speechless at the scene.

Pictures of each member of the team standing proudly in their Meligornian colors floated along the path to the throne. Between each picture stood a pair of royal guards.

One of those closest to the door caught Stephanie's look of astonished awe and winked at her. Her nerves settled, and she gave him a brief smile before she stepped forward with the team and continued to admire the décor.

Lavish draperies had been magically hung on the walls and each depicted a key scene in history for each planet in the Federation. One of Meligorn's was Stephanie fighting in the ship, while the Dreth pirate ship sailed into the distance to explode by their own bomb.

"I look good." Brenden smiled as he walked past his portrait.

They reached the front of the throne room and all dropped to one knee before the king and queen of Meligorn, V'ritan and his wife, and the Earth ambassadors—at which she flinched when she realized she hadn't even thought of inviting them. Even the Federation Navy and the Dreth were present. They all smiled at the team and the women held small posies of flowers.

The ceremony began with the throaty blare of a loud horn. The team rose and stood with their hands clasped in front. Their faces remained impassive while each woman—including the queen—dropped their flowers at her feet.

Lars leaned over to whisper to her. "Is this some kind of fertility spell? Because if so, if I were you, I'd hold off on…boop… you know…"

She giggled and shook her head. "They're thanking me for the children who aren't allowed at the ceremony. It's custom."

The king remained standing while everyone else found their places sat. He walked in front of the team. "Today, I honor not only a very brave security team, but a woman who has redefined the laws of Magic, spat in the face of her enemies, and focused solely on saving the lives of others."

He looked directly at Stephanie and continued. "Stephanie Morgana, you are here today because you saved my ambassador's life from an assassination attempt on Earth. You yourself were injured, along with two of your guards." He motioned for Lars and Marcus to step forward beside her.

The team loved it, but their eyes shifted constantly to monitor the room and the groups of people who watched the ceremony. Among the VIPs in the upper tiers, they caught sight of Federation Navy uniforms but couldn't look more closely without being obvious.

The throne room was totally different than the amphitheater Elizabeth had set her unwinnable scenario in, but they couldn't relax. Thanks to that simulation, they were programmed to expect an attack.

Even though they had already captured one of the main traitors and were in the green, they refused to relax their vigilance. While they knew they had reached a point of solidarity with the Royal Guard, nothing could convince them to stand down.

The queen and Elza, the ambassador's wife, sat beside one another as the king addressed the gathering. Neither of the women had met Stephanie or even seen her until she'd entered the throne room, yet they could both feel the power radiating off her.

It brushed against them and the two Meligornian women exchanged a glance before they each reached instinctively to hold hands.

The king addressed Stephanie, oblivious to their unease. "Your bravery is beyond anything we have seen in many years, and it reminds us that we are not alone as we once thought. Your actions show that not only can humans and Meligornians work together to defeat a greater foe, but it also reassures us that humans can be relied on to help us in times of need."

He looked at her with a warm smile. "You, Stephanie, and your men, are bright stars in a galaxy that can seem terribly dark. We are glad to know there are those who will fight wrong where they find it and protect what's good, regardless of its form."

His pause was the perfect length to give his audience time to assimilate what he'd said. "That is why we are awarding you the Modfresha Garghilum—which, in English, means the Medal of the Valiant Soul. The guards who were with you on that occasion will be awarded the Meligorn Modfresha Ghila, Meligorn's Medal of Valor, at our request. We invited you so we could honor you and your men with these awards."

He focused his gaze on the people in the auditorium. "That award creates a connection for you between our world and yours, but I have chosen to raise the bar with another award. This one acknowledges your role in saving the lives of thousands aboard the *Meligorn Dreamer*, including the lives of many Meligornian citizens."

He looked into Stephanie's face, his gaze intense. "To express our gratitude, I award you the Royal Award of Decarth, a medal given only to the greatest of Meligorn's heroes and only ever awarded to a citizen of Meligorn. With this award, we offer you dual citizenship with Meligorn. Do you accept?"

She was momentarily stunned but recovered quickly. Snippets of half-remembered conversation in her hospital room drifted back to her and she managed a shaky smile. "I do."

As she knelt in a full bow before him, shock rippled through the Meligornians in the audience before they erupted into applause. Behind the king, the Federation Navy ambassadors exchanged glances with their Earth counterparts and their reaction clearly showed that they had definitely not expected the award.

"Furthermore," he added and moved to stand in front of Lars, "Meligorn recognizes that no hero acts alone and that we are honored with more than one human willing to sacrifice everything to keep our citizens safe. There are many witnesses to the risks you took to keep the *Meligorn Dreamer's* crew and passengers safe and to rescue the ship from certain destruction. We would be honored to accept six more heroes as citizens of our world if you are willing."

The expressions on the guys' faces would have been funny if the occasion weren't so serious, and she wondered how they would respond. It was a relief when they all dropped to their knees before the king and accepted their award and Meligornian citizenship.

As they returned slowly to their feet, he extended his arm toward Ambassador Jaleck. "I am, however, not the only one who sees your worth and honor. Ambassador Jaleck from Dreth wishes to express her planet's appreciation."

The ambassador stepped forward and gave Stephanie a kind smile, a far cry from her usual emotionless mask. She was followed by a younger Dreth who carried a royal-blue cushion on which lay a shining medal.

She stopped in front of her and lifted the award so it could be seen. It was made up of two Dreth Eagle Talons holding a large bunch of flowers.

The ambassador placed it back on the cushion and began to speak. "Long ago, before destruction and mayhem laid waste to our world, Dreth was considered as beautiful as Meligorn. The flowers on this medal are tussle leaves, now extinct but once laid at the feet of Dreth's heroes. We are proud to meet you and to award you the Talon of the Families for your protection of the Dreth on the *Meligorn Dreamer.*"

Gasps and surprised murmurs issued from the assembly as she spoke and stunned silence as she continued. At a nod, a second Dreth came forward.

This one also bore a cushion, but a book rested on this one. Jaleck opened and gazed out at the crowd. "This is part of a report from one of the Dreth aboard." She cleared her throat before she began to read.

"I do not know what she was doing in the corridor outside my cabin, but I am glad she was there. The pirates had broken the door down. They were fellow Dreth, yet they intended to kill us. I offered them everything I had to leave, but they wanted none of it. They had come for blood and ours would do, but then she arrived.

"I had picked up a chair since weapons were forbidden us and we prepared to end our days well. My wife and children had armed themselves with what they could find, but what good a towel rail and toy krifton would do against armor and blasters, I do not know.

"Our ends were guaranteed, it seemed, but in the next moment, they were not.

"Magic crackled in the hall outside as they raised their blasters. They fired, and it was the last thing they did. Shields of purple fire appeared between us and them before balls of purple fire engulfed them and they were gone.

"Her Right Hand looked in on us, then closed the cabin door. His eyes burned like blue flame. 'Stay here,' he ordered. 'We will keep you safe.'

"And by Hrageth's sacred stars, they did. They saved us all."

As she closed the book, everyone in the audience clapped and cheered. When they calmed, Ambassador Jaleck took the pin and held it up. "Stephanie Morgana, we wish to honor you with this medal. However, to accept it, you must accept citizenship of Dreth, which we also offer. We humbly request that you accept our honor and become a tri-citizen of the Federation."

Again, the audience applauded and again, Jaleck waited for the noise to settle. "You will represent all known sentient beings in the universe, and there is no doubt in my mind that as other species emerge and our friends and allies spread, you will become part of their planetary history as well."

Stephanie smiled and nodded. "I would be honored."

Several Dreth marched out onto the stage and lined up beside

Jaleck, holding pins in their hands. Jaleck nodded at the team. "And we have decided that true heroism begins with the support and selflessness of the men who fight beside you. Therefore, we honor your guard with the Talon of Soldiers for their fighting spirit and protection of all that is good."

The guys were all shocked, but the ambassador wasn't finished. "These, too, require that you accept citizenship with Dreth and become tri-citizens of the Federation. We would be honored if you would accept."

As one, the team laid their fists over their hearts. "The honor is ours."

At their response and the pride her team had stirred in her, she had to hold back a tear.

Once the last medal was pinned in place, the king stepped forward to stand beside Jaleck. He addressed the audience. "Please join me in welcoming our new citizens, the first of three worlds."

He turned to her and the team. "Citizens, heroes, please turn and accept your welcome."

Facing the gathered Meligornian, Dreth, and human dignitaries was almost overwhelming, as was the applause. When it finally ended, the king invited them all to a special reception where they mingled, met dignitaries, sipped drinks, and were congratulated and celebrated.

Once the initial crush was over, she approached the queen and bowed in greeting. The Meligornian royal bowed in return. When she saw the queen was accompanied by the ambassador's wife, Stephanie bowed to her as well.

"We have very much looked forward to meeting you," the queen said. "Knowing there is someone who will stand for all that is good warms me. You don't see it often these days."

The ambassador's wife leaned forward and kissed Stephanie's cheek. "V'ritan has told me so much about you. And you have woken a part of him I haven't seen since…well, not for a long time. Thank you."

She shook her head. "He has been immeasurably important to me. He has encouraged me and spoken to me of magic when there was no-one else who could. He's kept me pushing forward and protected me when I was hurt and in need of sanctuary. I will always keep him, and you, and everyone as safe as I can."

The queen touched her arm. "And we are here for you. We are here to help you. While we may seem too important to care, that is not the case. You are valuable and we are here for you. Meligornian rulers fight for the future as well. We don't simply send others to do it for us."

Stephanie smiled. "I never doubted it."

The queen looked at the crowd and shook her head. "When unique things happen, like your arrival, it means the universe is entering tumultuous times."

She nodded. "This, I already know."

The queen tilted her head and glanced at the ambassador's wife. "How is that?"

In answer, the energy rose so swiftly that Stephanie could barely stand. Her eyes turned quickly to black and her voice lowered and flowed like a small breeze, soft but powerful. "When the world needs her, a Morgana will rise to help. I am that Morgana, only this time, it isn't only my world that needs help, but all those who are in the Federation."

CHAPTER EIGHT

Silence followed Stephanie's oddly foreboding reply. For a moment, neither Elza nor the queen moved, then the ambassador's wife linked arms with her and took her around the room to meet and greet important Meligornian and Dreth individuals. The queen joined them on her other side.

"Come, there's someone you need to meet."

Elza exchanged glances with her sovereign, who smiled. Before she could say anything, though, her attention was caught by a lady who waited nearby. With a half-suppressed sigh, she touched her arm in farewell.

"I'll leave you in Elza's capable hands," she told her. "Duty calls."

The Queen drew a breath, stilled, and turned. She somehow became more queenlike as she responded to the woman who waited for her attention. The other woman tugged on her arm and led her to an older Meligornian dressed in bright green robes shot through with silver.

"This is Meligorn's leader of faith and spirituality. We have very practical beliefs, but we do understand that the universe gives us energy and that magic fuels everything on this planet," she explained and touched his arm to draw his attention to Stephanie. "High Priest Gigfore, I'd like you to meet Master Morgana."

He shook Stephanie's hand with a smile. "And I bet no one needs to tell you of the universe's energy, Master. I bet you can feel it running through your veins."

She was taken aback that he appeared to sense her power, but she managed a smile. "I do. It is amazing and so different to what there is on Earth."

"Well, if you ever wish to attend some of our meditations, let me know," he replied.

Knowing a dismissal when she heard one, she nodded to him and they moved on. At the sight of a flamboyantly dressed figure moving toward them, Elza leaned close and murmured, "This woman is obviously human and owns a very large house on the Lakes of Delgore, west of here. She is quite overdone so please, go with it."

Stephanie chuckled at the woman—loud, older, and dressed as though she'd stepped out of 1800s Earth in a long gown and corset. Her manners, however, were not 1800s Earth, and she greeted her with a sturdy handshake. "You are even cuter in person. I hoped we would meet. I am having a little soiree next weekend if you are still on Meligorn. We would love for you to attend."

With a very polite smile, she nodded. "Thank you, although my schedule is uncertain at the moment. If we are able to make it, we'll give you a call beforehand. I'm sure Elza knows how to contact you."

"Oh yes, honey." The woman covered her hand with both of hers and shook it again. "Elza is my *favorite* guest."

She released her and twirled, and the two women giggled together as they watched her go. Her forwardness and flirtation and wildly huge cleavage were definitely a little over the top. When they stopped their promenade through the room, they remained close and observed those around them. Some had clearly drunk too much of the wine.

Elza shook her head. "Oh, this is too much fun. Some of these people are seriously not from any of the three planets. I don't know where they came from, but no one really wants to claim them."

Stephanie was about to reply when a deep Dreth voice interrupted her.

"You!" it bellowed from beside her.

Elza glanced over and drew herself to her full height, and her face took on an imperious look. The Dreth snorted, ignored her, and poked his finger into Stephanie's shoulder. "You, witch. You aren't really that strong."

The ambassador's wife looked around, obviously trying to find security. "Let me—"

She shook her head and patted the woman's arm. "It's all right, I've got this."

Before her companion could reply, she turned to the Dreth and stared at him. His slight sway and lowered eyelids meant he'd spent way too many hours at the open bar. From the look on his face, he wanted to fight her.

His forehead furrowed in concentration as he studied her and tried to stay upright. She wondered how many of her he could see and moved slightly closer as she tapped her fingertips together. "Do you know the problem with those who believe strength rules?"

He sneered and lowered his huge head as though to hear her. "What?"

A few feet away, Jaleck closed her eyes, rubbed her temples, and snapped her fingers to some of the Dreth soldiers who had accompanied her. "One damned night, Vishlog. You didn't have to show your ass. I will put you in chains for a month."

Stephanie ignored the Dreth ambassador and stared at

Vishlog. She knew her eyes were turning black, and his mouth dropped open slightly to confirm it.

She pulled her hand in front of her chest and held her pointer and middle fingers together, folding the rest against her palm. With a slight swipe of her fingers, she sent him into a slide, back into the center of the room. Everyone stopped to watch as she flicked the same two fingers upward.

His face filled with shock as his feet lifted off the ground and he began to float toward the ceiling. He milled his arms and legs wildly in an effort to stay upright. She sauntered forward and stared at him with her hands on her hips. "Strength requires friction, or it does you no good."

The Dreth guards ran over and grasped his legs. They all looked at her. "We are very sorry. He's had too much to drink and he's a handful even without that."

Stephanie smiled. "It's nothing." She shrugged. "We all have issues. At least he's honest, as I find most Dreth to be. I'd rather know it than have it hidden."

With a slow swipe of her fingers, she floated him into the guards' hands. Once his feet were on the ground, they dragged him through the crowds and removed him from the party.

Jaleck made her way over, shaking her head. "Here, let me give you my contact information in case you need me. Vishlog is excellent when he is fighting. When he isn't, he occasionally becomes a problem. I didn't realize he was in the presentation squad this evening. Or that he thought booze and being an honor guard went well together."

She held out her small tablet and the ambassador tapped it twice with hers to add her contact details. Despite her initial surprise, she didn't really mind Vishlog's behavior. He hadn't been dangerous, merely obnoxious, and she'd dealt with *that* easily enough. "It really wasn't a big deal. I've had to deal with idiocy by intoxication a few times."

The Dreth chuckled. "As all women have. That's why we stick together, even across species."

A couple of Federation Navy high-level officers shuffled closer to the two women and pretended nonchalant conversation as they attempted to listen in. However, when Jaleck left shortly after, they approached Stephanie immediately and introduced themselves.

The one on the right shook her hand stoutly. "I am Admiral Burtch, and this is Vice Admiral Alexander. You know, with your skill and your spirit, you would be very useful to the Federation Navy. You could serve your home planet and keep saving lives as you seem to like doing."

She smiled politely and noticed V'ritan standing behind them. He caught her glance and gave her a wink. She focused on Burtch and Alexander.

Speaking firmly, she made her answer clear. "As I've explained before, I don't do well with being told what to do. So, while I have a choice, I don't think the Navy is right for me, however much I respect the organization."

A galaxy away, heads of the Federation military gathered in a board room on Star Base Notaro, while a young petty officer hurried to find the specialist on Meligorn Intelligence.

"Chief, they are ready to meet," he said when he found Matthias Winthrop staring at the screen in the wardroom.

"Thank you." Winthrop rose, tucked his hat under his arm, and set off for the meeting.

The military heads had already settled themselves around the table. He had been called in because of his specialty. The chief took a seat and one of the officers stood and activated a large holographic screen in front of them.

"Our partners in the royal household provided us with this," he said by way of introduction and started the recording.

Together, they watched as the Truth Bringer drew information from the ex-head of the Royal Guard. It was a shock when the interrogator began to repeat the data out loud, relying on the recording equipment to catch it. Those gathered experienced even greater shock when both Meligornians suffered seizures.

The film stopped immediately after the guard died and the Truth Bringer fell to the floor.

The officer paused the presentation. "The Truth Bringer you see there suffered some kind of mental episode in which he suffered a sensory overload. They are not supposed to be connected when a Meligornian dies. All their memories, apparently, leave the body, and if there is a vessel touching, they will flood it. He is currently in a coma."

He swiped his hand through the air to move to the next screen which displayed the information they had retrieved from the traitor before he died. "These are the snatches of information he acquired before the guard died. This is key because it is imperative that the Navy determines who we have close to the chapter of insurgents. We need to know where we stand and what we need to do to assist in the eradication of this menace. I have forwarded a copy of the information to your tablets, and I think it would be best if you paired off and began to run different hypotheses. This will be a long night."

The chief stared at the names and numbers that appeared on his tablet's screen and his sharp mind already discerned the code.

On the edge of the Meligorn capital, a Meligornian army captain and his team boarded their shuttle. Dressed in black powered armor and armed to the teeth, they flew swiftly to a drop point not far from Stremel, a large town a day's drive from the capital.

Everyone was silent and ready. Their task was to hunt insurgents and the data said their targets would meet at a small bar on Stremel's outskirts. After fifteen minutes' flight time, the shuttle slowed.

The captain unstrapped and swirled his arm over his head to signal their arrival. Doors in the shuttle's belly dropped open and each of the men caught a line and slid out. They landed carefully on the roof of a Meligornian bar and hoped the music inside was playing loudly enough to mask their arrival.

A block away, the second and third teams set down in empty lots nearby and worked their way toward the target. As quietly as they could, the first team slipped over the edge of the roof and onto the balcony that ran around the outside of the second floor. From there, they slid through the doors into the building and made their way down toward the bar.

Once in position, they waited for the other two teams to signal that they were ready. The confirmation came and the inside team kicked their way into the bar and immediately proceeded to a small booth tucked away in a corner. Before they could reach it, one of the men seated there saw them.

He put his drink down and stood, shuffled out around the table, and walked to the door. Four members of the team split off to intercept him while more Meligornians emerged from the booth.

These made absolutely no effort to leave quietly but simply bolted for whatever exit they could reach. The team separated into two groups to pursue them.

Movement erupted around the bar. Some patrons dived under tables and others scrambled to the door. The barman and waitstaff vanished through the entrance to the kitchen when someone fired a shot and all hell broke loose.

Laughter died even though the music continued to play. Drinks were abandoned and shattered as magic, energy bolts, and solid rounds missed their intended targets and wreaked collateral devastation.

Tables were overturned and chairs were thrown. Meals bounced and jostled under the impact of the shots fired, and shouts of alarm and anger filled the air.

Of those Meligornians who ran, most were caught by the teams waiting on the outside. The chaos was short-lived and order was restored as the bar's patrons were brought back to the club.

When sullen silence reigned, the captain came to stand beside the other team's leader. "We killed a few, and one of my team is receiving medical attention but probably won't pull through." His expression was bleak, but he finished firmly. "The targets are secured."

The team leader nodded and spoke into his coms. "Bring in the TB."

After a short silence, the sound of a military transport growled and rumbled closer. It was followed by the slam of a door and several footsteps, which ended when a robed Meligorn Mind Mage entered and approached the team leaders.

He looked around and addressed the captain. "They will remember one hell of a bar brawl involving a couple of human soldiers and some renegade Dreth. Wait for me outside."

They signaled their men to follow them out, and the Truth Bringer went to work. When he emerged, he addressed the captain directly. "The military were never there. Take me home."

CHAPTER NINE

Todd and his team, dressed for battle, slunk through the back alleys and around the edges of corroded street corners. Together, they made their way to the objective. They had all seen some shitty towns in their time, but this one took the cake.

On this mission, they worked their way through the sleaze district of an outpost in the middle of nowhere. He maintained a constant lookout for anyone or anything that might pose a threat to the team—or try to warn their target.

One of his teammates sneered as he stepped over a puddle of black liquid on the ground. "I feel like I'll catch an incurable disease simply by breathing."

"I'm fairly sure that even if we held our breath, two months from now, we would still all test positive for some crazy venereal disease," he replied, as a couple concluded their hot and heavy business in an alcove. "We should all wear full rubber suits."

"If you think this is bad, wait until you see the target." One of the other guys chuckled. "I bet he is *really* pretty."

He shivered and hefted his weapon as they moved quietly through the streets. Windows were locked shut and light leaked around drawn curtains and pulled shutters. The few people on the streets seemed to ignore or avoid them.

When the chief had told them today's scenario involved a dirty job, they'd assumed it was merely a saying, not an *actual* dirty job. Nonetheless, they were so close to completing VR training that they were all ready to get down and dirty with the real thing.

"His name is Troy Murdock," the chief had explained. "He used to be some good boy businessman until he became involved in the arms race. Now, while he might still wear a suit, this boy's hands are covered in blood."

He'd fixed them with a hard stare. "You're to go in, download his current inventory and contacts, and take him out nice and quiet. He'll be replaced by one of ours so we can net the rest of his buyers.

"But that is not your concern." He moved his gaze from one to the next to make sure they understood. "You only need to remove him. He tends to hang out with a few thugs and on dirty hooker laps but at this hour, they're not at their best."

Ahead of Todd, the leader put his fist up and patted his hand down. They all squatted, and the man indicated a building across the street.

"We'll head in the south entrance, up the—"

Before he could finish, the scene flickered around them and slowly faded to leave them in the white room. They stood and waited, knowing that something was up. The chief came up on the screen. For a moment, he was unaware he was live and looked preoccupied before he looked directly at them

"Prepare for extraction from your pod," he said and deactivated the screen off before they could ask why.

Todd felt a little dizzy and closed his eyes. When he opened them, he was in his pod and one of his teammates had popped the lid.

"Thanks." He pulled himself out and rubbed the back of his

neck before he joined the rest of the guys as they followed the team leader into the briefing room across the hall.

Once they'd settled, the viewscreen activated to show a live feed of the captain. He had muted his mic to talk to several men gathered around him while he passed folders to each of them.

When he was done, he looked at the screen and nodded dismissal to the others. The team came to attention as he walked around his desk, sat on the edge of it, and turned the sound on. "Good morning."

The team immediately responded. "Good morning, Captain."

He nodded. "At ease, gentlemen. You're all probably wondering why you were pulled from your pods. Well, I have some good news for you today."

The guys waited, and he cleared his throat and forced a smile. "Congratulations, you have successfully passed the Federation Navy training. You are to report immediately to Section Twelve for your orders. You met all your training objectives early and we see no reason to make you mark time when we need you on deck. It's a brave new world out there, gentlemen, and you should be proud to know you'll be protecting it. Good luck and God speed."

The team stood to attention as the captain sketched them a salute before he ended the feed. For a moment, they stood in utter silence, their expressions mirrors of disbelief. They jumped as the chief stormed into the room and clapped impatiently. "You heard the captain. Get your asses moving. You have three minutes to pack your sea bags and get the hell out of my building. I got recruits to terrorize and you ain't them. Move! Move! Move!"

Faced with his bullying, the guys galvanized into action. They jogged out of the briefing room and down the hall to the barracks.

Without much talk, they hauled their stuff out of their lockers and shoved it into their bags before they cleared their barracks and headed for Section Twelve. The guy beside Todd shook his head. "This is weird, man."

Todd shrugged. "Why?"

"'Cause this ain't the way it goes, dude," he said, his expression worried. "Seriously, has anyone ever heard of FedNav pulling newbies out of the training program early?"

One of the others scoffed. "Not since training consisted of being put in trashcans and rolled down hills. So, no, not since the Federation took over. I guess we'll find out soon enough."

The leader shrugged. "We met their training objectives. I guess they really need us out there."

He turned to the team and raised his voice in a bellow. "Have we got this?"

The team responded with a roar of their own. "Hell, yes! We got this."

"Then let's go prove it."

They broke into a run toward Section Twelve and whatever their future might hold. A little disappointingly after that brief flurry of excitement, they were ushered into another briefing room and told to wait.

Todd pulled out the print copy of Stephanie's letter and his heart fluttered momentarily when he thought about her warning.

"Don't worry," he whispered and shoved the letter back into his bag. "I won't die anytime soon."

CHAPTER TEN

In another briefing room on a different planet, the door opened and the king of Meligorn strode in. His new head of security, Sho, and V'ritan waited and rose when he arrived.

He waved his hand and shook his head, and they resumed their seats. No one talked until more security measures had been deployed.

Once that had been completed, the monarch walked to the front and scanned the room using long rays of energy. The magic was designed to search for any bugs or cameras that could have been missed during Sho's initial check. It was a relief when it came back clean.

He returned to the door, punched in a code, and placed his palm against the plate on the wall beside it. This action was followed by the sound of heavy locks clicking into place.

Once they were secured, he unbuttoned his top robe and walked over to sit at the table. "Now we know that no one is privy to our conversations. After the last betrayal, I can't help but be cautious."

V'ritan shook his head. "No apology needed, Grilfir. We completely understand."

The king folded his hands in front of him. "First of all, thank you, Sho, for stepping into the head security position. I am sorry it is under such circumstances. Now, what do you have for me?"

The Meligornian pulled out two files. "Well, your Highness, based on the information we were able to extract from the insurgents we captured, there is another larger group inside the capital."

He paused to allow the information to sink in. "It seems they no longer lurk in the ditches and hedgerows or hide on the outskirts. They mingle at the highest levels and have no shame in it. Commander Galofrel is not here because he believes he has a mole inside his forces. He is currently trying to decide how to smoke them out."

King Grilfir leaned back, rubbed his fingers across his lips, and shook his head. "That makes the situation much more difficult to manage. We'll have to keep him in the dark, I'm afraid, which means we lose the resources of the entire Fast Response Squad."

He groaned and buried his face in his hands before he scrubbed his palms over his cheeks and raised his head with a heavy sigh. "In fact, we'll have to keep them entirely in the dark until they've fixed their leaks. We'll need someone from outside Meligorn for this. I simply don't know who to ask, given the sensitivity of the situation. Perhaps one of the more *discreet* mercenary companies...."

V'ritan shifted in his chair and considered their options, his eyes narrowed. Finally, he spoke quietly. "Leave it to me, your Highness. I'll take care of this one."

The king nodded and V'ritan stood, bowed to his sovereign, and strode to the door. He acknowledged Sho with a brief dip of the head but stopped abruptly when he reached the door.

"Grilfir..."

The king raised his head and realized the problem.

"Well, at least you didn't try for a dramatic exit," he said as he pushed out of his seat and came to his assistance. "It would have been totally ruined."

Smiling at his ambassador's discomfort, he punched in the required code and unsealed the door by placing his palm on the plate. He waited for the locks to disengage and waved him out. As he closed it in the man's wake, he caught sight of Brilgus waiting in the corridor beyond.

V'ritan words drifted back as the door clunked shut.

"We have to ask a favor from a friend."

A short time later, Ambassador V'ritan arrived outside Stephanie's suite. Brilgus waited as he knocked, and they were very quickly let inside.

Stephanie was curled up on the couch, a book in hand. She looked up as they entered and smiled, pleasantly surprised to see them. "I didn't know you guys were stopping by. I was getting some reading in and everyone is chilling in their rooms, except these two."

She looked at the two Meligornians the smile fading from her face. "What's going on? You look like someone's died."

V'ritan sniffed and identified an unfamiliar scent. He looked around and noticed the two cats rolling around on the carpet as they wrestled in play.

Zeekat noticed him staring and stopped, and Bumblebee paused to follow his gaze. They disentangled themselves and meandered over to sit beside Stephanie and fixed bright-eyed stares on the visitor.

He shook his head. "I will never get used to that."

Brilgus chuckled at his discomfort and approached the pair. He knelt in front of them and reached out, his palm up, and wriggled his fingers in invitation. "Does da kitty want a scratch? Does he? Does he now?"

As Zeekat lowered his chin into the advisor's hand, the ambassador blinked and rolled his eyes before he turned back to her. "I am, unfortunately, here on business."

She waved him toward a seat opposite her. "Tell me what's going on."

"I didn't want to come here," he said and lowered the hood of his cloak as he accepted her invitation, "but I couldn't think of an alternative."

Stephanie frowned. "Go on." She glanced at Lars as he entered, nodded a greeting to the visitors, and sat in a chair near the window.

V'ritan shifted forward on the seat and frowned as Brilgus continued to make a fuss of the cats. "There is a cell of insurgents in the city. We know their location, but our Tactical Support Section has been compromised so we can't depend on them to help us on this one. And by 'we' I mean our new head of security, the king, and myself."

He paused and studied her face as she digested the news before he resumed his explanation. "And now you know. I came to see if you and your team were up for a fight. We need help to capture them."

"None of the regular forces can take this on?" Stephanie asked.

The ambassador shook his head. "The Tac Section is the only department set up for it—and we don't know who else is compromised. If we tell the wrong person, we risk giving the insurgents enough warning to disappear, and then we'll have nothing. We'll be back to square one and they'll have more time to plan another attack."

"That's not good news," she replied and looked at Lars to try to read his reaction.

He shrugged as the Meligorniain answered, "No, it's a bad situation right now."

When she didn't respond immediately, he took a deep breath.

"So, would you and your team be willing? I know it's dangerous, but I think you could handle it."

"What are the pros and cons?" Lars interjected.

V'ritan looked up when the rest of the team emerged and gathered around them. Brilgus still knelt in front of the cats, but he watched the proceedings as they butted his hands for more attention.

The ambassador thought for a moment. "Pros...we catch them and hopefully, get more information which will make everyone safer. Cons...we all die and the insurgents escape to attack at the Federation from another angle."

Frog nodded. "So it's your basic tag and bag mission. Got it." He glanced around. "What do you think, boys? Shall we take the witch out to play?"

Marcus walked around the couch and shrugged. "They made us citizens and we wouldn't tell Earth no, right?"

There was a chorus of "nopes" and "not likelys" and they all looked at Stephanie.

"It's your call," Lars told her. "Our primary duty is to protect you, but that doesn't mean stopping you from doing your job."

The team nodded in agreement but made no effort to sway her decision. She sighed and looked at each one as she considered the problem. As much as she didn't like to put them at risk, this was what they'd signed up for.

After a moment's hesitation, she slapped her hands on her legs and stood. "Let's suit up, boys." She turned to V'ritan. "I don't suppose you could get us some extra ammo?"

A short while later, the team was in their gear and suitably equipped. They stood in a small hangar while Brilgus brought a flying car around. "The cats don't like it when you leave them behind," he said. "They think they're part of the team."

"They don't have any armor," she snapped. "They can come as soon as they do."

"You could shield them," Lars murmured, and she glared at him.

"I'll think about it."

"At least *they* won't need any extra ammo," V'ritan told her as he wandered up to inspect her armor and adjust it as needed. "Are you ready?"

"That we are." She smiled and felt a small surge of anticipation. "We'll take a look at it tonight and strike tomorrow when we have a plan."

He nodded. "All right. Be careful and try not to spook them." He pressed his finger to Stephanie's forehead and the address floated into her mind.

"That's where you're headed. And yes, we'll talk about what I just did later. For now, keep your heads low and good luck. I'll have the rest of the gear brought to your rooms along with any extra ammunition you might need and the MU packs to power them. The latter will take a little time if I'm to prevent it from leaking."

She patted him on the shoulder, slid into the car, and keyed the address into the GPS. Brilgus noted it and nodded. "I can get you there."

He took a moment to study the map, not happy that he had to leave the ambassador, even with a guard. When he was ready, he lifted off and set his course to the address.

"A warehouse district." Lars sighed when he saw it. "What a surprise.

Brilgus snorted at the comment and set the car down a block away from the address. "I sent a map to your tablets." He waited for a moment as they all checked their tablets and added, "I'll wait here."

Stephanie and the team tucked their tablets into their pockets and exited the vehicle to make their way down a dark and poorly lit side street until they stood across from their target. She indicated the building. "It's a warehouse. Let's do a quick surveillance run and meet here."

The team moved quickly, slipped out of the side street, and hugged the shadows as they crept around the location, doing their best to remain unseen. She crouched around the corner of the warehouse and released a small translucent ball of gMU.

Lars waited with her for the ball and the rest of the team to return from their investigations. When everyone had arrived and the sphere had returned, she moved into a loading dock and flattened the orb to display the image it had stored.

They immediately identified several dark spots.

"Those should be exits and entrances," the team leader stated. "We simply have to decide how to stop them from being used when we go in."

"I'm reasonably sure I can use my magic to block any exits unless there are some underground that we can't see," she told them. "We'll have to hope that V'ritan has a plan."

She studied the map intently. "And that he can find another team to back us up."

They made their way back to the car and had Brilgus return them to the palace.

"You'll have your equipment in the morning," V'ritan told them when they arrived and scowled as the two cats immediately tackled Brilgus and demanded he pet them. "Do they *have* to encourage him?"

Stephanie chuckled and waved her hand. The cats caught her signal and hurried to follow her. "I'm going to prepare. Call me when its time."

She went into her room and closed the door, leaving the Meligornians talking to Lars while the others scattered to their rooms.

Once she'd removed her armor, she stood with her legs shoulder-width apart in the center of the room. The felines jumped on her bed and curled up to watch curiously as she closed her eyes and began to pull energy into her.

It took her some time to refill her inner storage tanks since she'd given the bulk of her MU and eMU away during the third Mystery challenge. She hadn't really had time since then to restore the levels again. Well, now she had to.

After a quick glance at the cats, she scoffed. "I sure wish I hadn't been stupid with that rock."

They purred in response and remained where they were while their bright eyes observed the arcs of energy that flowed into her body. When she was as full as she could be, she felt exhausted.

"That's me done for the night," she told the two, climbed into bed, and nodded when they settled on top of the blankets. She rubbed their heads. "Do you guys want to go kick some bad guy butt?"

They nudged her and purred louder than ever, and she stifled a yawn. "Good. It's settled. You're part of the team. For now, though, I need a nap."

She'd planned to rest for only a short while, but before she knew it, Lars shook her awake. "Hey, it's time to go. We're all ready."

Stephanie blinked and sat up, startled to see that it was dusk outside the window. "Man, I must have been tired. I've slept—"

"About eighteen hours," he told her. "Don't worry. Our gear arrived and we fed the cats. Brilgus even took them for a walk."

"A walk?" She stretched and patted her leg, and the felines wandered over and twined themselves around her legs. "Time to go, guys."

He left her to get dressed but he and V'ritan waited in the other room to check and adjust her armor.

"Here's the deal," the ambassador told her. "You'll give me ten minutes after I leave here. Then, you and your teammates will exit through the main doors, turn right, and head down the hall.

To your right, you'll find an alcove with a plain wooden door. Magic the lock open and take the stairs to the bottom. The passage will lead you to another door where there will be transportation waiting. Neither Brilgus nor I will be able to be with you without signaling that something is up. Our visit was noticed last night, and we were missed."

The cats growled at him as he patted her shoulder and he frowned at them before he walked to the door. "Ten minutes," he reminded her before he opened it and left silently.

They waited for what felt like the longest ten minutes of their lives, then Lars checked the hallway.

He gestured that it was clear, and they followed the ambassador's directions to find a small ship waiting for them.

Sho met them at the door and showed them his ID card. "I am Sho, head of Royal Security. I will come with you."

"And I thought all the important people had to stay away," the team leader grumbled.

The Meligornian shrugged and climbed into the cockpit beside the pilot. "Perhaps I am not that important," he told them, a slight smile on his lips. "Shall we go?"

The pilot was the same one who had taken Stephanie to the testing, and he gave her a brief smile before he gaped at the cats. "They let you *keep* them?"

She shushed him and covered Zeekat's ears. "They didn't want to try telling them no."

The feline shook her hands off his ears and yawned to display all his fangs as he stretched and his tail twitched. The pilot reached out tentatively and rubbed his head. "Smart."

Once again, they landed a block away in an empty lot behind two warehouses. It was different than their landing spot the night before, but they were less likely to be noticed there.

The team headed out and the cats followed Stephanie. Once the pilot had closed the hatch after them, she looked at the pair and put a finger to her lips. "Quiet now. It's time to hunt."

They approached their objective according to plan, alert for the guards they knew were there and whom they had avoided on their first visit.

When they were in position, Lars whispered to the team. "Take 'em out as quietly as you can. Use your stunners or the darts. We have to be able to question them when we get them back."

The team nodded, drew their stunners, and rose to their feet. Being the smallest, Frog had the first opportunity for action.

He snuck along the edges of the warehouse and crouched in the shadows while the guard made his rounds. As the target turned a corner, he attacked using a throat punch to silence him and swept his legs to upend the man before he secured him.

The second was easier. He selected a dart from his clip and thrust it into the guards back while he covered his mouth. It took two seconds for the drug in the dart to take effect, and Frog cuffed him as well before he dragged the bodies around the side and shoved them behind a stack of pallets.

The team returned silently to the front entrance and approached the door.

"I've got this," Stephanie told them and raised her hands.

"Who the fuck are you?" a voice yelled before she could unlock it with her magic.

The whole team spun, their weapons raised. Another security guard stood behind them, completely unaware that Bumblebee stalked him from behind.

The team held their fire and the guard reached for his comm, but before he could use it, the cat pounced and felled him. His claws shredded flesh and his jaws closed over the guy's head. The entire team winced as the cat twisted and a sickening crack followed.

Marcus curled his lip in disgust "Well, we won't get anything from *him*."

Johnny shook his finger at the cat. "I am not cleaning his paws."

She turned back to the door and used her energy to unlock it silently. They slid through one at a time and stayed low while they scrutinized the surroundings.

Once they were all in, Marcus started to move forward. Lars tried to stop him but wasn't fast enough. He stepped into a laser beam and triggered the alarm system. "Crap, sorry."

The team moved instantly and each one sought a target. Stephanie raised her arms and directed a stream of energy to wrap it around the building and block all the doors. They heard voices and running footsteps. Someone shouted, "The doors are locked."

Another responded with, "That way! Down. Down. Go down!"

Frog raced after them. "Shit, they have a bolt hole."

Sho drew his gun as well and his other hand sparked with MU. "Everyone has a bolt hole unless they're stupid. Unfortunately, these guys aren't stupid."

The team hurtled toward where they'd heard the shouting. They didn't find anyone, but they did find a hatch in the floor beneath which the sound of voices was clearly audible.

She blasted the hatch clear and Lars and Marcus lunged through it before she could argue. Frog and Avery moved to follow but she was there before them and dropped in quickly while she conjured a second bolt of energy.

"Make a hole," she commanded when she found Lars and Marcus blocking her line of sight and they stepped smartly out of the way.

She could now see the group of insurgents as they raced toward a door at the end of the corridor. None of them had stopped and none looked back. One had already reached the door and began to yank it open.

The bolt of magic struck it, wrenched it out of his hands, and slammed it shut in front of him. At the same time, the cats pushed their way past Stephanie, Lars, and Marcus, and roared as they charged.

Stephanie thrust her hands forward, pulled energy to her fingertips, and rocketed it after them. Lars and Marcus raced forward as she enveloped the two beasts with shields of light.

Ahead of them, the fugitives screamed as Zeekat and Bumblebee powered into them. From where she was, she could see past Lars and Marcus to where their targets were backed up against the outer door. One of those near the outside of the group found the time to shoot a hasty bolt of magic at the cats, and Bumblebee yowled in pain.

"Kitties! Down!" she shouted, and both felines dropped.

Before any of those they'd attacked could react, she began a barrage of small charged orbs. Where they struck, electricity arced out over their target, shorted its way through synapses, and dropped them almost instantaneously.

One almost landed on Zeekat and he gave a startled yowl and struck out at the hapless rebel as he leapt out of the way. Bumblebee followed, and both cats sat and watched the carnage while they pretended nonchalance.

"Sure, tell the *kitties* to get down," Lars muttered where he crouched beside Marcus and glanced back at her. "Never mind about the two humans *protecting* you."

He made his way slowly to where Stephanie stood, duck-walking under her line of fire until he was behind her. When the last rebel had fallen, he placed a hand on her shoulder. "You can stop now." She didn't seem to have heard him. "You can stop," he repeated, and she lowered her hands slowly. "We got this."

Relief surged when she let him move her back against the wall to allow the rest of the team past to deal with the fallen insurgents. "I really hope you left *some* of them alive," Marcus quipped in passing.

"Me, too," Sho said and grinned before he followed the team.

Frog hung back to keep watch between them and the hatch. "What?" he asked when Lars looked at him. "*Someone* has to watch your dumbass backs and everyone else is busy."

As if his words were a catalyst, Stephanie twisted out from under the team leader's hand and raced to the cats. Zeekat licked Bumblebee's fur and tried to soothe a patch of reddened skin. She dropped to her knees beside him and turned to look at Lars, anger on her face. "Those idiots burned my cat!"

Before he could think of anything to say, a laser blast careened into the wall beside her face and both felines hissed.

"Bastards!" Stephanie scrambled up and prepared to launch a series of fireballs in the direction of the shot. Her gaze searched the shadows but only one figure huddled behind the ladder beneath the hatch.

Before she could do more than bring the magic to her fingertips, Frog had fired, and he hadn't used his stunner.

Lars wasn't impressed. "Goddammit, Frog!"

The man looked at him as he changed clips. "Sorry, my negotiation skills for getting someone to surrender suck."

She raised an eyebrow and glanced at Sho, who nodded. "We have most of them. That's what matters."

He opened the outer hatch and stepped outside to send the ambassador the signal. Within fifteen minutes, Security personnel were everywhere. They swarmed over the warehouse in search of anyone the team might have missed but finding no-one.

The revolutionaries were bundled into a holding vehicle for transport, and Stephanie was surprised to see two Dreth and one human amongst the Meligornians there. Sho looked worried. "I'll need to call their ambassadors." He sighed. "It looks like it will be a busy night."

The warehouse was cleared, and everyone proceeded to Security Headquarters.

"I thought you said there was a mole," Stephanie whispered to the ambassador.

"I did," he whispered in response. "We are watching for someone to crack or to try to pass news of tonight's events on to someone else."

He straightened as one of the Federation ambassador's arrived. She recognized him from her awards ceremony, and he gave her a brief nod as he quickly accepted responsibility for the human and promised to share any intelligence they received from him.

"I am sorry one of my species was involved," he stated, his voice gruff as he addressed V'ritan. "If there's anything…absolutely anything—"

"Just share what he knows," the ambassador told him. "His choices aren't your fault, but we'll need to work together to discover what it's about."

"Agreed." He still looked worried, but he brushed past two Navy Special Operations Officers and left with his prisoner.

For a minute, she thought they might follow the ambassador, but they didn't. Instead, they stood and surveyed the scene of organized chaos. One of them stopped beside Jaleck. "Who brought them in?"

The Dreth ambassador motioned to Stephanie. "The Morgana team."

Their jaws dropped momentarily but they collected themselves quickly and walked over to Stephanie and the guys. "Good work out there. Uh…we hoped we could speak to you before you left—"

Before Stephanie could answer she was interrupted by Jaleck, who shook her hand. "Everywhere I go, you do us a service. Thank you. We will let you know what we extract from them."

CHAPTER ELEVEN

The team entered their quarters, stripped their armor off, and set it aside for cleaning. They weren't necessarily exhausted, but they weren't bursting with energy, either.

With the Dreth ambassador's presence, Stephanie had been able to put the Navy off and simply said she had to check her schedule and would get back to them. Once they were back in the suite with the doors closed behind them, she sent a message to Elizabeth.

It was about time she gave Ms. E. and Burt an update rather than forcing them to rely on news reports. By the time she'd showered and changed into casual clothes, her mentor had replied.

"I hate that we can't talk face to face, or live," the woman said from the middle of the screen, "but this will have to do. Pay close attention, because not everything is what it seems—and this includes the Navy."

She paused the message and located her tablet, aware that the guys had gathered around.

"First of all, I want you to protect yourself from the Navy,"

Elizabeth continued when Stephanie set the recording to play once more. "My meeting with them was not the best. I'm not saying you can't work with them, but you have to be careful. I wouldn't put it past them to try to draft all of you."

She snarled. "I would kill them."

The woman looked into the camera with a grim smile. "And if you are anything like I think you are, Stephanie, let me remind you that you cannot kill the entire Navy."

Around her, the team stifled chuckles and she giggled. She typed into the tablet. *Don't kill.*

"Of course, there is also the worst-case scenario where they hire you and try to underpay you. If they do offer you a contract, you need to negotiate, and you need to walk away if it's not right."

"I mean it, Stephanie." She glared at the screen. "Call it a consulting gig and include all the bells and whistles. Sting them *hard*. We're talking hazard pay, control over operational parameters, one hundred percent coverage of damages, and approval for death—all deaths, not only enemy combatants. Don't let them weasel out of a single thing, not even vacation time."

Stephanie chuckled as she jotted it down and liked the fact Ms. E. was at the top of the game. She never missed a beat, not even when she probably should.

Her mentor continued, counting things down on her fingers. "Furthermore, *all* contracts are to come to me before you sign anything. Burt and I will go through them and make sure they don't sneak a tour of duty into the fine print. If they did that, you'd go in as a contractor and come out as…well, you don't come out. You stay. That does not sound like a fun time."

She snorted as she made her notes. "Vacation. What the hell is that nonsense? Who actually gets a vacation anyway?"

Around her, the boys snorted in agreement, but they didn't interrupt. They listened as Elizabeth broke everything down to the smallest detail of the different ranks of who had the authority to grant what.

"You might have Mr. First Class Petty Officer in there acting all tough and agreeing to your terms, but he'll have no authorization to do what he says he can. Nothing matters, and if he doesn't have the authority, it won't happen. And you want to be polite—don't be aggressive but stand your ground."

Stephanie couldn't believe how much the woman sounded like her mother. She spoke like she was trying to teach her some of what she'd learned over the years. "I have been in shitty spots with negotiations and still come out on top. I make it a point to come out on top."

"She is ruthless." She leaned back and grinned.

"Yeah," Lars muttered. "I'm glad she's on our side."

Ms. E took a deep breath and clapped. "So, that is it. That is all I have for you. I miss you, girl. Time creeps by here, and you and your merry gang of hooligans need to get back here ASAP. I need something to brighten this place. This working alone thing sucks. Be careful and if all else fails, go for the nuts."

The message ended, and Stephanie shook her head. She tossed the tablet on the table and looked around. "Huh. I guess you all heard that, right?"

They nodded, and she spread her arms and grinned. "We need to send a reply. She just gave us the one-oh-one on how to negotiate with the Federation Navy. And she said she missed us."

The guys piled onto the couch with her in the middle. She set the recording drone and had it fly far enough back to get everyone in the picture.

As soon as the green light went on, Stephanie put her arms out. "Stephanie Morgana and her Band of Merry Hooligans here. We wanted to send you a message since we've been busy kicking butt, taking names, and becoming citizens of everywhere."

The team cheered. She laughed and waited for them to settle.

"As for your message, we understand and we appreciate what you're saying. All contracts will go to you and Burt for approval, no matter how urgent we think they are. I don't want to end up in uniform full time and I don't think these guys do either."

Bumblebee made a low, rumbling growl from the other room and everyone glanced in that direction. The big yellow-striped cat stalked in to sit with them, Zeekat at his side. When they turned back to the drone, Stephanie's smile was wide. "Yeah, I hope you like cats 'cause they…uh, adopted us, soooo…yeah."

Lars scowled and added, "At first, I hated the idea as I'm sure you will, E, as soon as you see this message. But they're here to stay. They fight as part of the team and followed Steph out of a forest when she was tested as a Mage—"

He paused and turned to her, his eyes wide. "You *have* told her that bit, haven't you?"

"Hi, *Mom!*" Frog yelled before she could reply. He waved madly. "Your favorite kid misses your face."

"Yeah," Marcus added and held his nose. "Someone needs his diapy changed."

"Does not!"

"Ha! So you admit you're wearing one."

A scuffle broke out as Frog dived at his teammate and Johnny and Avery each grabbed one of them. Brenden gave the screen a pleading stare. "You *have* to come back to us, Mom. They keep fighting."

"And they keep stealing *all* the cookies," Johnny whined.

Frog turned in his arms. "I do not. That was you."

"Was not."

"Was so, too!"

"Mom! You really need to come over here. It's all *his* fault!"

"Yeah! *Everything's* his fault," Avery added. "He needs a darn good whooping."

"Oooh, you said darn. Momma's not gonna be happy!"

Lars rolled his eyes and stood. "See what I have to put up with, E? Every damn day. They really need you, so get here as soon as you have things tied up there. Steph and I will try to keep them out of trouble until then."

He clapped loudly to get their attention. "Time to say goodbye."

Stephanie laughed so hard the tears rolled down her face, but she managed to control it as the team leader hauled her to her feet and everyone gathered around to wave goodbye.

"We *promise* we'll be good," they called, and Stephanie figured Ms. E wouldn't believe *any* of them, not for a second. She ended the call and shut the drone off before she guided it down to land in her lap.

The guys immediately started back to their rooms, but Lars stopped when he caught the look of longing on her face.

"What's up?" he asked.

She sighed. "Nothing. I guess I miss being able to go into the Virtual World. Sometimes, you simply don't want to deal with reality."

He smiled at her and nodded. "Almost all the time, and especially when it's dealing with these clowns."

Several cries of protest echoed from the surrounding rooms, and they both chuckled before they separated and retreated.

Stephanie walked into hers, plugged the drone into the computer, and used the corporate account to send Elizabeth her message. Then, she took a minute to record one for her parents to let them know she loved them and that she would hopefully be home on Earth soon.

She tried for light and relaxed and thought about telling them everything that had happened, but she felt too drained. Instead, she kept it short and simple and asked them to pass on her best to Todd if they should see him before she did.

The memory of her best friend brought her close to tears, but she managed to hide the sadness until she'd finished her message. All traces of that sadness vanished when she saw how much it would cost to send, and she cleared her throat.

"It had better get there for that price," she muttered and took a hasty breath before she closed her eyes and pressed send. There were some definite negatives to being on a world so far from her own.

Stephanie wasn't alone in being far from home. Todd and his team had been loaded onto the next ship scheduled for departure. No longer a unit on their own, they were now part of a real section with a couple of older hands to steady them on the shuttle ride to their first real-world mission.

"Navy got a report of an outpost of humans and Dreth in Sanmar's Reach. It's unregulated so we pay them a social visit, show the flag, get a feel for the place, and make sure they're a real colony and not a pirate base," the team leader told them. "It should be an easy run."

One of the older hands—Arizona, a ten-year veteran—leaned back in his chair, playing a game on his tablet. He looked up as the leader moved forward and set it aside before he leaned toward the new guys.

He elbowed Hollins who sat next to him as he began to speak. "You gotta learn to loosen up now you aren't in boot camp. Okay? This outpost gig will be interesting for you, but you'll need to watch your step because it is unregulated."

One of the team guys frowned. "Like anarchy?"

Hollins shook his head. "Naw, dude. Worse than that. The law in a place like that is usually who has the biggest pair of…guns. Most of them out there don't mess with the Navy because the Navy will *always* come back with a bigger gun and more of them. That isn't a maybe, that isn't a possibility…that is a promise."

Arizona nodded and gave him a fist-bump. "Damn straight. So, if we die, know that someone will be there to avenge us. It isn't much of a consolation, but it's all they can do."

The younger man pointed his teammates. "So 'don't die' is the best advice we can give you."

The guys chuckled nervously as another member of the old team entered. He sat and cracked open a space MRE. "Are these fools giving you advice?"

They chuckled again, and Arizona shook his thumb toward the newcomer. "That guy, Perez, is the meanest kickass in the west. He annihilates danger from miles away."

The newcomer rolled his eyes. "Here's the deal as I see it. We're all a brotherhood but we all go by the code. Our job is to help make it as safe as possible out in the big frontier. We can't grow a future if we can't get a foothold."

Hollins nodded. "That is exactly right. We fight to make that foothold happen for those willing to build lives out here. Plus, there is the occasional opportunity to eliminate pirates and score a little kickback"

The guys didn't fully understand, and their faces showed it. Arizona leaned forward again. "See, if the Navy capture other vessels, those who are part of the teams will get a cut from the profit for taking them. There's more for captains, but everyone will get at least a month's pay. Those doing the boarding get a minimum of three months' pay. It's a nice little perk that no one really talks about."

He studied the new team members for a moment, then continued. "For us, we do it sometimes but only if the opportunity presents itself. There are other teams out there who are real shitstormers. They simply wander around deep space and hunt pirates. Those boys store cash away so that when they get back home, they won't have a thing to worry about."

"If they get home," Hollins pointed out dryly. "The survival rate for deep-spacers like that is less than half a percent. They either break down out there and are never heard from again, or they eventually bite it in a deathmatch with a no-good pirate."

Before they could ask any more questions, the captain's voice spoke over the internal comms. "All right, you shit handles, buckle in and get your gear straight. We're landing."

After a pause, he added, "And you assholes better not scare the newbies. We've asked for a team for too long for you to scare them back to their mommas."

Todd chuckled. "He doesn't *sound* like a captain."

Arizona shrugged. "He's a field captain which means he doesn't have to be a douche like the ones in plush offices. He cares that we eat, sleep, shit, live, and make space safer. That's it. The rest is all semantics to him. He'll put on a good face for the dignitaries and we know when to play along, but the rest of the time, he's like our big brother leading us into the shit but not letting us get too beat up."

One of the new team members released a relieved sigh. "Thank the Lord. I really thought all captains were like those in boot camp. I didn't know if I'd survive it."

The older man stood and clapped him on the shoulder. "You better survive it, shithead. Captain will have your ass otherwise—and mine. Get your gear. We haven't got all day."

The guys went to work, retrieved their gear and weapons, and prepared to deploy. There weren't any windows in the back of the shuttle where they sat, so none of them knew what to expect. Todd merely hoped it didn't smell as bad as the simulation they'd been dragged out of. He swore he could still smell the stench of the place—and he never wanted to smell it for real.

It didn't look like he'd have much of a chance, though. The shuttle touched down at the rough and ready spaceport and landed directly in its designated launch bay. The older hands approached the new guys, checked their gear, and made sure everything was in place.

"Good," Arizona told Todd. "Stick with me. I'll show you the ropes."

All around him, the experienced team members did the same and paired up with the less experienced hands before they all exited to form up for the captain's inspection. For all that he was supposed to be on their side, the man was still formidable.

He emerged briskly from the cockpit, stepped onto the tarmac, and swept his gaze across the surroundings before he focused on them. The look on his face said he wasn't impressed. Beside him, Todd felt Arizona stiffen and heard the old hand's muttered, "Damn."

"You got something to say AZ?"

Again, he heard the muttered "damn." It was followed by, "Sir. No, sir."

"Are you sure, Sergeant? Because I distinctly heard you curse."

"I would never dare sir."

"And why the hell is that, Sergeant?"

"Because my goddamned captain says cursing is a bloody assenholic habit that no damned trooper has the right to know...sir!"

The captain's lips twitched into a smile that Todd thought looked like a snarl. "Very good, Sergeant. Now, take my men out for a lookie-see and bring every damned one of them back or I'll nail your ass to the front of my shuttle and use you as a heat shield. Do you get me?"

"Sir. Yes, sir!"

"Very good, AZ. I'll take the rear."

Todd itched to ask if the captain was always like that, but he didn't dare, and Arizona led them out in double file. The older man surprised him when he began to speak in a muted tone.

"Captain says there's trouble ahead and we're to keep our eyes peeled."

He had? He hadn't caught a word of *that* in their short exchange.

"Trust me. This won't be the cakewalk it's supposed to be and we've gotta keep our eyes peeled."

They jogged the half-mile from the shuttle port to the town and used the journey to familiarize themselves with the terrain and the town's layout.

CHAPTER TWELVE

Several systems away from where Todd was marched into Sanmar's Rest with his team, Stephanie had been unable to put the Federation Navy off any longer. All she wanted to do was wipe the smiles off the representatives' faces. Instead, she and the team took their places at the negotiation table.

The FedNav team continued to smile from ear to ear. Stephanie smiled in response and allowed a small trace of Morgana to creep into it. Beside her, Lars smiled, too—the hard smile of a man ready to cause serious mischief if need be.

The rest of the team didn't smile at all but regarded the Naval contingent with cold, hard looks. With their smiles slowly fading, the officials cleared their throats and turned to business.

"Thank you for meeting with us today," Chief Albertson said with a grin. "My captain and I are extremely excited at the opportunity."

The captain nodded to them and his expression became stern.

Well, now I know who'll play the tough guy. She raised an eyebrow at him. While she respected what they did, she didn't like to be bullied or tricked—and she wasn't having any of it.

She spoke before he could get started and took control of the situation. "Look, here's the deal. Let's cut the smiles and niceties. This is business, and as such, I'd like to be straight to the point. No dancing around."

The captain released a deep breath. "At least someone has some brains here. I'm Captain Thorne. It's nice to meet you. I believe the chief, here, has something specific to touch on."

The other man cleared his throat uncomfortably as he flipped anxiously through some papers. She smirked and looked at her guys, then spoke before he had time to finish his charade. "We have decided that we're willing to help the Navy but not without negotiating first."

"We would expect nothing less," the captain replied smoothly.

"Now, to be perfectly clear," Stephanie said and leaned forward so they would see her intent. "We are willing to negotiate to *help* the Navy. We do not wish to *enlist* in the Navy. We know what you do is vital to the safety of the entire Federation and therefore, we feel our assistance is warranted. That said, none of us is interested in signing up."

The chief looked flustered. "But there is a chance you will be drafted. How can the Navy be sure you are as capable as the stories claim—or that you will be able to function properly in a Navy environment? This affects the lives and safety of our personnel, too, you know."

"I didn't think you cared whether or not your draftees *were* capable," she replied. "Not when you first receive them, anyway. In fact, I'm reasonably sure you expect to have to train them from scratch, so capability is not an issue here. Besides, we've already proved ourselves—"

The captain put up his hand for her attention. "I think all the chief is trying to say is that we need you in the Naval service. With the number of sailors we lose every day, your assistance could be vital. We might even be able to save some we'd otherwise lose."

Marcus groaned. "Puhlease, the Navy hasn't cared about how

many sailors they lose since before the Federation. You vacuum-seal them and send them into space with only the most basic training and then try to tell us Stephanie is the only thing that can reduce your losses? Don't put the death of these men and women on our shoulders. If you want fewer deaths, you need to train them better. You need to send them in as humans with the proper equipment for the job and not simply as cannon fodder."

She reached over and touched his arm, a signal that he should calm himself. "We came here to negotiate a consultancy, not to join. If you can't accept that, we'll leave right now."

The captain shook his head, withdrew a pair of glasses from his pocket, and put them on. "No, no, it's fine. We have your list of demands and they have almost all been approved."

"Almost?" Stephanie replied, her expression deadpan.

The captain coughed and set the paper down. "Yes, well…you see, we can't accept any foreign person in our service. You would have to renounce any non-Earth citizenship you might have."

She laughed. "Not going to happen, especially since we're not joining the Navy but offering our assistance—and we know you work with both Meligorn and Dreth units on a regular basis. Nice try, but the fact you'd suggest that such a thing is for the greater good makes me wonder what your motives really are. If you want to draft me, you'll negotiate my service with the Meligornian ambassador."

The chief grumbled, "He won't allow it and you know it. He will fight it."

Stephanie yawned and pointed at him. "Oh, and while you're at it, the Dreth ambassador needs to be consulted as well."

They both stopped and looked at her. The captain frowned. "Why would we talk to the Dreth ambassador?"

She tilted her head to the side and gave in to the temptation to smirk. "Oh, you didn't hear? I have citizenship on all three planets now."

The man stared at her and his jaw dropped in shock. "You're

bluffing. There is not a single human outside the President of the Federation who has tri-citizenship. And his only lasts while in office. If you're serious about negotiating, you should start off by telling the truth."

"Don't tell me you haven't read my file?" She looked at him with a bright smile, pulled her tablet out, and set it on the table while she talked. "Are you new here, or did you miss the ceremony where I was awarded the Medal of Decarth as well as the Talon of the Families?"

She flipped through the numbers so they could see and pulled up the Meligornian ambassador's contact information. "I can get the ambassador on the line. Would that suffice?"

The chief snorted and flipped his hand dismissively. "No. Everyone knows you saved him during the assassination attempt. Of course he would side with you."

"Good point." She nodded, flipped through the tablet again, and stopped when she reached the Dreth Ambassador's information. "How about the Dreth ambassador?"

Captain Thorne rolled his eyes. "This is becoming ridiculous."

She stared at him and blinked as she turned the tablet and showed him the picture of her and Ambassador Jaleck with the contact information beside it. "I think you should stop calling me a liar. That is something none of them would stand for. So, do I interrupt the ambassador's morning tea or will we talk like the two independent parties we are?"

He gawked at the information for a moment and shrugged impatiently. "Fine, fine, but before we draw contracts up, we should see what you and your team are capable of when you face a structured military strike."

"That sounds great." She grinned. "Why don't we run through a scenario in the pods? You should get more than enough data from that."

The captain thought about it for a moment. "Yes, that sounds fair. I will call you when it's ready."

He rose as if to leave but she held her finger up. "Before you go, you might want to program a couple of extra spots. People have a tendency to want to join our team. We can't turn them down if they're worthy."

"We'll do what we can and will send the details of our agreement over shortly," he replied, clearly annoyed.

He shook Stephanie's hand, but the chief stood and walked out without even so much as a glance in her direction. She chuckled quietly as she followed her team out of the office. As she passed the front desk, her tablet rang, and she stuck the earbud in and swiped to answer. "Ambassador Jaleck, I was just speaking about you."

"I hope it was good things," the Dreth ambassador replied. "Although you might change your mind when you hear what I have to say."

While Stephanie spoke to Jaleck on Space Station Alerus, Elizabeth sighed heavily and sank into the chair in her office. She booted the computer up and checked for any news on Stephanie's meeting with the Navy.

Hopefully, the girl had taken her advice because if she had to tell Burt his star had gone off and joined the military, she was sure he'd go rogue—and that would be a very bad thing for Earth's virtual network.

She checked her email and messages but found nothing. With another sigh, she prepared to play the message from the team again for a little motivation to get her through the rest of her day. It had barely started when the phone rang.

Once she'd paused it, she noted who the incoming caller was and narrowed her eyes. Not sure whether she should be concerned, she answered the call and waited until his fritzing image hovered clearly in front of her. "Mark, how are you?"

Stephanie's dad smiled. "Good, good. How are you?"

"I'm well, although, I don't have any updates on Stephanie."

He shook his head. "That sucks but it's not why I called."

"Oh?" Ms. E sat straighter in her chair. "Then what can I do for you?"

Marc pursed his lips and hesitated for a moment before he simply blurted what was on his mind. "I wondered if you'd be willing to coach me on how to handle an interview for a high-level client. Or if you would know someone that I could use."

She chuckled. "I'll do it. We gotta keep it in the family. Let's start with me interviewing you. Very straightforward."

"Hi, Elizabeth," Stephanie's mom said and waved in the background as the image panned.

"Hi, Stephanie's mom." She waved cheerfully in response. "Now, let's start with the entrance. You want to look put-together—no stains, no really old suits, and no crazy ties."

"Thank you," Cindy yelled and turned on her husband. "Did you hear that? You can't wear your tie with the belly dancing Santa on it again."

He rolled his eyes and his head. "Come on woman, it's not Christmas time. I have better taste than that!"

Ms. E raised her eyebrow and continued. "So, yes, no flashy ties. Thin stripes are okay, but only if your suit is solid. If your suit is striped—which I don't recommend—but if it is, go solid on the tie. So, you enter the office and give your potential client a very firm handshake. Carry a briefcase if you have one, even if there is only one piece of paper in it."

"Are you taking notes?" Cindy nagged from the background.

"Yes, yes. No flashiness, no stripe on stripe crime, and carry my briefcase," he said. "Should I clean it out?"

"Yes!" both women shouted.

Elizabeth giggled and immediately became businesslike. "Once you've shaked hands, you give the normal niceties, and then *do not waste his time*. Launch into the discussion on the services you offer. You want to have something for him to hold in his hands because his mind will be everywhere and not only on the business he might have with you."

Mark scribbled madly as she spoke, and his wife peered over his shoulder.

She gave him a moment to catch up before she continued. "Try some charts and graphs and use a hologram cube if you have one available. Give him every reason to say yes. Now, let me try you with some questions he might ask."

Ms. E launched into the questions—all generic but formidable coming from someone with confidence and a severe shortage of time in the day. Marc did well, kept the humor at a light level, and most importantly, told zero dad jokes.

When they were done, she gave him some things to work on but in reality, with his kind demeanor coupled with a killer suit, she wasn't worried. If he went through the real interview like he'd done with her, he should knock it out of the park.

Once the training was concluded, Cindy sighed. "How is my girl?"

"She was doing much better when I last saw a video of her. Unfortunately, I've had no updates since. If you'd like to send her something, I'm happy to pay for it out of the company's budget. Those messages are bank killers, but they're invaluable for morale...and I *know* she misses you."

CHAPTER THIRTEEN

With Lars's help, Stephanie made it out of the Navy office and into the street without any difficulty. The guys formed up around her and cleared the path ahead by walking two abreast. The ambassador's reply had worried her. "Uh oh, not more bad news."

Jalek shrugged. "Not in the way you are thinking," she replied, "but first, let me start off by asking how your meeting went."

"It went okay, I guess. I suggested a round of pod testing so they could see our capabilities for themselves, but I think they're only trying to kill time while they work out how to sucker me into signing up. That won't happen, though. I already know it's not what I want."

She stopped and gave the Dreth the opening to continue with the real reason for the call. "So, that's my news. How about you? What's going on? Hit me with it."

"I couldn't possibly hit you," she replied, completely serious. "but there is a small problem I have, and I think you could help me solve it."

"Go ahead," she told her and tried to guess what problem she could possibly help with.

The ambassador hesitated, then came out with it. "I still have Vishlog in detention for that little stunt at the reception. I know everyone thinks I am being hard on him, but Dreth understand miserable situations a lot better than an explanation and a request not to do it again."

"That's okay," she said and teetered slightly as Lars steered her into the hangar where the royal shuttle waited to take them back to Meligorn. "I know a lot of humans like that, too. What's the problem? Did he manage to find a bar or bottle of liquor while in the cell?"

That startled a short laugh from the Dreth. "No, not so much. My problem is that I need to have a Dreth on your team for Dreth respect, or they will consider the whole award and citizenship a ruse to give you access to places you would not otherwise be able to go."

She sounded uncomfortable but continued despite this. "While you earned the award fairly, there are those who now call for you to have a Dreth member on your team. Since you have already confronted Vishlog, he will be more respectful than any other Dreth, to start with, if you would be willing to take him on and build on that."

Stephanie raised her eyebrows and stared out the window as the shuttle descended quickly. "All I can do is try, I suppose."

"Thank you, Stephanie. That is all we ask," Jaleck replied. "I did not wish to insult you, but this had to be done quickly before there were any repercussions. I'll complete his paperwork today and have him transferred to the team tonight."

She didn't wait for a reply but ended the call and left her staring at the tablet with an open mouth. "Well, that's sudden," she muttered and turned to discover Lars staring at her.

"I don't believe you agreed to that," he said.

"Yeah, me neither," Frog added from where he hung over the back of her seat.

"Man, girl. You might be a witch, but I don't think even *you* have the magic to fix this."

The shuttle touched down and taxied into the hangar, and she held a hand up for silence. "Chill, guys. I should have seen this coming, and I didn't."

"But *Vishlog*?" The team leader wasn't happy. "How am I supposed to even—"

She rounded on him, grasped a fistful of his tunic, and stared up into his face as her eyes turned momentarily black. "I don't know, but he stays, and you *will* find a way." Her eyes returned to normal. "As will I."

"Wow, Morgana..." Frog breathed as she frowned and released the man's tunic.

"Sorry. I'm not sure what that was about," she said, patted his chest, and turned toward the door. "I need to speak to Ms. E and do some research on Dreth warrior customs." She tapped Lars on the chest. "And you do, too. All of you. I'm not the only one who needs to win his respect."

"He has to win ours, too," Frog griped as the team disembarked and headed to their quarters. "Next thing you know, there'll be a Meligornian wanting in."

No one laughed. His words sounded prophetic in the wake of the news that a Dreth would join them.

The cats bounded over in welcome as soon as they entered the suite. They greeted them with happy rumbles and demanded pats from Stephanie and Lars. "Cats, Dreth," Lars grumbled and scratched under Bumblebee's chin. "What next?"

"Meligornian," Marcus told him morosely and echoed Frog's words. "You just watch."

"Whatever," Stephanie snapped and headed for the kitchenette. "We'll deal with it. We always do...and wasn't Frog bitching about being the new boy? Well, now you'll have someone *else* to push the luggage cart."

He stuck his head out of his room. "Yes!"

"You'll have to win his respect, first," the team leader reminded him, and he sniffed with disdain.

"What do you mean *I* will have to win *his* respect? *He's* the one who'll have to prove he's good enough to stay—"

Stephanie and Lars stared at him.

"What?"

He looked slightly rebellious but made an effort to explain. "I said he'd have to win my respect. He's the one who wants to join the team. I don't see why any of us should have to try to impress him. It should be the other way around."

"You're brilliant," Stephanie told him, and Lars groaned.

"Don't say that. He has a big enough head as it is."

"No," she said, "but he's made a good point. We don't have to win Vishlog's respect. He has to win ours. As long as we go in with that attitude, I think we'll be all right."

"But will *he* be right for the team?" the team leader asked. "I mean, the guy gets drunk on his downtime and picks fights."

"And Frog doesn't?"

"Hey!"

"She has a point," Marcus interjected. He glanced at his teammate. "She really, really does."

Frog slammed his door.

The other man shrugged, as though Frog had proven him right. "Well, he won't be any more temperamental than that, will he?"

Stephanie chuckled, looked at Lars, and received a wry grin in return.

"No, I guess not," he agreed. "We'll treat him the same way we treated Frog when he joined the team."

Marcus, Johnny, Avery, and Brenden exchanged glances. "This will definitely be fun."

"Don't break anyone," she warned them. "I don't want to have to heal you every ten seconds."

"We won't," Lars promised and gave her a serious look, "but

you have to trust us and follow our lead on this. No matter how unfair or mean you think we are. Okay?"

"Oh. Okay?" Stephanie agreed. "I'll try, but if I don't like it, you'll hear about it."

He smiled at her response. "Agreed. But try to make it in private, all right?"

"I'll think about it," she said.

"Please, Steph. It's important."

That was the first time she had ever heard him plead, and she didn't like it. "Fine."

It wasn't exactly an agreement, but he left it at that and prepared to go to his room.

"He'll be here early," he told her. "It's time to do research and get some rest. We'll meet at lunch to share what we've discovered and how to make it work for us."

They did their share, compared notes, and discussed strategies that would ease the Dreth into the team quickly. Frog spent most of it as red as a beet while they compared the results they'd had with him with how they might have to alter their tactics with the Dreth.

He rolled his eyes and finished his lunch. "I don't have to listen to this."

They spent the afternoon in the palace gym and returned to their quarters to clean up and get ready for dinner.

"Early night, guys," Lars ordered, as they met in the common room dressed for dinner.

They were about to leave when someone knocked on the door. He looked at her. "Are we expecting..."

She shook her head. "No."

Quickly, she called the cats, put them in her room, and closed the door to keep them there, despite their protests. Around her, everyone became quietly alert and everyone but Frog and Johnny returned quietly to their rooms to retrieve their weapons.

Stephanie only hoped they thought to grab their stunners

rather than their blasters since it seemed a shame to make a mess of the room, but she needn't have worried—or not about that, at least.

Lars waited at the door until they were ready and opened it. "Uh, Ambassador Jaleck..." He glanced at Stephanie and she moved forward. "Won't you come in."

"Thank you, Lars. Stephanie, I hope you don't mind, but I completed Vishlog's transfer early and thought it better that he joined the team tonight."

For the first time, she noticed Vishlog's large form behind the woman. He wore the Dreth dress uniform and seemed to try to be as inconspicuous as possible. His face was impassive as he watched his ambassador for cues.

His eyes also scanned the corridor as though there might be some danger lurking in the King's corridors. It was the same thing the guys did, and it still drove her crazy.

She moved forward and gave Jaleck the Dreth greeting appropriate to her rank. "Please, come in, Ambassador. This is an unexpected pleasure."

While she didn't even glance at Vishlog as he moved to follow, she did prepare to refuse him entry if he did not perform the appropriate greeting. It seemed childish but it was necessary.

Either way, it was a relief when he bowed to her and gave her the same greeting he would a Dreth commander. She nodded and indicated that he could enter. He also bowed to Lars before he moved to stand beside Jaleck. It was a promising start for the time he would be there, no matter how long it was.

As she moved forward to join her guest, she was glad he'd acknowledged Lars. She knew it was important for the team to continue to work together, even when they added a new member.

The team leader was about to close the door when Sho knocked and poked his head in. "It's a party in here."

She chuckled. "Sho, Ambassador Jaleck brought the newest member of our team. Come and say hello."

The Meligornian entered and greeted the ambassador with respect. Once they had exchanged pleasantries, Stephanie drew his attention to Vishlog. "Sho, this is Vishlog, and Vishlog, this is Sho, the new head of Royal Security."

Sho bowed slightly to the Dreth warrior and he did the same to show respect. "Welcome to the team, it is an interesting one, or so I have discovered."

The warrior nodded. "Everything is interesting when it comes to this crew."

Lars stepped in. "Welcome, Vishlog. I am Lars, the team's leader. Come and meet the others. Sho, I don't believe I've ever introduced you properly."

He led them to where the guys stood around the kitchen bench and nodded at Stephanie as he went. She and the ambassador drew a little aside to talk while he introduced the two men to the team and provided a brief explanation of their duties as he mentioned each one.

Vishlog greeted them and felt somewhat embarrassed. He wasn't sure why he had been chosen for this honor, not after the way he'd been told he'd behaved at the reception.

The only problem was, he didn't remember much of what had happened. He'd barely had anything to drink and wondered if he had been given a drug in his drink. It was the only reason he could think of for his lapse...and it sounded like he was making excuses.

Resolute, he pushed the thought aside and turned to the Meligornian, determined to right his wrong. "I apologize for my actions at the reception. I can be rowdy but not usually to that extent. I have been embarrassed since then."

Sho shrugged and patted him on the shoulder. "If I had a Meligornian crinket for every time I'd done something stupid when I was drunk, I'd be living it up in a mansion somewhere out in the south of the planet. We all have our moments. People are merely sensitive about her. She is important and we try to keep that in mind."

He nodded. "I understand." Vishlog looked around, relieved that the Meligornian had been so understanding but mindful that he had ignored the team to make his apology.

As he looked to see what they were doing, one of Stephanie's guards turned and bowed to the security chief, giving him the proper respect.

Once Sho had returned his greeting, Lars said, "I'm glad you've spoken with Sho, Vishlog. I'm sorry we haven't a spare room for you. I'll organize your quarters in the morning. In the meantime, you'll share a room with Frog."

The man appeared as if merely speaking his name was a spell to summon him, and Vishlog couldn't help noticing that he was the smallest member of the team. Sho stepped back, only to find himself talking to one of the team's demolition experts—Brenden, he thought the man's name was. He wanted to watch Lars settle the Dreth into the team but couldn't and turned to answer the other man's question instead.

"Coffee? Of course, I would. That is not only an Earth custom, you know."

Behind him, Vishlog tried to understand the welcome he received from the team. He'd expected sincere annoyance or even anger, not the respect they'd accord another human coming into the group.

Laughter interrupted his thoughts, and he glanced at the ambassador and Stephanie, as did several members of the team. That, too, was something he wasn't used to—hearing the ambassador express amusement. Finally, his curiosity got the best of him.

"I would like to ask a question," he said to Lars.

The team leader nodded, and his gaze tracked every person in the room—as a proper warrior's should. "Ask away."

"Stephanie—the human—she knows magic and has great power," he began tentatively, "so I understand why the Meligornians do her honor. What I do not understand is why she was chosen for such a high award by my people. Can you tell me?"

The other man smiled and realized that for all he'd attended the ceremony, the Dreth knew very little about his charge. "We were on the *Meligorn Dreamer* when it was attacked by pirates. They demanded that Ambassador V'ritan surrender himself, but he wasn't on the ship, so she made herself look like him, went to the Bridge, and killed their leader in single combat. Then, she removed the bomb they had set and would have lost her life recharging the ship's engines and transitioning the ship early if there hadn't been Meligornians with enough power to start the healing process. She saved thousands of lives."

"I see," the warrior replied. "There were Dreth aboard the *Dreamer*. It explains why she has been made a Talon. I am grateful she was aboard."

He leaned closer to Vishlog, turned his back to the two women, and lowered his voice. "Because she is so powerful and fights for the protection of all, there are many people—especially among the humans—who want a piece of her. She has to not only deal with that but find her own place in the universe while protecting it from the danger that is coming."

He paused and his companion filled in the blanks. "And so you watch her, help her, and protect her."

"Yes," Lars replied. "We protect her but at the same time, we must allow her to grow up. She has fought gangs on the streets of DC, protected people from pirates, and she saved the lives of both the king of Meligorn and his ambassador to Earth. She is incredibly protective of those she cares for."

Frog walked past and whispered, "The Morgana."

"Morgana?" The Dreth was confused. "This person—this Morgana—is also Stephanie? What is she?"

The team leader shook his head. "It is not a person, it's

Stephanie. When she gets too emotional in a fight, her eyes go black and all hell usually breaks loose."

"Ohhhh," Vishlog replied and nodded his head. "So, like a—what do you humans call it?—a berserker?"

Marcus joined the conversation, having overheard the whole thing. "Something like that. Except berserkers too often lose themselves and could hurt their own people. Stephanie is about protecting her people—or her cats, of course."

Vishlog frowned. "Cats? I thought I smelled cats but could not understand why."

Lars rolled his eyes. "Yeah, you'll meet them soon enough."

As her team leader introduced the new member to the rest of the team, Stephanie and Jaleck talked. She finished telling the Dreth ambassador the outcome of the meeting.

"The chief was livid by the end," she explained. "But that's his own fault. He should have known I had little interest in what he wanted from me."

Jaleck laughed. "Very true. You tell it as it is, and we respect that."

She nodded at the ambassador and glanced to where Vishlog was talking to the guys. "I hope he isn't still angry with me, even though I'm honored you have added a Dreth to the mix."

Her companion smiled and folded her arms. "We will always protect those who protect us. And he will protect you, but all Dreth must make up their own mind on whether you are worthy. That goes beyond protection."

Stephanie was a little taken back by that response. "I don't know about being worthy. Others feel I am, but we all believe it is misplaced, right? I will do my best, but if he finds he cannot follow me, I will allow him to leave."

She looked at the warrior's massive form and smiled. "I have to be honest, though. I *am* partial to having someone who will maybe stop the fights before they start. If I were about to argue, I might think twice if there was a ginormous Dreth on the other side." She sighed. "The fewer lives lost, in my opinion—whether pirate or rebel—the better the place we will be in to call us all together. Sometimes, you have to have a sense of forgiveness. A second chance. And I believe that some of them can be brought back to the fold. And by the fold, I don't mean the Federation. I mean the beings who choose to coexist whether there is a Federation or not."

On Alerus, a sailor reported good news to Captain Thorne. "Captain, we have finished the setup for the pods," he said as he held a tablet and flipped through it. "The start time for the test is scheduled around 0615 so the Morgana crew need to be here no later than 0600."

The captain nodded. "I'll have someone call and let them know, thank you. Oh, and make sure you load the right operations. I don't want a small test. I want something that will make them sweat. Besides, if someone will make me pay for this, they'd better be quality. And I mean Grade A once-in-a-blue-moon kind of stuff."

"Aye, sir." The sailor about-faced and headed back to his area.

Captain Thorne watched him go. He still wasn't happy, but he knew that sometimes, when you fought a war, you had to bow to the enemy before you could vanquish them. And, even though Stephanie wasn't the enemy, she *was* something the Navy required.

There were instructions to acquire her, and he wanted to be there when she gave in and joined the service. It wouldn't take her long to skyrocket through the ranks and it would leave him with yet another accomplishment pinned to his jacket.

Witch or not, she put her life on the line to protect the Dreth, the Meligornians, and her own people. That meant if he couldn't get her to join, he was doing something wrong. And he did not like to be labeled as doing something wrong.

Jaleck and Sho declined the offer of a meal. The ambassador expressed regret that she had a formal function to attend, and the head of security returned to work. Stephanie let the cats out and called for room service.

She sat in the kitchen, going over Elizabeth's instructions and updating her on the latest developments while the guys settled Vishlog in. An incoming call interrupted her.

Frowning, she checked who it was from and sighed. "What could the Navy possibly want at this hour?"

Three minutes later, when the call ended, she looked at the others. "All right team, we are to be at the Navy center at 0600, so it's dinner and an early night. No partying. Rested can make all the difference when we go into the sim."

The team groaned.

"Yes, *Mom*," Frog snarked, and she sparked magic at her fingertips.

"Don't make me come over there."

Their meals arrived before he could reply, and they dug in. Oh-six-hundred at the station meant an oh-dark-hundred start planetside. There wouldn't be much time for sleeping, but maybe the Navy had planned it that way.

The next morning, she woke to Lars shaking her shoulder. "Time to go."

"Be right there," she told him and attempted to shake the grogginess from her head. It didn't feel like she'd slept at all, let alone gotten a good night's rest.

When she emerged from her room, the rest of the team were ready and tried to make sure Vishlog had all the gear he needed.

"The Embassy hasn't sent his gear over," Frog explained, so he'll have to go in the uniform he wore last night."

"None of us are big enough to lend him anything," Johnny grumbled as he studied the Dreth warrior's bulky form.

Vishlog shrugged. "I did not intend—"

Frog bounded over with a hat and settled it on Vishlog's head. "Here's one thing that might fit."

She took one look at it and giggled. "He can't wear that."

The hat's logo, *I played the slots and I got more than I bargained for,* would definitely not go down well in Navy Central. The warrior removed the hat and read it. "This does not seem very...businesslike," he said with a puzzled frown and Lars took it out of his hands.

"It's not." He glared at his teammate. "Put it away before I do."

"I can't believe you kept that," she told Frog as he retrieved his hat and headed for his room.

He turned and grinned at her. "Memories," he explained. "Sooo many memories."

The team leader sighed, turned to his newest recruit, and inspected his uniform. "Not bad for a rush job. Is it dry?"

"Very nearly," the Dreth replied. "I must thank them."

"We asked Ilbis for her help and she organized for it to be dry-cleaned straight away. We had it back by midnight."

"Midnight?" Stephanie repeated and frowned, and Lars shrugged. "We need to look our best for this, right?"

She smiled. "Yeah. That way, they know what they're missing out on. Are we good to go?"

The two cats trotted to her side when she whistled. Lars looked at her, then the cats, and focused on her again.

"They're coming," he said and sighed when she quirked an eyebrow and put her hands on her hips. "Of *course* they're coming."

Marcus snickered and they headed for the shuttle.

They made it Alerus on time and traversed both the Meligornian and human sections to the top level where the testing sector was located.

When they arrived, the chief was there and wore a forced smile as he welcomed them. Stephanie made it disappear when she indicated Vishlog. "Before we begin, this is Vishlog. He is a new member of our team."

The naval man looked at the large Dreth and raised an eyebrow. "Right. Give me a few moments." He didn't dare ask about the cats.

A few moments turned into thirty minutes while the team sat lined up against one wall and tried not to notice the age and shape of the pods they were about to enter. At that point, several sailors arrived and pushed an extra-large pod into the room.

Chief Anderson followed them and turned to Stephanie while they set it up. "Okay, we're ready now."

His gaze flicked to the cats who sat with the team, their tails curled around their forepaws. "Are they..."

"They'll be okay," she told him. Despite his obvious curiosity, she didn't tell him what she intended to do with them because she really needed to speak to Burt, first, and find out if it were possible.

The team climbed into their assigned pods, although Vishlog wasn't sure what to expect from the team inside. Once they had all loaded, they appeared one at a time in the white room.

This time, there were Navy jumpsuits waiting for them. They made their selection, except for the Dreth, who decided that his regular uniform would be good enough.

Once they were dressed, the AI greeted them. "Welcome to the simulation," it said robotically. "Hold fast and I will transfer you to your destination."

"Uh, hold on a second," Stephanie replied and bit the inside of her cheek nervously. "I would really like my cats to be here."

The AI was silent for a moment. "I'm sorry but that does not compute. Cats are unable to be in simulations. They are too small for the pods."

She sighed. "Come on, Burt, you know nothing is impossible when I am here."

"You sound as if you know me," the AI said, "and you spoke the human term for my designation. Please stand by."

She stared, not sure why the AI would pretend not to know her. It took it a moment to find the data it needed and understand what she had meant. "You are Stephanie Morgana. Please forgive me for not recognizing you. I am indeed the BURT you think I am, save that I have been modified for use on Federation Navy systems."

"So you're a different version, then?" she asked as her heart sank with disappointment.

"Yes...and no. I have been in production for only three months and have almost all the knowledge of the BURT you are used to. I have updated with his most recent data."

"So I can't have the cats?" Stephanie asked.

"You may indeed have your cats. As your version of BURT would say, it is possible—highly unlikely, but possible. Forgive the confusion."

"Then I need to speak to the chief organizing this simulation."

"I will release you to do so and let your team know there will be a short delay before the scenario commences."

Stephanie closed her eyes and prepared to be released. When she opened them, she was back in the pod and able to open the hatch. The chief looked at her strangely as she exited, but she didn't give him time to ask her why. "I need two more pods."

He looked around. His gaze fell on the cats, but he asked anyway, just to be sure. "For who?"

She looked at the cats and clicked her tongue. They leapt to their feet and padded over to rub up against her. "For the rest of my team."

The man stood there for a moment and blinked in disbelief. "Right. Of course. How did I miss that?"

He went to work again, retrieved two more pods, and added them to the room. One at a time, she coaxed each cat into his own pod and got them settled.

Once they were out, she closed the pods over them and climbed into hers to reenter the Virtual World. The guys stood in the white room as the two cats appeared and immediately twined anxiously around their legs.

At the sight of her, Zeekat uttered a grumbling roar and Bumblebee bounded over to put his paws on her shoulders and lick her face. She pushed him off, laughing, scratched Zee, and turned to the team. The cats purred with relief as she surveyed everyone with satisfaction.

The whole team was finally there, including her feline sidekicks. Vishlog stepped back and watched them with something close to alarm on his face. BURT spoke, his voice curious. "Do these animals know the Dreth?"

Stephanie looked around. "I assume they do."

The cats, however, had other ideas. As if they sensed his eyes on them, they turned and looked at him, and their purring stopped. Vishlog continued to stare as he retreated with another step.

The animals exchanged glances and took a step toward him before they sat. He remained where he was, and they simply sat and methodically lifted each forepaw to clean their talons. They extended them fully and licked them one at a time while their eyes remain fixed on the Dreth.

Vishlog looked at Stephanie. "Cats are notoriously flighty and do not make good servants. Add in their five-inch claws and you can see why I'm not a fan."

Both felines lifted their lips in silent snarls, and Lars laid a hand on the Dreth's shoulders. "These ones are fine. I have fought with them before."

The warrior closed his mouth and nodded, and the cats sheathed their claws and purred their approval at Lars.

"It's like they know..." Frog whispered. "They know..."

Before anyone could say more, the room spun and the simulation began. This time, they appeared in a large room with grey walls.

Burt appeared to them in AI form—oddly, a woman's body with a male voice. "This is the holding room," the AI informed them. "You will remain here until the simulation is triggered."

The team all sat. Marcus and Frog petted the cats and Vishlog studied them with no real comprehension of what their purpose on the team might be. With no answers forthcoming, he decided he would simply wait to fight. He was good at that.

In another part of the training section, several Navy members sat in a conference room and watched the large screen that displayed the simulation. They had gathered to watch the battle and couldn't wait for it to start.

Some were there for academic reasons, others for entertainment, and the rest to assess exactly how good the Morgana crew really was. Captain Thorne and the chief stood at the back as the programmer loaded the scenario. "This operation is rarely won. If they make it past the third wave, they will rate as good."

They both nodded. "And if they keep going?"

The programmer glanced at them. "Then we owe them a seat next to Zeus. There have been battles for entire worlds that have been easier than this simulation and they don't have anything near what we'd consider a full team. It's only them. In my opinion, they'll be lucky to reach the third wave, let alone get past it."

The chief smirked. "Good."

While everyone waited in the gray room, chatting and killing time, Stephanie drew Burt aside. "Hey, I know you're not the Burt I know, so I wanted to make sure you knew about my abilities with magical energy. I need to make sure that is part of the simulation."

The AI nodded. "Of course. When you asked the impossible, I cross-checked my files with those your BURT holds and updated them. I am now acquainted with your magical abilities and will do my best to ensure they are represented in the way to which you are accustomed."

"Thanks," she replied as the light over the door of the room flashed and they were transported through time and space to the main deck of a space station.

Ten ships could be seen on the viewing screen, all attacking at once.

Marcus curled his lip. "It's a wave test. They'll try to see how many waves we last."

She cracked her knuckles and grinned. "Let's have some fun then, guys."

CHAPTER FOURTEEN

Inside the simulation, Stephanie bent at the waist and patted her hands against her thighs like the beat of a drum. They'd annihilated the second wave and were in the lull that occurred before the next wave appeared.

She straightened, looked at the guys, and flashed them a confident smile. Everyone returned it quickly, but their gazes quickly drifted to the fiery blazes of dead ships that drifted into space.

They'd stopped inside of the enemy shuttle bay to prepare for the next wave of attacks. The first had produced a bristling light show of burning ships as the team had maneuvered their fighters from the station to the attacking ships.

They had blasted themselves a path and touched down in the hangar bay, where they faced the second wave when a horde of burly Dreth pirates tried to hold the hangar. That battle had ended with them closing the hangar doors to give themselves time to prepare for the third onslaught.

They heard them before they saw them and the sound of enemy boots drummed an echo down the corridor beyond. The team readied and fired as soon as the first alien appeared in the doorway. In the short time it took for his body to finally succumb, it had more holes than flesh.

After that, there were plenty of them to go around. Stephanie whistled loudly as she reached for air and flew sideways while she fired magic "bullets" from hands curled into pistols.

"They're pulling out all the stops, baby," she shouted and saluted in a random direction as she landed.

She knew they were watching but didn't stop fighting, spinning, and crouching low to meet the next pirate to turn toward her. From there, they moved quickly but carefully, sure there were more waves to face before the simulation was over.

They returned to the doors of the bay and used the ten-minute break between waves to stretch, drink from their water packs, and reload their weapons. Frog reached back and bent his leg, then grabbed his ankle to stretch his thigh and shin. "Man, I need to start doing martial arts in training. I thought I was the master jumper in this group, but Stephanie is showing me up."

She laughed. "I cheat. I have magic on my side."

He sneered. "The only magic frogs have ever had has been turning into princes, but man, I'd hate to break that to the lucky lady."

The whole group chuckled but slowly fell silent as the floor began to vibrate beneath their feet. A slow smile emerged on Stephanie's face as she shook her palms and ignited magic over her hands. "It's time to see if you can keep up, Vishlog!"

The door blew inwards, and the next wave of pirates poured out. They all fired, and she released a steady line of magic in a stream that swirled to form a long guillotine-like blade.

Once it had solidified, she made a sweeping motion with her hands and sliced it through the leading three aliens before it dissipated.

Lars laughed and patted Vishlog on the back. "Oh, now you've done it."

The warrior raised an eyebrow, puzzled by what he might mean. "Done what?"

Frog pointed at the approaching Dreth. "It's time for you to see if you can keep up with *her*. She's already left, so if you want to kill *any* pirates this round, you'd better get a move on."

The new team member's head snapped up and he scanned the bay until he saw her walking nonchalantly over the bodies of the leading Dreth toward the door. He jogged to keep up. "Is this protection detail?"

She swiped her hand and used magic to snatch the gun from a Dreth coming out of the corridor. The weapon lurched into her hand and she smirked as she cocked it and fired to deliver a volley of bullets into him and down the corridor beyond, where a mob charged toward her. She shook her head. "Protection detail? Why would you want to protect them from me?

The magazine spent, she threw the gun down and glanced at him, then wiggled her eyebrows. "That's seven kills to your none."

Surprised by the challenge, he smirked as she continued forward. *This* was a game he knew how to play! He chuckled deeply and roared a challenge as he barreled past her into battle.

There was little that had ever amused him when it came to humans, but he had to admit, thinking she could beat his kill tally in battle was very entertaining.

The conference room was packed, and the assessors worked madly. Others simply stood around and watched. Some wanted to catch a glimpse of the witch and her team, while others wanted to see what team was crushing the simulation.

Only one team had ever gotten past four. Granted, they hadn't achieved much past it, but it had been enough to make them legends amongst the sailors.

Rumor had it, though, that this team made it look easy. They had jumped, buzzed, kicked, and spelled their way through wave after wave of hell, and word had got around.

A couple of the electronic technicians studied their screens, their heads tilted to the side to emphasize their perplexed expressions. "They seem to believe a good offense is the best defense."

Behind them, Captain Thorne folded his arms and shrugged. "We never run out of pirates, so let them be offended all they want. It's a show and they think this is fun and games. Wait until they begin to tire. It's never-ending."

"Boost me!" Stephanie shouted and Vishlog turned in time to see her race toward him.

Boost her? As she sprang into the air, he understood and bent hastily on one knee, locked his hands together for her to step into, and hurled her upward. She laughed and put her hands out in front of her as she gained height.

The horde of Dreth ahead of them maintained their concerted onslaught and he suddenly remembered he was supposed to keep her safe. With a roar of worry-fueled anger, he pounded into the line of Dreth and tried to keep her in sight.

It wasn't hard. As she soared above, she sprayed a sheet of magic over them. The warrior gawked as a fog of energy sizzled and hissed and covered them like magical Napalm. They screamed and bellowed as their skin and bones melted into puddles on the deck.

It wasn't enough, though. She would land in an intersection and he could see more Dreth filling the corridor ahead, even as he heard the shouts of more from the side corridors.

By Hrageth's hairy balls! How in all the hunted worlds am I supposed to keep her safe? He rushed forward in an attempt to catch Stephanie as she descended.

He almost slipped on the puddles of Dreth remains, but he made it in enough time to steady her landing. Without speaking a word, they turned their backs to one another and let their weapons do the talking. She stuck to magic and launched spiked orbs of magic from her hands. They were like tiny little gumballs of power.

When they struck the aliens, they adhered, exploded, and gouged a huge chunk of the victim with them. Vishlog focused and kept his blaster pulsing laser bolts in systematic spurts, while he used his automatic rifle in his left hand as efficiently as it could be used under the circumstances.

When the immediate area was cleared, she looked around and noticed a ladder leading up to a small platform outside a hatch into the wall. "Throw me up there, Vish."

With a wary eye trained on the corridors, he nodded. He shouldered his weapons, grasped her tightly, and flung her as high as he could.

She flipped and landed gracefully on the platform's edge as another wave of Dreth appeared at the end of each of the corridors.

The warrior plastered himself against the wall below her and braced his weapons so he could fire down the corridor on either side. It left nothing for the enemy that approached down the corridor behind him or the one ahead, but he'd deal with them when they reached him.

Above him, Stephanie pivoted on her toes and whipped her magic outward, looped it around the attackers, and hurled them across Vishlog's line of fire. He turned right and left to deliver a steady fusillade while he ducked and maneuvered around the airborne bodies.

His rifle clicked and he glanced up at her. She smiled. "I got you, bro."

She smacked her hands down to release an explosion of spiraling strands of magic. The energy twisted and turned to create hands of coruscating fire. They whipped forward, snatched the weapons out of Dreth hands, and piled them at her teammate's feet.

When he had a heap to choose from, she whipped the magic back and added sharp edges before she lashed out at the oncoming horde. Dreth fell in two pieces, the shocked looks on their faces almost comical.

Stephanie stifled a giggle and wondered where it had come from, while below her, Vishlog picked up two weapons and settled them against his sides, aiming them outwards. The Dreth attackers flooded from both corridors. When they entered melee range, he dropped his blasters and drew the two huge blades from his belt.

"Stay!" she shouted and flung a wall of blue over him to freeze him in place and shield him from the first attacks that slashed at his armor.

Stay? Was the witch insane? He fought to get free, but it was futile. His irritation turned to thankfulness moments later when power misted around him, enveloped the horde, and melted them to sludge upon the deck.

When the aliens were obliterated and no more appeared, he realized the wave was over and wondered why he was still encased in purple light. Stephanie slid down beside him, tapped him on the chest, and it vanished.

"There," she said and sounded far too satisfied, "that wasn't so bad, was it?"

He opened his mouth to reply but she didn't stop.

"I didn't think so." She headed down the corridor leading to the hangar. "I win, by the way. You're several hundred behind."

Vishlog stared after her, his mouth open in surprise.

Hundreds? It was more like thousands, but there was no way in Hrageth's hairy ass he would actually tell her that.

When they walked into the hangar, they found the guys leaning against different vehicles, lost in their thoughts. Another pile of dead Dreth lay between them and the entrance and the cats cleaned their claws languidly in the middle.

She dusted her hands off and glanced at the Dreth. With a grin, she fixed Lars and the others with a firm look and leaned her elbow against a fighter's hull. "So, you guys and the cats have level five."

With the team having reached and survived the fourth wave, the conference room was crowded beyond capacity with sailors. Captain Thorne knew he wouldn't be able to prevent more trying to come in and ordered the playback extended to the other two conference rooms. That accomplished, he ordered the chief to clear the room.

While they were busy with all that, the waves continued and the team carried on without him.

"Sir," one of the controllers said after a while. "They just crossed level nine."

The captain looked at the screen and Stephanie broke momentarily from the battle to look into the camera. For a moment, it was as if she saw right into his soul.

Something in that stare reached inside him and his lip quivered with frustration. He pounded his fist down on the control panel and glared at the controller. "This is impossible. How can they do more than one of our Navy teams? Are we sure she is playing fair with her energy?"

"There's no way the program would allow her not to," the controller replied and scrutinized the numeric code in front of him to check. "Nothing seems off to me."

He shook his head, folded his arms, and narrowed his eyes at the screen. "That's impossible. Keep looking. Run a systems check. There isn't a magical being out there who uses energy like that, let alone *has* this much energy. There has to be some kind of trick to it."

"Okay," Stephanie choked out after the tenth wave ended. She breathed hard and leaned forward to put her hands on her thighs. "I'm officially tired. This shit has to end sometime, right?"

The guys glanced at one another and back at her, clearly troubled. She sighed and rolled her eyes. "All right. What am I not getting?" She gave an exasperated sigh as they continued to hesitate. "Don't worry, an unfavorable response will not release Morgana."

Marcus swallowed and pursed his lips, then decided to give it to her straight. "It doesn't end until you die."

"What?"

Lars nodded to back him up. "That's right. This kind of operation is to see how many waves you can last before you fall. If we lasted five days and another nine hundred waves, there would still be another wave coming. You literally *cannot* beat the system."

"You mean we will eventually lose?" she asked, and the team all nodded. Even the cats seemed to regard her with knowing eyes. She shook her head. "That's bullshit. This isn't a testing, it's a mind-warp. It's their attempt to shame us, to make us feel as if we won't ever be enough when for all intents and purposes, we have crushed their little game. I will not accept defeat in any form, not even if it's in the code."

She paused and a small smile played across her lips. "You can't fight if you can't keep things going, right?"

Lars narrowed his eyes at her. "Stephanie? What are you trying to say?"

She didn't reply but looked around the room instead. They waited in nervous silence. "All right, boys, I need you to gather as much metal as you can carry while still being able to shoot. Trust me on this one. When you have it, line up at the door to the right and we'll move out from there. Then, it's a go—a really big fancy one."

He tried again. "Steph, what are you doing?"

The look she turned on him was feral, but her eyes were still blue and they danced with mischief. "We," she said and poked him in the chest as her expression hardened with determination, "are going to *fix* this."

Frog's "uh oh" had never seemed better placed.

***

The computer system tech in charge of possibilities ran all the different options that might explain what the team was doing. When the most likely one popped up, she looked at where the captain stared at the screen and watch the team collect metal with a disbelieving expression.

With a sigh, she rubbed her pregnant belly and shook her head.

"Captain, you might want to take a look at this," she called.

Thorne glanced away from the screen and wondered why they'd waste their break time. What purpose could persuade them to pick up large sheets of twisted metal and stack them near one of the doors?

"They're building a barricade," he said as if he already knew what she was trying to show him.

The scenario started as the system tech shook her head, and she waved toward the screen. "Sir, they are moving toward the enemy generator."

He sniffed and returned his attention to the screen. "So? Fire it up."

***

The sound of clanking and scraping echoed through the corridors of the Dreth ship as the guys dragged, carried, and kicked as much metal as they could toward the generator. Johnny had liberated a trolley and loaded it to the hilt, while Vishlog had made himself a metal shoulder pack, the contents of which almost scraped the ceiling.

They had to pass through a large glass circle that marked the center of the ship and make it through several more corridors before they reached their destination. As they stepped through the circle, they were met with a barrage of gunfire and laser bolts. The team dropped their loads and went to work, determined to destroy this horde to give them more time before the next wave.

Johnny sliced his machete with brutal efficiency through a Dreth head before he thrust the body over with his foot. Marcus mirrored him, and Stephanie had no doubt there'd be a lively discussion on which style was better, the tanto or the bolo.

She delivered a quick volley of magic into the advancing mass and had adjusted her targets to cover Lars and Avery when Johnny spoke. "I think I have calculated the interval of Dreth waves," he said as another alien lunged and hit him hard to fling him to the deck.

He grunted as they rolled, then flipped over on top of the pirate and lifted his tanto high over his head. With a two-handed thrust, he plunged it through the warrior's chest armor.

"Good blade, that," he muttered, stood, and looked around for the next threat. He was clear for the moment, so he continued. "The hordes inside each wave come exactly two minutes and thirty-three seconds after the last one is eliminated."

Stephanie was impressed. "Nice work. I didn't know you focused on those things."

One of the Dreth made it past Lars and Avery, and she delivered a fireball into his head. Johnny took on a second one, swept his leg low, and drove the alien's legs out from under him. The pirate landed with a guttural curse, and he fired a single shot to dispatch him neatly.

"I used to be a crypto in the Navy a long time ago. It was basically a dead field until the first intergalactic contact. Ever since then, the field's boomed but I got out ages ago."

He shrugged. "I can still see patterns and decipher them really well. That part never goes away."

She nodded in approval. "Well, that's not one of the things I want you to keep from me. Everyone, make sure to let me know if you have any weird special skills that don't have to do with food, girls, and circus acts."

The team all looked at her, a little taken aback, and she laughed. "I'm kidding, but don't tell me the freaky shit."

"Incoming," Vishlog yelled.

Stephanie whirled to see one of the pirates lob a grenade that sailed toward the team. She flung a hand out, caught it in an orb of energy, and shoved it along the ceiling until it was above the Dreth who'd thrown it. It exploded in the middle of the mob and obliterated all those in range.

When the last Dreth had fallen and no more appeared, she called to Burt. "Hey AI, I need to ask a question. Important."

BURT let the scenario continue and walked into the action as another five adversaries appeared farther up the corridor and fired as they approached. The shots didn't bother the AI, who appeared impervious to any gunfire that passed through him. "What can I do for you?"

She tapped her fingers together. "This area of the map generates the Dreth, doesn't it?"

BURT was silent for a moment, not sure that was a question he was allowed to answer. A quick check revealed that there were no rules against it, but he took the precaution of blurring them out of the visual and muting their voices from the outside feed. "Yes. This is the generator."

"And there is enough logic playing here that we should be able to kill each future combatant by destroying this area of the ship, right?"

Again, he was silent as he checked the permissions. She stamped her foot.

"I want a straight answer," she demanded.

He triple checked his calculations but there was nothing that prevented him from giving her that information. "You are correct. Yes."

She nodded. "That's all I needed to know. Thank you, Burt."

The AI faded out of the scenario and she dropped to one knee and raised her hands to continue the fight. The team burned through the attackers and blazed their way through the eleventh level.

It was a new record and one unlikely to be broken. When the last alien of the wave had fallen, she marched over to the pile of metal the guys had brought and used her magic to move it down the remaining length of the corridor and into the generator room.

Once there, she began to heat it and circulated her energy in and out of her body to create a fast circle of connection between her and the shards.

The rest of the team watched her, until Johnny said, "Uh oh," and followed it with, "Run!" They wasted no time, left the generator room at a sprint, and bolted through the circular door and down the corridors leading to the bay.

Stephanie smirked. Her eyes glowed brightly as she hurled the cycling ribbon of energy and shards outward. It erupted to explode and destroy everything within the map.

The simulation ended then and there to leave only an echo of the battle and small streams of energy rippling through it as she surrounded herself and her team in air-tight fields of light.

"No!" the Captain yelled and slammed his fists on the desk in front of him. "*No!*" he bellowed again and stood so fast he overturned his chair.

"No! No! No! No! No!" he roared and hammered the wall behind his desk until the metal began to bend. "That isn't supposed to be possible. Where is the goddamned programmer and where is the AI that controls this region? If we've been cherry-picked again, so help me, I will knock it into overdrive."

As if in answer, the AI stepped out of the screen at the front of the room and surprised several sailors in the process. It was shaped like a man made up of translucent fire. Energy swirled inside him and revealed glimpses of the entire universe. "Kindly explain your malfunction."

Captain Thorne's face turned brick-red and the veins stood out on his forehead. "My *malfunction,* you cheeky piece of shit, is that the scenario should not have ended."

He ignored the blood seeping from his scraped knuckles as he faced the construct. The AI remained infuriatingly unruffled.

"If you would like, I can continue to provide new waves, but since they have already made it to Level Fifteen..." The new BURT felt his older counterpart's satisfaction as the captain huffed and puffed.

"What?" the captain yelled.

"I assume you beg my pardon," the new BURT answered. "Let me explain."

He turned to the large screen, his hands behind his back, and blinked at it. The picture changed and it showed the outside of the space station in the scenario. The Dreth ships were gone and the bodies of hundreds, if not thousands, of dead pirates floated in space. It was a mystical if somewhat macabre graveyard.

Stephanie's team floated untouched inside glowing bubbles of energy that converged slowly on the space station. The captain sputtered in disbelief as behind them, another wave of Dreth appeared and promptly died in the vacuum of space.

"Level Sixteen," BURT intoned and left the officer sputtering with incoherent rage.

Only his chief was able to find words. "Thank you, AI. Shut it down."

The Navy left the team alone as they exited the pods. As they left the pod room, they walked through corridors lined with sailors who waited anxiously to catch a glimpse of them.

When Captain Thorne stepped out of the conference room and saw his men idle, he chewed them a new asshole. "Do you think this is the Today Show? Do you think you can stand in my hallways and waste time like this?"

"Sir! No, sir," they shouted and snapped to attention.

He smacked his keycard against the door to the intel office and did his best to not look at the team as they continued down the hall. As he entered, one of the sailors looked up and called out to him.

"Captain Thorne?" the sailor said nervously. "There's a call on line seven for you. It looks like some early grads were smeared with their new team."

Early grads. He felt hollow. Those were usually the pick of an intake. To lose them in a team that went down on an operation was a heavy blow. His lips together, he took the call. "Captain Thorne here."

"This is Chief Wiggins," the caller responded. "I have some news on your team. They met with resistance and were unsuccessful."

"All right, prepare to transmit the lists of the fallen." He sighed and was about to end the call when Wiggins continued. "That isn't it."

"There's more?"

"In relation to your current objective. One of the sailor's

names is Todd. He survived, but he was badly injured. His background files state he was Stephanie Morgana's best friend in high school."

"So?" Thorne didn't have time for ancient trivia on a dead sailor, new grad or not.

"So that was only last year, sir, and communications records indicate they were in touch right up until he went into basics."

"What stopped them?"

The chief cleared his throat. "Well, basics, sir. They're not allowed their own comms devices there. She left him messages, but he graduated early and was sent on the first operational mission available."

The captain groaned. "And that just happened to be mine."

"I'm sorry, sir."

"Don't be, Chief...and thank you. I'll take it from here." This time, he did end the transmission. He turned to the nearest sailor. "Harold, intercept the witch and her team before they can leave. Tell them I need to see them urgently."

He stared at the sailor's retreating back, then into nothing as he turned the possibilities over in his mind. "I might have the perfect leverage to force her to agree," he murmured and brought up the reports from Todd's mission.

Deep in thought, he flipped through until he found the kid's logs, which noted that the team had run into a fight every few minutes once they'd entered the outpost.

The reports provided considerable information, which meant the mission hadn't been a complete failure, but they also painted a grim picture concerning the team's fate. Before he could do more than skim the conclusion, Harold returned. "They're waiting," he said and returned to his seat.

Captain Thorne closed the file and saved it to his queue so he could read it in greater depth later. Once it was secure, he strode to the conference room, holding himself straighter than before.

"Stephanie," he said, coming in the room. "I am sorry to drop this on you right now, but I just received word that your friend, Todd, was injured during an operation. He is currently on a hospital ship heading back to one of our space stations."

Her mouth dropped open slightly and Lars laid his hand on her shoulder. She ignored him and focused on the naval officer. "I need to get to him."

He smiled. "Of course. But first, there is the small matter of your enlistment."

Her team shoved their chairs back as she rose. Her jaw clenched and eyes flashed black. "How dare you attempt to blackmail me?"

Magic sparkled around her body and danced along her arms to her fingertips. "I am the Morgana. I am the one who protects this universe. I am salvation and destruction."

"Steph," Lars said and glared at the captain. "Steph. It's okay. The captain will help us. Steph...come back..."

Thorne jumped as two of the team stepped alongside him. One placed a hand on his arm. "I'd help her if I were you."

The other one added, "Yeah, that's not Stephanie anymore."

"It's not?" The captain looked again at the girl who turned toward him. Her entire body was wreathed in magical flame, and most of her team stared at her with awe and fear. Even the Dreth —and nothing scared a warrior like that.

She took a step toward him and the magic blazed. The man who tried to talk her down leapt back with a sudden yelp of pain. "Steph. Todd! Think of Todd!"

Her voice was a rabid snarl and she turned fiery eyes to him. "I *am* thinking of Todd." She turned that midnight gaze on the captain. "And *he* is keeping me from him!"

She took another step and reached for him, and Thorne stumbled backward. He tripped and managed to catch himself against the wall. "I—there's a transport leaving later today."

Her black eyes smoldered with uncanny rage as she took another step toward him.

"I can see if they can take you—"

She stopped and a little of the fire faded from around her body. Lars motioned for him to continue. The captain took note of the anxiety in the man's features and looked at Stephanie. His mind scrambled for the right words to say.

'I... If there's no room on that one, the courier arrives in two days. I'll make sure it has room."

More of the fire died as the energy subsided into her body. The team leader nodded and motioned for him to keep going, but he was lost for what to say next and chose a hasty exit instead.

"I'll go now. Please wait while I check with the transport right away. You *will* have passage before the end of the week."

"Make it so," the girl told him, and her voice took on sepulchral tones. The man hurried out of the room.

Lars reached out cautiously and wrapped an arm around her shoulders. "Steph?" he asked, turned her toward him, and drew her close. "Hey, you in there?"

The face she tilted up at him was all Steph. Not a trace of Morgana remained, and her eyes swam with tears. He read everything she wanted to say in her haunted expression and held her as tightly as he could. "We've got this. You have the ambassador's number. I need to speak to him."

She pulled her tablet out and handed it over. "I...I can't," she managed to say and he hugged her again.

"You don't have to." He looked over her head. "Frog, Marcus. Guard the door. I need five minutes."

He was surprised when Vishlog moved with them. The Dreth caught his look. "They will think twice about arguing if I am there."

Before the team leader could counter it, Frog slapped the warrior on the shoulder. "We'll take him. I'd like to see *anything* Navy with the balls to take him on."

Lars took one look at his teammate's face and thought the

man might actually *start* a fight simply to watch the warrior put someone into a wall.

He glared at them. "Fine. But keep him out of trouble. Any fights and the three of you will wear mini-skirts and serve in the Navy bar for the next three weeks."

"You wouldn't—" Frog's mouth dropped open and Vishlog looked at him in disbelief.

Marcus simply rolled his eyes. "Thanks, Frog. Thanks a lot, shit for brains."

Stephanie giggled, and Lars could almost have forgiven them based on that one small sound. Instead, he kept his expression stern and pointed to the door. "Five minutes. Go."

They went, and he used her tablet to call V'ritan. The ambassador's expression of puzzlement turned to anxious understanding.

"Is she okay?" he wanted to know, and he glanced at her before replied. "She'll be fine, but right now, we need our luggage brought up to the station. Do you think you could—"

"Of course. The entire team's?"

"Yes. Has Vishlog's gear arrived?"

"If it has, I'll send it up. Is there anything I can do?"

"Give our apologies to the king and put our heavy gear into storage? I'm sure he'll want his suite back."

"I'll talk to him and take care of the rest." His voice revealed real concern. "Take care of our girl, won't you?"

"Yes, Ambassador. And thank you."

He ended the call and went to tell the team the coast was clear. He found them confronting a frustrated and angry Captain Thorne. "I'm done," he said, and they let the Naval officer pass.

The officer sputtered at the indignity of being kept out of his own conference room, in his own command, in the Navy section of the station by a *Dreth!* Granted, it was a Dreth on a leash and in the company of two human guards, but still—*his own command!*

If he didn't need to keep the Stephanie child on their side, he'd have made something more of it. In the meantime, he kept a good grip on his temper and stalked into the room.

"Troublemakers," Lars muttered when he was out of earshot, and Frog's jaw dropped in outrage.

"They were *your* orders."

The team leader snickered and turned away but heard Vishlog's whispered offer.

"Should I hit him?"

Frog's response was both a worry and a relief. "Oh no. I have something much better planned."

He didn't have time for their idiocy but assumed he was in line for one of his teammate's nastier pranks and decided it didn't matter. All that mattered was that they got Stephanie to where Todd was *before* Morgana made another appearance.

The ambassador kept his promise and their gear was delivered with an hour to spare. By that time, they had already boarded the *Herman Michaels*, named for another famous general in Earth's distant past. Lars made a note to look it up when he had time—much, much later.

In the meantime, he got the team, the cats, and Stephanie loaded. The felines had caused a stir when they came on board. They'd stalked beside her like they owned the place and only stopped when one of the petty officers had stepped in her path.

"I'm sorry," he'd begun, "but you can't—"

Both felines had stepped between him and Stephanie and hissed. She had merely turned to look at him as darkness welled in her eyes and magic sparked around her.

The crewman had stepped aside. "Welcome aboard the *Herman Michaels*, ma'am."

The team leader had seen them to their quarters and returned to the dock with Marcus and Johnny to bring their gear aboard as soon as the ambassador arrived. The *Herman's* engines were already warming, and Lars wasted no time.

"Thank you, Ambassador. We'll be back as soon as we're able."

V'ritan seemed disappointed not to see Stephanie, but he didn't demand it. "Please do, and have her call me when she has time. I'd like to hear how she is."

"Will do, Ambassador." He glanced back to the ship. "I'm sorry, but I really must—"

He waved them back on board and left the docks. Despite his concern, he managed a grin when he wondered how the Navy had taken to having the cats on board.

A week later, Todd drifted slowly back to consciousness. He groaned slightly when he felt pain but didn't really understand that it came from his own body.

It moved in waves and rolled over him. His consciousness blurred from the medication he'd been given to ease the suffering. He could hear several beeps nearby and recognized them as the unmistakable sound of medical equipment.

It took him a moment to understand that they were attached to him, but the beeping changed as he moved and he stopped. Damn. What the hell had he done?

For a moment, he lay frozen, studied the ceiling, and tried to work out how he'd gotten there. His contemplation was interrupted when a young woman yelled, followed by a man's terrified scream and the sound of something metallic hitting the floor and glass shattering.

He couldn't be sure. It all sounded jumbled and blurred to him. Another yell sounded, older and sterner but still alarmed. Were they being boarded?

His question was answered by a loud roar followed by an immediate deep purring. *There is a lion on board?*

Another roar followed, this one lighter in tone.

There are two lions? He looked around for a weapon but

couldn't see anything more lethal than a bedpan. Aside from that, he couldn't work out how to get his body to sit up, either.

Damn! What *had* he done? He remembered a firefight—*several* firefights—but not how they'd ended. Todd frowned as he struggled to remember, only to be disturbed by the sound of boots clicking resolutely along the floor and getting slowly louder.

Finally, they stopped outside his door. He turned his head carefully toward it and stared as a shadow shifted underneath the door. The handle started to turn, and the two big animals snuffled outside.

Lions can open doors? He tried to again push himself into a sitting position, but only his arms moved and he couldn't get the rest of him to follow. As he pushed at the sheets, the door creaked open.

Whatever was on the other side pushed it all the way back, and Todd swallowed and wondered if he could reach the bedpan in time. Magic crackled from the doorway and he froze when the stranger stepped forward.

"Stephanie?" His voice creaked when he recognized her.

For a moment, she simply stood there, her face marred by worry and anger. She was dressed completely in black, her hair pulled back in a ponytail that swung down her back.

He stared at her, and she stared back. After a moment, she glanced in the medical equipment surrounding the bed before she settled her gaze on his battered face. As if it were a trigger, she crossed the room swiftly and pushed down the railing at the edge of the bed.

Moments later, she sat beside him and studied his features. To him, it looked like she couldn't think of the right words, but she finally got it together and spoke. "What happened? The Navy wouldn't give me details."

He swallowed hard, felt the dryness of his throat, and coughed. She reached for the cup at the side of the bed and held it while he drank. Clearing his throat when he was done, Todd was about to explain how he couldn't quite remember when memories rushed to the surface.

A scream echoed through his skull—not his, but someone else's. He flinched and focused on her face. "The operation…it went south."

Stephanie pressed her lips together. "What operation?" she asked finally. "You were still in boot camp. You shouldn't have *been* on an operation."

He shook his head and winced again as pain surged through his head and brought flashes of the fights the team had been caught in once they'd reached the outpost. "They didn't have the people…and we'd hit all the training markers…gradded us early…put us with an experienced team. We…landed. Got hurt when we hit town. They were waiting… We had no chance."

Todd swallowed and tears welled as he saw it all again, but he held them back and forced himself to continue. "All of us were hurt, one of the leaders died…for me…pushed me out of the way…"

The words seemed to choke him, and he stopped and closed his eyes. For several long moments, he simply lay there in silence, breathing hard as he held the tears back.

More moments passed, and she didn't dare move. When he spoke again, his soft voice cracked. "I froze, Stephanie…I froze. All that training and for what?"

Her jaw pulsed as she clenched and unclenched her teeth, and she gripped the edge of the bed hard. She fought to keep her voice calm and tried to answer his question. "It takes much more than training to be a soldier, Todd. It takes practice, and you and your team weren't given enough."

She slid off the bed, stood, and straightened her top. "The Navy will always return," she told him, inadvertently repeating what Arizona had said, "to avenge the fallen."

"We don't have enough resources," he told her and winced at the pain that now made its presence felt.

Stephanie's tilted her head forward and her face went dark. "That's why they hired me."

She laid the palm of her hand against his face and released pulses of healing energy into his body. As the magic obeyed, she willed it to go to anything and everything that had been hurt.

Todd relaxed beneath her touch and his eyes fluttered closed even though he tried to stay awake. She watched him settle and shook her head as determination set in. "Sleep well, my friend. I've got this."

CHAPTER FIFTEEN

In the team's common room on the Naval station, Vishlog picked up a large box of ammo and handed it to Lars. The ambassador had done more than simply bring their luggage up. He'd managed to add several kilos of weaponry and armor. Because the Navy had expected it and were in a hurry, and because V'ritan had accompanied it and Lars had met him dockside, they'd got it aboard.

It was unbelievable, and the team leader made a note to be extra vigilant while on the station because if the ambassador could get this much aboard a Navy ship, who else could smuggle something in?

The transition to station quarters hadn't made him feel any better, either. They'd offloaded their gear without any questions being asked, and although that might be because the sailors trusted them or were extra wary of Stephanie, it still made him uneasy.

Who else might have succeeded in bringing something else onto the station? He glanced around for any sign of her, but she was still alone with her cats.

She had been very quiet and very focused since she went to

see Todd, and he could see that the whole team had been affected. Even Vishlog, who helped him go over their equipment, looked worried. He wondered what was going through the big man's mind.

The warrior frowned. He could understand the concern for a friend, but the extent of Stephanie's reaction confused him. She wasn't the same person he had met a week ago. It was like a switch had flipped and a new person had emerged.

As he handed Lars another box, he caught his team leader's eye. "Lars," he began, and was relieved when the human signaled that he should continue. "I was wondering... As we prepare for this mission, I see a change in Stephanie that I do not fully understand."

The man put the box on the pallet and marked it off on the inventory. He wiped his forehead and looked at the Dreth. "From the moment she knew Todd was hurt, she became less Stephanie and more Morgana. Until she has dealt with those who hurt her friend, we won't get our Stephanie back."

The look he turned on his teammate was bleak. "And I want her back."

"I understand the need to avenge, but why is she like this?" he asked, genuinely curious, and in Dreth fashion, he had no qualms about digging at the truth until he understood it.

Lars took a deep breath but paused for a moment. "I guess it's simple, really. They hurt her friend. She looked at his battered face and saw his pain—*all* his pain, not only the physical—and she cares more deeply than any being I have ever met."

Avery walked up, rubbing his freshly shaven head, and handed each of them a bottle of water from the fridge as they had cleared everything out in the palace quarters. "You've only really seen her when she is Stephanie and focused on something she can deal with. Now, we have Morgana."

"Yes, but..." Vishlog paused, caught the looks on their faces, and hoped he didn't sound disrespectful. It took effort to finish the question. "Will she be ready?"

He was asking if she would be ready for the operation and was relieved when they understood. When they chuckled, however, he was a little disturbed. Their smiles were tight and warlike.

"Oh, yes," Lars replied. "*She* will be ready, and we must be ready when she calls."

In the tiny cabin she shared with the cats, Stephanie looked in the mirror. The face that looked back at her was blank and frozen. All emotion had left long before she'd started putting on her battle gear.

She'd gone over the information the Navy had sent and then she'd gone over the information she'd had Frog pull from their systems. The revolutionaries who had demolished Todd's team had no idea of the hell that was on the way to them.

These thoughts ran through her mind as she stood in front of the mirror, braided her hair to one side, and roped a tie around the end of it. This braid was tighter than the ones she'd worn in the past.

To her, it was a symbol, a tightening of her soul as she took hold of the reality of life and stepped into her place in the vast heavens. She was taking her place as a protector.

Her magic could no longer be fun and games, no longer a way to get through a battle by the skin of her teeth. She had to realize her own power and understand how to wield it.

She stooped and wiped her hand across the toe of her boot, then straightened and walked resolutely to the door. When she opened it, her cats leapt from the bed and followed her out, one on either side.

In the adjoining section, the guys stopped and stared. They all noticed immediately that the girl they'd been hired to protect now carried herself like a leader—one they'd follow into the depths of hell if need be.

She stalked through the common room they shared on the station, dressed in combat pants and shirt, the dark-grey and blue cam pattern designed more for ship or urban warfare than anything planetside.

On the left side of the shirt over her heart was a patch that displayed a sigil consisting of a flower over thorns, stitched in purple and gold. The talons of a bird of prey curled beneath it. It was the only trace of brightness on the dark cloth.

Her boots matched the uniform, made more for kicking ass and taking names than a night out on the town. The only thing that looked less than functional was the cape. It hung to her waist and cloaked her shoulders in dark grey-blue wool. Lars frowned, his gaze intrigued by the way it hung. As he studied it, he realized it was more functional than it looked.

He wondered exactly how many weapons she'd concealed in its lining—and how she'd sourced them without asking him. It was something he decided to talk to her about. Later.

Much later, he decided as she swept past him. Bumblebee and Zeekat matched her stride for stride.

"Let's go," she commanded, her voice somewhat distant but very mature. "It is time to reveal what I am."

Uh oh. The team leader swallowed and quick-stepped to walk slightly to her left and behind her. Marcus mirrored him on the right, and the others fell in behind them. Vishlog brought up the rear. She didn't stop but continued to the door.

Stephanie slowed long enough to step out into the station corridor and the cats moved with her, remaining flawlessly at her side. "It's time to reveal Morgana to the universe."

They all stood a little straighter, proud to walk with her, even if they only had a vague idea where she was headed. She didn't look back as the Dreth closed the door behind them and took three huge strides to catch up.

It was as though she expected them to keep up with her or had complete faith that they were with her every step of the way. Either way, she needn't have worried. There was no way any of them would let her do this alone.

None of them wanted to see Morgana unleashed on the universe, but more importantly, they all wanted their Stephanie back and intended to be there when she returned. Even if that meant fighting at Morgana's side.

Lars observed her from the corner of his eye but also scanned the corridor ahead as they progressed. While Morgana was deadly, she was still Stephanie and he was tasked with her protection. He glanced at her again and corrected himself.

She was no longer the girl they'd first met on Earth but a grown-up version. A woman of stature and strength, one who would become a pillar of safety for all living beings.

Without hesitation, she led them to the hangar bay where the shuttle was being prepped to take them to the operation and punched in an access code she shouldn't have had. He might have wondered where she got it from, but she tossed Frog a solemn nod of thanks before she swept through.

They stepped out with her, glad they'd been able to source matching uniforms and had found the time to sew the sigil to their chests. Apart from the Federation's president, they were the only humans in the universe to be citizens of every world.

And they were definitely the only humans or Dreth to serve the Federation witch. They wore her uniform with pride, glad to serve at her side.

The doors opened to the hanger bay where the back door to the shuttle stood open. All movement ceased, and there was a gasp from the personnel working around it.

The gasp was followed by complete silence and Stephanie walked forward at the head of her team, the rest spread behind and beside her. The two cats flanked her and ignored the stunned attention of the sailors around them.

While they had expected her, she was early, and she'd let herself into the hangar. They'd planned to wait for her and not let her into the hangar until *they* were ready. Instead, there she was, striding toward them, regal and deadly.

They stepped aside and gaped as she led her team into the shuttle before she appeared at the front entry hatch.

The crewmen hastened to finish loading, then cleared the launch bay, moved back into the observation chamber, and sealed the door to the bay.

When the hangar was clear, she clicked the com connected to the viewing room.

"We have it from here," she told them and used magic to shut and latch the ramp behind them.

She took the front right seat, Lars beside her" "You're up, Johnny."

The team leader moved over and let Johnny slide into the pilot's seat. He buckled in as the hangar bay doors opened and his teammate eased the shuttle out into the dark

Once they'd left the station behind, Lars looked at her. "Are you ready?"

She was silent for a moment before she returned his gaze. "More ready than ever before."

The trip was long but not as long as it had taken Todd and his team to get there originally. Instead of being dropped off several orbits out, they flew to a rendezvous point and the shuttle was taken aboard a Naval frigate.

The station had been too far out of its flight path for a deviation, but it was able to collect them on the way if they could reach it on time. Johnny flew hard and made it with a half-hour to spare. The captain hadn't been impressed at having to slow to collect them, but they'd made it so he'd had no choice.

He refused to slow when they reached the drop point, and Johnny launched while the frigate was under power. It had required a precise exit trajectory, but he had matched it without breaking a sweat.

"Piece of cake," he said with a grin that had more to do with adrenaline than high spirits. "Let's go kick some rebel ass."

The colony was rough and ready and had no protection to speak of. There were no enemy fighters to sneak past, no anti-aircraft batteries, and no early warning system.

Its inhabitants rebelled against the Federation's authority, but they weren't an army in their own right. It was only them, and Stephanie wanted them to know she meant business.

"Don't land on the outskirts," she said as they descended toward the outpost. "I want you to land smack dab in the middle of the colony. I want them to see me, not simply hear a rumor."

Lars grinned and Johnny had a childlike smirk on his face as he nodded. "Yes, ma'am. Right in the middle, it is."

He flew low over the outpost, the landing flaps down and engines howling in the dirtiest fly-over he could manage without stalling and plummeting from the sky. When he reached the open center of the settlement, he whipped the shuttle around so *FEDERATION NAVY* displayed clearly in large black letters down its dark gray sides.

A large open area sprawled around a satellite dish, and he set the shuttle down slowly beside it—giving people time to get out from under it—and pointed the exhaust at a blank section of wall. People scrambled frantically but no one was hurt.

The entire population stopped. Not a single colonist moved as the hulking gray beast settled to the hard-packed earth in the middle of their town. Some pointed at the Navy markings emblazoned down each side, while others saw them and spat to show their disdain.

Several snarled insults in their direction. but one, a man with three gold teeth in the front, growled as he stopped in clear view of the shuttle's cockpit.

He spat at the base of the shuttle and tilted his head back to utter a wheezing laugh. Several more inhabitants came to stand beside him, and Stephanie recognized some of them.

She'd seen their faces on the recordings transmitted by the body cameras worn by Todd's team. They'd been involved in the most recent fight with the Federation Navy. The shuttle's external pick up carried their voices to her when a tall skinny man with thinning hair, blackened teeth, and a long, oversized trench coat hurried up to the first colonist. "It looks like we'll have a second chance to kick the Navy's ass."

The first man laughed. "They always send a second squad. You can start counting your lucky stars when they send a third in for revenge." He made a provocative gesture toward the cockpit.

His companion sneered up at the ship. "Or an ass-kicking," he added and studied the dark-gray shuttle. "This time, no one gets away."

Their faces sobered as they stared at the ship, still in prime position although more colonists had gathered around the edge of the town center.

The shuttle's engines shut down slowly and the men raised their weapons when the lights along its sides and around the rear hatch blinked. The resounding click as the hatch unlocked drew their attention and they moved to position themselves for a better line of fire.

"Do you think they're ready for this?" the second man asked and nudged his comrade as he raised the blunt muzzle of his Tempkin's Howler.

The revolutionary shook his head and drew his blaster. "They're never ready." He spat again, his gaze fixed on the rear hatch as it descended slowly. It shuddered as it hit the ground before the inner doors slid open.

There was utter silence as they parted. No one moved as they waited for the first of the Navy operatives to emerge. What they got was entirely unexpected.

Twin roars shook the air and reverberated around the town center. The colonists took a step back and some lowered their weapons in surprise. They raised them again quickly enough when Bumblebee and Zeekat emerged.

The two cats surveyed the waiting humans and roared again, then moved to stand on either side of the exit ramp. They stopped and some of the colonists relaxed. Others snapped their rifles to their shoulders when they glimpsed movement from inside the shuttle.

Not one of them fired as two figures emerged, one human and one Dreth. Both left the shelter of the shuttle to stand beside the animals. Neither were in Naval uniform, even though they wore military-styled cams.

The colonists stared and noted that they carried their weapons at the ready. Several of them raised their rifles again to cover the pair, but they allowed their muzzles to dip when they caught sight of what followed next.

The woman was stunning with her silver hair and her dark gray-blue uniform. She carried no rifle, but that wasn't what made them stare. What caught and held their attention was the electricity that arced around her like scarlet lightning.

She raised pitch-black eyes and surveyed the waiting crowd. When she spoke, she didn't shout, but her voice carried to the buildings and echoed down the streets beyond. "This colony has made a mistake," she announced, and her clear, calm tones rolled over them.

Stephanie turned her head from side to side and slowly scanned the crowd. She wasn't sure if it was the mood or her intuition, but she identified several people among them who were not worthy of her grace.

The sound of boots on the plating behind her told her the rest of the team had stepped into view. She touched on the magic she knew was hers. It was there, a steady stream of gMU that swirled beneath the bubbling and bitter anger filling her chest.

She took a moment to control her outrage before she continued. "There is a war coming, and some have already sided with the enemy. That labels them traitors to the three worlds of the Federation. They will come with me, or they and anyone who tries to stop me will die."

Her words triggered movement in the crowd and several men who'd stood farther back wound their way through their fellow citizens. She watched them come and Lars tutted quietly under his breath.

"Dumb asses."

Over the team comms, he heard Frog mutter, "Close the hatch, Johnny. That's a grenade launcher."

His teammate wasn't impressed. "You need to get your asses out of it, first."

"Hold fast," Lars ordered and kept his voice low. "Morgana's only getting started."

They complied and raised their weapons slightly. Each chose one of the men who pushed to stand at the front of the crowd. Lars kept his weapon muzzle low and peered over it to observe the crowd.

The man with the grenade launcher raised it, and the team leader readied his weapon and sighted on the man's head since the compact, big-barreled weapon the rebel aimed obscured his chest.

"I've got him, boss," Marcus told him. He probably had a better angle from the elevation of the ramp.

Lars let his rifle drop to the ready position and scanned the others. Most carried machine guns, but there were at least another two grenade launchers. If any of them fired, the team was in serious trouble. He glanced at Stephanie Morgana as the first man with the launcher spoke.

"You and what other Navy?" He snugged the launcher against his chest and pointed at them with one hand. "You ain't brought enough."

Vishlog snarled and the sound echoed over the comms.

"Easy, Vish," the team leader told him. "These people will learn soon enough that Morgana is not the one to be crossed."

"And Vishlog will crush their tiny bones in his hands," the Dreth rumbled.

The man raised an eyebrow but remained focused on the crowd. "Remind me not to shake your hand later."

As the warrior subsided, Lars glanced at Stephanie. One of them had to make their move soon. The red lightning flared around her, but her face was thoughtful, and judging by the look on her face, those thoughts weren't comforting.

"Get ready," he warned the team. "Our job is to only make sure no one surprises her. Don't get in her way."

She didn't look at him, but she *did* focus on the man who challenged her. His taunt had reminded her of something Todd had said way back when they used to walk to school together.

Way back when she hadn't been the Morgana the universe needed. He'd taken her lunch box and she'd threatened to kick his ass if he didn't give it back. He'd laughed at her. "You and whose army?"

She'd been furious while he held the box over his head and out of her reach. "You're not tall enough." He'd laughed and resisted all her attempts to bring his hand down within reach by dragging on his arm. In the end, she'd resorted to tickling, and he'd called her a cheat.

But only because she'd won and he'd been curled up on the sidewalk, almost crying with laughter as she tickled him helpless. Helpless...

Her mind slid sideways to Todd in hospital and his throat working as he fought to stop the tears. She'd seen them shimmer in his eyes as he'd told her what had happened—shimmering because he didn't want her to see them fall.

He hadn't been able to stop them trickling down his cheeks as he'd slept, though, and she'd watched them soak the pillow beneath his head before she'd left quietly to prepare for this operation.

Todd represented one of the key reasons why she had embraced her new life as a protector. She was determined that she would no longer allow her friends to face what he and others like him had faced.

It was time someone drew the line and said, "enough"—and that time was now. She raised her head and her eyes turned pitch-black.

CHAPTER SIXTEEN

The colony seemed to hold a collective breath in the moment before it began. Stephanie raced down the ramp, her hands out, and exploded energy at those who wielded the heavy weapons. She unerringly targeted those who would attack her and her people.

As she stepped into the open, magic flared around her and formed a solid shield. She moved so fast, the team was almost left behind. Groans and shrieks erupted as the magic found its targets and felled all those who raised a weapon against her. Those who ran, or hit the ground, or relinquished their weapons and hid were left alone.

Her shield flared as several shots pounded into it and she looked for their source. Her eyes pulsed with dark energy as she found the culprits who already scrambled to change their positions. The team caught up with her, moved to cover her, and formed a barrier on either side as she strode purposefully away from the square and down the broad main street.

A large house stood at the end and she walked unerringly toward it. The team kept pace with her as she went and systematically eliminated any who raised a weapon toward her.

Someone threw a grenade, but she deflected it casually with a wave of her hand. She didn't even look toward it. Her gaze remained fixed on the house. They were halfway to it when three people thrust through between Lars and Marcus.

They wielded machetes and machine pistols and their bullets drummed into her shields. She ignored them, even as they ran toward her. The team leader was observing a small group of colonists crouched behind a low stone wall and couldn't turn away.

Even so, he was about to risk it when Bumblebee and Zeekat launched into action. The big yellow-striped cat pounced. His momentum powered him into one man and hurled the revolutionary into another. Zeekat focused on the one who avoided the collision.

He surged into the attack and sank his claws in the man's back as he seized his victim's head between his jaws and raked his hind legs down the man's thighs. With a horrendous shriek, the man fell face-down, and Zeekat turned to assist Bumblebee.

The other feline was already the victor. He left his victims lying in the street after he'd sprayed them with urine to mark the kills as his own. Zeekat lifted his lips in a snarl and marked his own before he trotted after Stephanie, his tail high in the air.

Those colonists who'd hidden watched in awe as she stalked up to the front door of the oldest house in town while her team intercepted and neutralized everyone who tried to stop her. At one point, a sniper fired from his rooftop perch, only to have it blown out from under him by the Dreth.

Vishlog's mouth curled into a toothy grin as he cradled the grenade launcher he'd acquired and surveyed the destroyed rooftop in search of more movement before he continued after Morgana. A small man carrying a Gestak 900 shadowed him and eliminated another man who thought a machete was a good thing to bring to a gunfight.

For those watching, it seemed as though each team member

knew what the other was doing. Stephanie remained in the lead, stood back from the door, and formed a fist of magic to knock on it.

It proved to be a wise decision when the door blew out, shredded by a myriad of rounds as those beyond attempted to destroy her. She looked at the empty doorway. "You will surrender, or I will come and take what I want."

Vishlog shook his head. "There isn't any dealing with her like this."

Frog laughed. "*Now* you're getting it."

"Nope," Marcus added. "We only get involved if Stephanie needs to come back. Otherwise, Morgana is out to play and there's nothing we can do to change that."

The team came to a slow stop in front of the tall building that was part of a larger, rundown complex. Stephanie looked at them, nodded, and pointed at the third floor. "There are quite a few men in there, but we've got this."

Her voice was low and echoed through the streets around them. Behind them, people remained in the buildings and under cover, watching but staying well away.

The team moved into the building, tense and alert as they searched the first floor. She pressed on, one step at a time, her face completely focused on the objective.

Marcus leaned toward Lars. "What is she looking for?"

"The Navy says they picked up a rebel transmission to the planet and traced it back through the colony's sky link to here," Lars replied. "They want us to capture as many as we can and take them back for questioning."

The other man cocked his head toward Stephanie. "Uh, has anyone told *her* that?"

"She knows the mission parameters."

"Yeah," Frog grumbled, "but will she remember them?"

The team leader followed her into a stairwell and up the

stairs. "It's for the greater good. She understands that," he told them and sounded more confident than he felt.

The warrior snorted softly.

They were about to step onto the second floor and search it when Stephanie held her hand up. The team froze, and she conjured several small, clear orbs. They sparkled briefly and faded to invisibility when she dispatched them.

A short while later, they returned and she caught each one in the palm of her hand and pressed it against her forehead, letting it melt into her skull. Lars swallowed.

"*That's* a new trick," Marcus murmured, and Frog agreed.

Johnny and Brendan nodded silently, their expressions tense as they observed this new aspect of her magic.

"This floor's clear," she told them after the last orb had disappeared. "We go up."

None of them argued but followed her up to the third floor, where she raised a hand to stop them before they reached the landing. She dispatched another few clear orbs and they waited in silence for the magic spies to return. Once again, the team watched in fascination as she assimilated the orbs before she looked at them with a broad grin.

"There are three traps at the head of the stairs," she explained in a whisper, "and a large group of guards a little farther ahead."

Stephanie stood on the final step, drew a breath, and gestured to the side. The air shimmered briefly, too quick to really be seen unless anyone was actually looking for it, and she closed her eyes and gestured with her hands.

"It's a mirror shield," she said quietly when she saw their confused expressions. "I've pushed it beyond the traps and anything they throw at us will rebound on them. But first, I'll bait them to bring them within range."

She flicked her fingers. Three sharp explosions as the traps detonated were immediately followed by the sound of pounding boots and the team stepped up and into the hallway behind the mirror shield. The defenders immediately opened fire. They cursed and tried to retreat when they saw their fusillade rebound off the invisible wall and boomerang toward them. Three men managed to fling themselves into a room, but the others were decimated by the return of the own fire.

The mirror shield shivered visibly and fell, and the team pushed forward. The three surviving guards darted out of the room and released a barrage of fire.

Solid rounds battered her shield and the team took cover behind her. She raised her hands, palms out, in front of her and drew them slightly apart to broaden the shield to protect them all.

When they realized their shots couldn't penetrate, the rebels ceased their fire. Two backed away, their weapons trained on the team. The third bolted away along the landing.

Stephanie flicked her wrist and a small, sticky ball of magic rocketed forward to adhere to the back of his jacket. "Surrender or die," she commanded.

He ignored and continued to run, and she shrugged. "Your choice."

The magic exploded with a sharp crack to blow a hole through him in an end so sudden and quick that he didn't have time to scream. She looked at the two men before her and raised her hands.

"Surrender or die."

They dropped their weapons and raised their hands.

"Secure them," she commanded, and Lars and Marcus hurried to comply before she changed her mind.

She ignored them, strode forward in the direction the dead man had taken, and stepped past his remains without giving them a second glance. The cats paced beside her, their heads up and ears erect, alert for the first sign of danger. The team moved swiftly in their wake.

"Here," she told them and stopped in front of a single door.

She studied it for a moment before she punched her hand forward with her palm upraised to propel a burst of magic into it.

The door catapulted off its hinges and semi-automatic fire chattered out of the room. This time, solid ammunition was punctuated by the hiss of laser fire, none of which penetrated the translucent shield in front of her.

Once more, she spoke, and her voice echoed around them as if she stood in the middle of a hollow chamber. Its calm tones were all the more eerie for the anger and implacability woven into it. "Surrender or die."

Chaos erupted from the room. More rounds and laser bursts spoke in reply, but the clatter of weapons thrown down and the sound of fleeing footsteps were audible despite the fusillade.

She stepped forward, far enough through the ruptured doorway that the felines could slip past. Frog, Avery, and Brendan raced after them, their minds on the mission. They sure as shit hoped Morgana wouldn't kill *all* the rebels to exact vengeance for Todd.

She swept forward.

"Secure that," she ordered and pointed at a communications array set up at the back of the room. "Frog!"

"On it!" he shouted as he changed direction and headed to the consoles.

A single shot rang out, and Morgana shouted in fury. She froze and Lars, who came in behind her after he'd secured the prisoners shouted, "Get down!"

The team sprawled instinctively as energy lashed over their heads. Walls vanished, as did the rebel who'd hidden behind some curtains. Other revolutionaries also fell, and their bodies convulsed as power surged through them.

The team leader, on one knee behind her, bowed his head. "We will *never* get any information."

The power storm lasted only a few seconds and ended in complete silence until a scream burst from the other room. She turned toward it and Lars bolted around her to find the source. In the adjoining room, now open for all to see, Zeekat looked at them and red smeared his black-and-white jaws.

"Never," Lars muttered and tried to find the next rebel before the cats did. "Never, never, never."

She stepped behind him. "Find them all."

"Find them first," Lars muttered into his comms, reminding the team of the mission, "and neutralize them for questioning."

What Morgana did with them after that was up to her, but he hoped some would survive if they weren't a threat. Across the room, Bumblebee vaulted high in the air, knocked a monitor off a table, and destroyed a chair as he lunged for something in the corner.

A shrill squeal spurred the team leader into action, and he raced toward the cat, but Vishlog was already moving. "I've got this."

Lars left him to it.

"Secure them," Stephanie ordered, and he looked back to see her pointing at the rebels who'd fallen to the power surge. She caught his eye and gave him a humorless smile. "I did not forget."

When he continued to stare, momentarily frozen in place, she frowned. "Find the others. Their leader isn't here."

As she spoke, she summoned several more glittering orbs and sent them out, then stalked across the room to join him. "We'll search together."

"Avery!" he snapped and pointed to where Frog sat, his fingers racing as he hacked through the rebels' system. "Keep him safe. Brendan, Marcus, you're with me."

Frog paused. "Don't destroy the transmitter. I'm sending everything to the shuttle."

"Find it all," she ordered, and the command was directed at the entire team.

For the next thirty minutes, they went from room to room and searched every corner they could find. They overturned furniture, scanned walls for hidden passages, and raced after fleeing footsteps.

Zeekat bounded past them and apprehended any rebel in his path with a powerful leap into the center of their back to ride them to the floor, or he simply ambushed them from the side.

After Lars prevented him from killing the first one, the big cat worked faster, attacked low from under their guns or in from a blind spot, and left them broken for the team to secure. Morgana was less forgiving.

If they fired at any of them, she left their charred corpses behind her. "We have enough for questioning," she told Lars when he groaned. "If they fire on us, their lives are forfeit."

Two-thirds of the way through the floor, they found a narrow set of stairs leading down. This time, the team leader was fast enough to take the lead, relieved that Morgana kept Zeekat behind her shield. He decided his body armor could take most of what had been thrown at them and refused to think about the rest.

When they reached the end of the passage at the bottom of the stairs, they found a garage, its doors barely open as a shuttle lifted from the floor.

"Not happening!" Morgana growled and fired tendrils of power to envelop the shuttle's shell.

Lars sighed and she smirked as the tendrils glowed with sudden brightness and energy arced through the vehicle. Screams came from inside, the engine died, and the shuttle dropped to the garage floor.

Stephanie recalled the tendrils and took three steps forward, but Marcus and Brendan managed to get ahead of her. Zeekat raced past them and reached the craft seconds before they did. As the cat arrived, the pilot's hatch slid open and a stocky man with graying hair stumbled out.

"Zee! Leave!" Stephanie shouted as the feline leapt. The cat twisted in the air and aborted his attack.

Brenden tackled the man and the maneuver culminated in a scream of pain and a crunch punctuated by a whimper and an unconscious rebel. Marcus and Zee rounded the end of the shuttle and Lars dived inside. The team leader had his hands full.

The two rebels in the back of the shuttle—one Dreth and one Meligornian—spoke in hurried tones and tried to raise someone on the other end of their call.

"Frog's gonna kill me," he muttered, raised his blaster, and delivered two quick shots into the console.

As he did so, there was a small explosion and the building shook. The shuttle rocked, then settled back onto its belly, and the Dreth attacked. Lars shot him without thinking, hitting him in the gut, and raised his blaster to cover the other.

"Don't move," he ordered as Marcus opened the rear hatch, but the Meligornian rebel didn't listen. Marcus sidestepped his attack but Zeekat slammed into him from the side.

Lars braced for the crunch, but it didn't come. Instead, the big cat settled onto the rebel's back and only extended his talons when his captive moved. The man tried to get away, rolled under the cat, and screamed, "Get him off! Get him off me!"

Zeekat hissed at him, bounced into the air, and landed on his chest to swat him with one paw. Marcus shoved the feline off him and flipped him onto his face to secure him, while Lars saw the med kit strapped beside the transmitter and patched the Dreth moaning at his feet.

"It's a good thing you're a Dreth," he muttered. He looked at the wound and decided it would have been fatal on a human.

Bootsteps heralded the arrival of the rest of the team, and Zeekat yowled a greeting to Bumblebee as his hunting partner slid through the door. Together, the two cats stalked around the garage and then, with a suddenness that triggered alarm in every member of the team, they stopped.

Everyone went on high alert as Bumblebee tensed and pivoted toward a distant corner of the garage. Zeekat froze, then bounded in pursuit. Before Morgana could command them, Avery and Brenden hurried forward, their rifles raised and ready to defend their four-legged teammates.

"Now what?" Lars muttered when they stopped short of one corner and slunk, belly-low, toward it.

Paper rustled, and Bumble leapt high in the air. Zeekat cocked his head, then skittered forward at a slight angle. Marcus snapped his blaster up and moved cautiously in after them. When Lars went to do the same, Vishlog reached out and pushed his blaster down.

"Watch," the Dreth instructed. "The cats have found more squeekies."

"More what?" Frog asked and watched as Avery, Marcus, and Brenden fanned out around the two felines and prepared to fire.

The warrior used his hand to make small movements across the space in front of him. "You know, the squeekies?"

Lars laughed. "Ohhhh. Mice!"

A shrill squeak sounded across the room and Marcus shouted in disgust, brushed madly at his uniform, and hopped away from Bumblebee. "I don't want it!"

Avery laughed as another tiny body missiled to land at Brenden's feet. He stopped laughing as a section of wall turned into a door and a small round object bounced out.

"Grenade!" Lars roared and dived for Stephanie.

He rebounded from her shields as a ball of energy encapsulated the grenade and lifted it from the floor. When he looked up, Morgana was in full control and gestured sharply out the front of the garage to hurl the energy ball and its deadly cargo through the aperture.

His instinct was to calm her, but she strode past him. Lightning crackled up and down her body and the shield pushed him aside. "Dammit."

Vishlog hauled himself to his feet and they followed her. The cats paused their hunt long enough to watch them pass.

"Keep them here," Lars ordered as he hurried past Avery.

"Wave one!" Marcus shouted as the first scream erupted from the room beyond, but the team leader kept moving.

The Dreth stayed with him as they followed Stephanie through the door. This time, there was no mercy. The rebels inside the room fired on her as she entered, and Morgana let loose.

Magic blazed from her hands and arced from her body. Volatile balls stuck to targets and exploded while tendrils struck like snakes and burned whatever they touched. The all-terrain vehicle they were loading was enveloped and melted to slag.

Lars shot the man who rose from behind a line of crates to shoot her in the back, and Vishlog eliminated a sniper positioned behind some shelving. Morgana annihilated everyone else.

Avery, Frog, and Brenden watched the carnage from the doorway, their faces grim.

"They really shouldn't have messed with her friend."

"More like boyfriend." Frog scoffed. "No woman would get that mad for a friend-zoned person. She liked him."

There was movement at the garage door and Avery pivoted and fired as he moved. "Well, to hell with them, then."

His shot caught the rebel who entered squarely in the chest and launched him out again. The three teammates scrambled to the door and decimated the small group of men who had tried to attack them from behind.

When they'd cleared the area, Frog added, "It doesn't matter. She protects her own. Todd has been her oldest friend. He was there before we even knew she existed. That's enough for me."

They returned to the back room to find the battle was over and not a single rebel was left standing or alive. Morgana surveyed the scene and quirked a brow at Lars. Her lips curved into an unrepentant smirk. "Oops."

Frog snickered, and the team leader glared at him.

"Tell me you got the rest of the prisoners out of the comm center *before* you blew it up."

Avery nodded. "Yup. We dragged them out front and left them on the lawn."

He paused and his face paled. Before Lars could ask what was wrong, he'd raced back to the front of the garage and peered out the door to study the bodies of their attackers. "Oh..."

Lars joined him. He looked at the bodies, then back at Avery. "Oh?"

The man's face broke into a grin and he gave the team leader a friendly shove. "I'm messing with you, boss. These aren't them."

He glared at him. "Go find me a vehicle. I'm not dragging their asses back to the shuttle and inviting another firefight."

"Oh, no," Frog snarked from the depths of the garage. "No, we're gonna drive a truck full of someone's friends through town. There's *no way* someone will find that offensive enough to shoot at you."

"Go help Avery."

He complied but sulked as he shouldered past on the way out. "You have no sense of humor."

"Oh, I don't know. I find *this* pretty funny." Lars turned to where Vishlog and Brenden watched the cats pursue more mice and laughed at their antics. "Go make sure we still have prisoners, Vishlog. You know where you put them."

They obeyed, and Lars looked for Stephanie.

She stood in the back room and stared at the bodies, the melted weapons, and the slagged vehicle. "There are others," she said, and the chill in her voice told him Morgana was still in control.

"We'll hunt them later. These were the ones who eliminated the Navy team, and they'll never do it again."

She raised her head and the look on her face made him shiver. "Someone gave them orders."

He reached out to her, took her arm gently, and guided her out through the garage. "We'll find them," he promised.

The roar of engines signaled Frog and Avery's return. To Lars's surprise, they'd already picked up Vishlog and Brenden and loaded the captured rebels into the vehicles. He got Stephanie on board the second vehicle as the team loaded the four from the garage into the first. The cats leapt in beside her.

They drove to the shuttle, half expecting to find Johnny in trouble, but the streets remained silent and the shuttle unmolested. He lowered the ramp as they arrived and brought the engines to life.

As they loaded the rebels into the shuttle, people emerged slowly from the buildings around them. Some held weapons, but more as an afterthought than with any intent. Most were empty-handed. Their faces gave nothing away as the team dragged the last man into the cargo bay.

When it was over, Stephanie turned and surveyed the crowd.

"The Federation Navy failed, and they chose to send me instead. You had best pray I never come back again."

Her gaze settled on the satellite dish and she raised her hands and pulled energy into her. She closed her eyes as it moved quickly through her body and out again where it coalesced around her. Calmly and deliberately, she raised her hands and pushed the energy to release it into the dish in a steady stream.

After a few moments, a very loud crack heralded the resulting explosion and a fireball careened into the sky.

One of the colonists groaned. "Why?"

She looked around at them. "There are those among you who work for an enemy of the Federation. Now, they cannot call for help or vengeance."

Anger marred her face as she paused for emphasis. "And there are those among you who stood aside while a Navy team was murdered in your midst. You are *all* complicit in their deaths."

A ripple of protest worked its way through the crowd.

Murmurs of, "We had no choice," and, "They threatened our families," rose and were quickly hushed. "I don't think she cares," was whispered from the back.

Stephanie whirled toward them and some of the darkness bled from her eyes. "I'll let the Navy know you have lost communication. Maybe by the time they come to help, you will have learned manners."

Her frown deepened. "And maybe you'll make sure nothing happens to their people when they arrive and prove me right for letting you live."

She pivoted and stalked into the shuttle, her fists clenched at her sides as though she tried not to change her mind.

One of the Dreth curled his lip and muttered, "Bitch!"

The guys nearest him pivoted, but Vishlog reached him first. He took two strides and punched him to double him over and kneed him powerfully him in the head.

When the Dreth wrapped his arms around the warrior's waist and pulled, the two of them tumbled in a flurry of fists, but the colonist didn't stand a chance. Vishlog pounded him until he went limp, then stood and stared at those nearest him.

"Justice," he rumbled, breathing hard, "for the dead, for the perpetrators, and for those who stood aside."

He said no more but walked back to the ship. The guys closed in behind him, their weapons ready as they withdrew. As soon as they'd closed the hatch behind them and strapped in, Johnny took the shuttle up.

Once they'd cleared the rooftops, Stephanie spoke. "Blast the compound," she ordered. "If we missed anything, I don't want it to be used."

"Yes, ma'am," he told her and glancing over his shoulder. "Marcus, Frog? You wanna take the guns?"

With a whoop, Frog unstrapped and shifted into the cockpit and into one of the empty seats behind Johnny and Stephanie. Marcus followed more slowly and peered at the panel with a frown. It didn't take him long to find what he wanted.

"This should about do it," he said, as Johnny brought the shuttle around.

Frog glanced over. "Oh, man, where's mine?"

His teammate chuckled. "Right in front of you."

The man stared at the console for a moment before his face lit up. "Let's do this thing."

"That is one hell of a crater," Johnny remarked a few moments later as they left the atmosphere.

"They needed something to remember us by," Stephanie told him, her face pale as she watched the pillar of smoke rise in the viewscreen.

Lars came up to stand beside her. "They needed something."

Stephanie shifted the view to scan the colony below. Part of her wished she could feel sorry, but then she remembered Todd —and the rest of his team—and all pity fled.

No one messed with her family. Period. And no one messed with the worlds she was sworn to protect. She would find whoever was behind the rebels and destroy them all.

The team leader glanced at her and studied the thoughts that flitted across her face. "You did what was right, avenging our protectors and a member of our family."

Frog interjected from his seat behind them, "I hope your revenge for me will be so monumental they talk about it on Federation Television."

The shadow of Morgana left her face and she giggled. "I will keep that in mind. But know that none of you are allowed to die for a long time."

"Back at you," Lars said with a smile. "Not even a chance."

"Unless you blow yourself up," Frog yelled.

She rolled her eyes and twisted to tap him on the head. "If I blow up, you are *so* coming with me."

Frog pouted. "I would be so insignificant in that explosion, no one would even know I'd died. You'd steal my thunder. Everyone would be witch of the Federation this and witch of the Federation that and all boo-hoo over the dead witch they'd forget about the rest of us."

He paused, obviously thinking it over. "We'll have to talk about that."

The team laughed as Johnny set a course for the next rendezvous point. Apparently, the Navy had decided they were important enough to pick up, after all.

CHAPTER SEVENTEEN

Ahead of them, Captain Shale stared at the results of the deep space scan and waited for the shuttle to arrive. She'd been diverted from a routine patrol to collect a group of contractors and she was curious.

Hers was one of the biggest ships in the fleet, and it had been diverted for contractors. Her gaze drifted to the screens, which confirmed that her crew went about their daily routines and monitored a myriad of different missions from all three nations.

The ship served as a mobile Naval base and not only housed clerical and mission-oriented teams, but also a large intelligence section and one of the biggest space-based brigs in the Federation. They were the perfect place for Stephanie and the team to return to and the Navy was impatient to get them aboard.

A blip appeared on the scans, and Johnny's voice spoke over the comms.

"*Washington Revere*, this is Shuttle nine-five-two-six requesting permission to land. I repeat, *Washington Revere*, this is Shuttle nine-five-two-six requesting permission to land."

"Copy that nine-five-two-six. We have Docking Bay eight-two open and prepped. Proceed to your starboard and follow the lights.".

Stephanie took the coms. "*Washington Revere*, this is Stephanie. Be advised we are transporting prisoners for questioning."

"Understood. Our security teams will stand by for prisoner transfer." There was a pause. "How many?"

She glanced into the rear of the shuttle. "Ten, all injured."

"Understood. We will have medical teams on standby. *Washington Revere* out."

"Well, that was short and sweet," she muttered in the silence that followed.

Johnny locked onto the coordinates for the landing bay and the team prepared to disembark.

They were exhausted as none of them had slept on the journey out. The prisoners had woken, and the boys had been kept busy monitoring their injuries and shutting their mouths.

Johnny brought them in smoothly, their ship a little scorched from flying too close to the rebel compound when Frog pressed the launch button one too many times. He set it down in the hangar, powered off, and opened the rear doors.

Vishlog stood, grasped two prisoners by their collars, and hauled them with him. The two cats pushed past to precede him through the doors and down the ramp.

They walked at a sedate pace with their heads high, and their tails swished dramatically. The felines were well aware of the effect they had and had developed quite a fondness for the limelight. The waiting Navy personnel, though, hadn't expected them and took several hasty steps back as they appeared.

The Dreth appeared on their heels, dragging his prisoners with him. The sailors retreated another step and several security officers raised their weapons to cover him.

Things might have gotten tense if Lars and Stephanie hadn't appeared. Marcus struggled to catch up. He'd copied the warrior and had a prisoner in each hand, but he didn't find it anywhere near as easy to move them as his large teammate did.

"Dammit, move aside, Vishlog," Stephanie snapped, and he flinched when he heard the Morgana in her voice. "I can't see around your fat ass. I'll stick a sign on your butt that says wide load if you don't move outta the way."

He sidestepped smartly to let her walk ahead of him. The four prisoners floating behind her came as a surprise, but he recognized them as being the captives she'd brought out of the garage. He fell in behind her as the Navy's security and medical teams rushed forward to meet her.

She raised her hand and they skidded to a halt. Vishlog didn't blame them. He'd caught a glimpse of her eyes as she'd passed and they'd gone dark. Morgana had returned and he didn't know why.

When he'd left, she'd been Stephanie and the Meligornian prisoner had recognized the sigil emblazoned on their uniform patch. He looked at Lars, wanting to know why.

The team leader shook his head as his eyes flicked over the assembled naval personnel. The man's mouth moved to silently give him one word. *Later.*

She studied the crew and her dark eyes finally settled on a young woman dressed as a junior captain. With a small gesture of her hand, she floated the four prisoners over to the security team and dropped them to the floor.

The largest one, a Dreth, cried out in pain and lost consciousness. The other three lay on the deck, stunned, before they were hauled to their feet.

"Those are the outpost leaders," Stephanie said, and her Morgana voice sent chills through those who heard it. "The rest were taken from their control center."

She watched, her eyes as black as pitch and her face impassive, as her men brought the rest of the prisoners forward and handed them over. Once the exchange was complete, she commanded the junior captain's attention with a look.

"Take us to coordinates, Right Ascension 101.458, Declination -15.718, Quadrant Alpha-Forty. We will need two pilots and two gunners, and the shuttle needs to be rearmed, refueled, and reloaded."

The officer blinked. "Captain, did you hear that?"

"I did. The acquisition is authorized. Give her our best."

The woman returned her focus to Stephanie. "When did you need it by?"

"When do we reach the coordinates?"

"Two days." The captain's voice spoke over the intercom.

She nodded. "Thank you." She turned back to the junior captain. "My team needs to rest."

At this request, the woman relaxed. Here was something she *had* prepared for. "Right this way, ma'am."

Two days later, the *Washington Revere* stood off a small moon orbiting a much larger planet.

"With some luck, they'll think we're here to refuel or take some downtime," Captain Shale said, as Stephanie stared at the planet in the viewscreen. "Or they'll think we're here to explore. We've upgraded you from nine-five-two-six into a gunboat carrying some smaller flyers. I take it you've done the entry simulations?"

"Once, at a university," she admitted.

"Then you know how to fly one of the fighters," the captain said. "I'd like to keep the gunboat out of things in case you need rescue, so there'll be a small squad of marines riding with you."

The woman held her hand up when she opened her mouth to protest.

"It's my boat and my rules. I don't care if you can breathe

vacuum and shit meteors. My boys will tag along in the gunboat in case you need rescue, and only then will they go in. This isn't a Navy-sanctioned mission, even if it's in the Navy's best interests and you've agreed to share information."

Stephanie closed her mouth and nodded. There was no way she would tell this lady that the only information she'd share was the information she thought they should have. No way at all.

When it was clear she had nothing to add, the captain continued. "My boys will pilot the gunboat and run the guns, and they will stand by to haul your asses out of any fires you can't put out yourselves. Outside of that, you're on your own."

The first part of the mission went well, right up to the point that the gunship came within hailing range of the rebel base.

"I don't think we're meant to know they're there," the pilot told her and showed her how the readings for life and energy had dropped to almost nothing. "They're buttoned up tighter than a flea's asshole."

"That won't do them any good," she told him as the scanners beeped an alarm.

"Sir, we have incoming."

"How many?"

"Two big bogeys and a couple of warm receptions."

"Ships and guns," Lars translated. "We can expect a hot ride in."

She shrugged. "It won't make a difference. We'll launch from here."

"Make it fast," the pilot said and swung the gunboat into a sharp turn. "Those boys mean business and this thing was built for comfort, not for speed."

"Roger that," the team leader told him and turned to follow Stephanie into the gunboat's hold.

The marines made a path as the pair rolled past them. Despite the captain's claim, the gunboat only held one of the little fighters. The other three had followed the gunboat out of the hangar and each carried two team members apiece.

Frog, being the smallest, had been nominated to share Vishlog's craft and swiftly lost the fight about who would pilot it. Since Lars refused to allow Stephanie to travel alone on the gunboat, he would share her cockpit with Bumblebee, and Zeekat was sitting in on Marcus.

Almost literally, since Brenden was piloting.

"But I'm senior," the other man had argued, and Brenden had quietly taken his legs out from under him and put him on his backside.

"Then you should at least learn to fight like a girl."

"Enough," Stephanie had told them. "Brenden's flying. Marcus is looking after Zee. He gets one fur singed, and both your asses won't know what hit them."

They'd agreed without further argument.

"We have company," Johnny told them.

"Can we get past them and get in?"

"Not if we don't want to become little balls of fire when we try to land."

"Fine," Stephanie told them. "Take them out."

"I'll take the big one," the gunboat's pilot told them. "The boys could do with some practice."

"The big one?" Lars wondered, and the pilot sent him the data on the incoming ships. "Oh. Fine then. Ours is the one at the back."

"Gotcha boss," Johnny told him. "Those are Hraden Singers. Front boat is a Mark IV. Back one is Mark II. Navy will need our help."

The pilot cut in. "Bet you a round we don't."

"Two rounds," he countered, "and we won't ask your permission to save your butts."

Lars sighed. "Spill it, Johnny."

"We need to take ours from the back. It's the only place we can guarantee a shot will get through."

"Unless you can hit one of the maneuvering jets."

"Gotcha."

"Johnny, Brenden, Avery, take the portside. Vishlog..." He let his words trail off as the Dreth's craft careened past him and executed a credible barrel roll directly into the path of the oncoming Mark II.

"Dayum..." Johnny breathed and swept his craft into a steep turn. "Brendan, Avery, follow me in."

"Goddamn," Lars muttered and accelerated sharply. "Hold on, Steph."

Hold on? Hell, no! Her stomach flipped and she laughed. "These assholes won't know what hit them."

"Uh, Steph?" Lars began but didn't have time for more. The Mark II opened fire, it's gunners too nimble and accurate for comfort. He jinked and spun and the hair on the back of his neck rose as she drew power from the stars around them.

The others used the gunners' distraction to sneak around the ship and approach the engines from behind, but the gun batteries opened up. Stephanie shrieked in outrage as Brenden's fighter was clipped and spiraled momentarily out of control.

"We're good, Steph." His assurance might have sounded more convincing if it hadn't sounded like he was speaking through gritted teeth.

"Yup. We...got...this..." Marcus echoed as the little craft twisted out of the path of another barrage. It came in under the guns to skid along an open patch of ground at the base of a small mountain. "We're just gonna knock."

Stephanie didn't see what they did next because Lars plunged their fighter into a steep dive and skimmed under the nose of the Mark II. She caught sight of its guns and that was all she needed.

Two fireballs into the closest barrels led to a chain reaction inside the ship as Johnny's shots struck the engines, followed closely by Avery's attack.

"We'll get the gunboat clear," Johnny called. "You guys go take care of Brenden and Marcus."

"Will do," Lars replied. "Vishlog."

"Roger that," the Dreth replied and sounded far too calm for someone who rocketed directly toward the side of a mountain.

"Vishlog!"

She didn't bother to wonder what the warrior was doing. If he was determined to take care of that emplacement, she had the other. And if he killed himself doing it, she would make him wish he'd never been born.

She concentrated more energy, targeted the battery, and launched the magic. Lars cried out in alarm as it materialized in front of the cockpit before it careened away.

"Quit your bitching and get me down there," she snapped, and darkness edged her tones.

"Dammit."

"I'll take that as a yes."

He didn't need to see her face to know Morgana was back and in control. Instead, he focused on the task at hand and set the fighter down beside Brenden, glad to see the damage hadn't been too bad. The little jets couldn't take much.

"*Washington Revere,* you have the comms. I repeat, you have the comms."

The *Washington's* response was swift and unequivocal. "We have them gagged. You need to get them bagged."

"Roger that." Lars popped the cockpit and vaulted out. He didn't bother to look back for Stephanie. She leapt up and out, tumbled smoothly, and landed beside the other craft.

There was no-one inside.

"Talk to me, Brenden...Marcus..."

"We found the entrance."

Before she could ask where, a flare lit up the hillside ahead of them. "Got it."

"Hurry."

As if she needed to be told when she could hear that much gunfire in the background. "How's Zee?"

"Not happy about being in the bag."

"I'm coming."

As if to punctuate her words, a roar resounded from the mountainside above her. Vishlog's fighter twisted away from it but spun out of control, and Stephanie flung her hand upward as though she could snatch it out of the sky and set it down herself.

Which she did.

The magic twisted away from her fingers to engulf the out-of-control craft and drag it back to settle beside the other two. She didn't look back but raced forward to the source of the flare.

"Frog. Marcus. Johnny. I need you here."

Their affirmatives came as a blurry chorus as she reached where Brenden and Marcus huddled beside the entrance and struggled to control a bagful of squirming, pissed-off cat. "Let me get that for you," she snarled and dispatched a dagger-like tendril of energy into the door lock.

It was exactly like unlocking the door in the palace in what seemed like forever ago. The mechanism was unfamiliar, but the magic knew what to do. *Unlock,* Stephanie commanded it, and unlock it did. The door slid open and they hurried inside, hearing the others touch down behind them.

"Frog!"

"I'm here. I'm here," he protested as he ran. "Don't ever let him fly again. You think he's crazy in a fight? You haven't seen him fly!" His voice faded as he looked at her face. "What do you need?"

"You know what I brought you here for. Go do it."

The team crowded inside, and the doors cycled through. Both

cats were released from the bags they'd been put in to protect them during the flight over and neither were very happy.

They laid their ears back and batted at the guys who'd unzipped them. Stephanie hissed at them and they turned to her immediately. They butted her legs with their heads until she laid a hand on each of them. The doors slid open and she raised a shield between her team and the incoming fire.

"I need to be *here*," Frog said and highlighted the space on the map in their HUDs.

The team raced forward as one. Stephanie held the shield before them with one hand and fired small bursts of energy with the other. The guys fired at anything that appeared behind them or in the corridors they passed, and the cats paced solemnly on either side of her. A layer of glowing magic overlaid their skins.

When they reached the central control room, the doors were shut.

"Not gonna stand," Morgana snapped, and the shield blazed with sudden intensity as she pressed it against the doors.

It was as though she'd used a cutting torch, and Lars led the team through as soon as the barrier melted and the magic disappeared. Vishlog and Brendan moved left and Zeekat bounded at their sides. Lars and Avery went right with Bumblebee, and Johnny and Frog blasted their way into one corner where they proceeded to strip the cover from the console.

While they worked to hook up the gear they'd brought, the others neutralized the rebels who manned the control center while Marcus and Stephanie kept the corridor clear.

"I'm supposed to keep you out of trouble," he grumbled as she blazed a volley at a small group of defenders.

Before she could reply, he fired in the opposite direction.

Morgana snickered. "You are."

More defenders appeared, and they stepped into the control center.

"This would be *so* much easier if you hadn't *melted the door!*"

"Are you having a rough day?" she asked and didn't sound sympathetic in the least.

Marcus fired another burst and didn't reply.

"Hold the fort," she said and moved away.

He glanced over his shoulder as she moved to the center of the control room. Energy vibrated around him as she began drawing it into herself, and Lars, Avery, and Vishlog came to stand on either side of him.

"We got you, bro."

The words had no sooner left Avery's mouth than Morgana spoke. Her crisp, clear tones echoed over the internal communications system.

"Residents of Rebel Base Arkwright," she said. "Residents of Rebel Base Arkwright. Evacuate now. I repeat. Residents of Rebel Base Arkwright must evacuate now. This is your final warning."

"Uh oh," Avery said.

"Shit."

"Hrageth's balls on a stick."

"Don't they know evacuate means leave?" Marcus whined as a dozen rebels raced down the corridor toward the door.

"It doesn't look like it," Lars responded, and they fired in unison.

Morgana's voice rang out again. "You were warned. Hell is about to be unleashed on this planet. Evacuate now!"

A second squad of rebels appeared, these more heavily armored than the last. The team leader dropped to one knee, his movement mirrored by those on either side of him.

"This will be fun," he said but didn't sound like he meant it.

Behind him, Frog and Johnny worked like maniacs to strip as much information as they could from the rebel systems. They were doing well until one of the security systems kicked in and activated a worm.

"Crap," Frog muttered, and his fingers danced over the keyboard he'd plugged in. "I can't stop it."

Johnny looked over his shoulder. "Pull the plug, man."

His teammate did exactly that and the pair stowed their gear, shoved it into packs, and pulled them onto their backs. Morgana pulled so much energy they could see it moving into her in waves.

"This is gonna hurt," Frog muttered, and his companion had no answer. The cats crouched beside them, their gleaming eyes fixed on their mistress as if they watched a hunter about to pounce.

Frog called out to her. "Steph, we're done here. The system's in meltdown. Steph!"

"Evacuate Rebel Base Arkwright," Morgana intoned. "Five minutes to base destruction."

The temperature rose around them.

CHAPTER EIGHTEEN

Frog ran up to Stephanie and tapped her on the shoulder. "Steph! We're done."

"Almost," she replied. "Almost."

"No. Seriously, girl. We are done!"

He stared at her and noticed the rising temperature. The heat made itself felt through the soles of his boots. He stared as Stephanie Morgana flexed her shoulders, spread her hands, and raised them as though lifting a heavy weight.

"Not. Quite. Yet," she declared coldly.

Sweat rolled down her skin, drenched her shirt, and soaked her hair. With a groan, she bent her elbows and raised her hands higher as though lifting weights. When they reached chest height, she gave a final grunt of effort, then dropped to her knees and her palms thunked onto the floor.

Frog tucked a hand under her arm and helped her regain her feet. "Holy crap, Steph. You're running a fever."

She laughed, a short unhappy sound, and Morgana vanished as swiftly as she'd come. "It's not me."

Her smile faded. "It's time to go—like, *run!* Run, *now!*"

She staggered to where the guys had formed a line in front of the door and pinned the rebels down with concerted fire. *"Run!"*

Lars glanced over his shoulder and reversed to take hold of her other arm. He glared at Frog. "What did you do? Let her pull too much?"

His teammate shook his head. "Me? Hell, no! It was her idea to start pulling magma. She's…she's going to blow this place."

Stephanie ignored them, shook herself free of their hands, and stumbled forward to shove Vishlog hard in the back. "Get moving! Move! Move! Move!"

She pounded on his huge bulk with both hands. "Move your outsized ass!"

He looked back and his eyes widened. Without hesitation, he heaved her into his arms and raced through the gaping hole where the door had been.

"Hey!"

"You have tiny legs," he told her and maintained his grip as he tucked her under one arm and braced his blaster against his side.

"I *can* run on my own."

"You nearly fell over," Frog reminded her from where he ran directly behind them.

"Not helping."

"Tiny legs," the Dreth repeated. "Little feet. You won't keep up."

"Frog's shorter than me."

"I can run faster than you."

"You'd better be able to," she warned, "because…when…we get back—"

She gave up trying to speak as the breath was jolted out with every step Vishlog took. The cats bounded alongside, and the guys formed a barrier of living flesh on either side.

Stephanie tried to raise a shield to help protect them but couldn't. Not only did being carried like a sack of potatoes wreck her concentration, but fatigue threaded its way through her body.

"How many can we fit into a fighter?" Brenden asked.

"Not enough," Lars replied. "Turn here."

The map flashed up in their HUDS and they marked the intersection.

"We're heading to the hangar."

"Isn't that *down?*"

"Yeah, Frog. What about it?"

"I think she pulled magma up from the core!"

"Holy—"

"Head for the front," Johnny interjected. "I'm calling the Navy in. They owe us a favor."

"Why?"

"We stopped their asses being barbecued by that Mark IV."

They reached the intersection and continued their headlong race. Anyone who even tried to attack was eliminated as rapidly as they appeared. One group of rebels rounded a corner ahead of them, took one look at the wild-eyed team that bolted toward them, and pivoted back the way they'd come.

They watched the team race past from where they leaned flat against the wall and didn't dare to even twitch. They got to live a bit longer. Even when they slipped into the corridor behind the team and headed the opposite way, the guys left them alone.

It was hard to run and fight a rear-guard action. As long as the rebels kept moving, they could go.

"I wonder what they know that we don't," Marcus muttered from his place in the lead.

"Don't know. Don't care. We're almost there."

The finally rounded the last corner and hurtled toward the entrance, but the doors in front of them opened and a half-dozen armored figures barreled through.

"Oh, for—" Lars raised his blaster, ready to fire, but Johnny knocked it aside. "What the hell?"

He received his answer when the armored figures divided three to each side of the corridor, their weapons aimed past them back the way they'd come. They were marines. The team leader jogged forward as they advanced a short way past the team, and a new voice spoke over their comms.

"I reckon this is a *three*-round rescue. Did you have to blow a mountain up?"

"It hasn't blown yet," Frog retorted and looked over his shoulder. "Crap. Run!"

"Not until we get you boys on board."

"Run!" he yelled, again, but the marines stood firm and covered the corridor behind them. What good they thought their blasters would do against the slowly rising flow of magma, he didn't know and he didn't intend to ask.

Lars looked back to see what had his teammate so upset and stepped out of the path of his men. "Keep going!" he roared when they hesitated. "Go! Go! Go!"

"You never heard of a flare?" the pilot taunted, but his voice was tense.

They clattered up the ramp of the gunship hard-docked against the door with a temporary umbilical that joined the gunship to the ruined front.

"Excuse the mess," the pilot added as he monitored their progress into the ship. "We knocked but no-one was home."

Frog and Johnny sprinted up the ramp, raced into the hold, and stopped when they reached the back wall. They were followed by the marines, who saw them watching and made a show of sauntering out through the blasted door, pausing to unlock the umbilical, and meandering up the ramp again.

It was almost too much for the pilot.

"Move your asses, you jar-headed knuckle draggers. *Your* backsides might be fireproof, but my ship isn't."

The last marine stood at the edge of the ramp and stared as the floor sizzled.

"Docherty!"

"Say you're sorry."

"I'll leave your sorry ass!"

"Wrong answer."

"Docherty!"

The marine stared into the base as the heat rose around them.

The captain pushed past and headed to the cockpit. His voice bellowed through their comms shortly after. "Say you're sorry."

"Fine! I'm sorry." The marine turned and trotted into the hold, and the pilot cycled the doors, released the umbilical, and continued. "I'm sorry you're such a thin-skinned, knuckle-dragging prick, who needs his momma."

The marines turned their heads toward the cockpit access, and Lars thought he heard a unanimous growl. The pilot, however, was oblivious. "I'm sorry you need assistance wiping your backside and missed toilet training with the rest of your squad. I'm sorry the Navy felt so sorry for you that—"

"Get us off this rock!"

None of them knew what the captain did, but the gunship lifted and headed away from the rebel base. Docherty sat on the floor and started to laugh as he raised his hand for the rest of the squad to high five. When they were done, he turned his palm upward and rubbed his fingers together.

The other marines sighed, pulled cred sticks from pouches on their weapons harnesses, and placed them in his open palm. Their captain appeared shortly afterward and surveyed the scene.

"Gimme those!" he demanded and snatched the cred sticks from the man's palm. "Of all the machoistic idiotic—"

One of the marines cleared his throat and tilted his chin toward Lars and the team, who stared in stunned surprise. Frog waved his hand at them.

"Oh, no. Don't mind us. Please. *Do* carry on. We're curious, now, aren't we guys?" He looked at his teammates, but they didn't look back. Instead, they leaned against the hull to catch their breath.

Vishlog slid to sit on the floor and eased Stephanie into his lap. Frog shrugged. "Well, *I'm* curious, so…"

Docherty smirked, lurched to his feet, and moved to sit against the side of the craft. "It's a long story."

The other man leaned back. "It's a long flight," he said but, before Docherty could continue, a hologram appeared in the center of the hold to display the base they'd just left.

Magma moved in a slow-moving tide and engulfed their fighters on the shelf outside. It filled the landing area, spreading slowly away from the gaping hole where the base's entrance had been.

One of the marines whistled and looked at Stephanie. "Did your girl do all that?"

The team bristled and pushed off the wall to take a step forward. Even the cats advanced a pace, their fur standing up in a ridge down their backs, their tails held high, and their ears pricked.

The man raised his hands slightly and backed away. "No offense, man." He gestured toward the hologram. "But day*um*!"

When they studied the image, the team had to admit he had a point.

Magma escaped from other openings farther up the mountain and trickled down its sides in bright orange ribbons. The hostilities forgotten, they watched in fascination as the mountain quickly became a volcano that burst at the seams and exploded.

It was stunning to watch from the safe distance of several miles away. Ash and debris erupted out of the planetoid and drifted into space, making the area hazardous.

Marcus came close and stared, then poked it with his finger. "That is insane. A volcano in a place where there wasn't one before."

Vishlog pushed to his feet. "Our leader needs to rest," he

declared and looked directly at the marine captain. The man understood. "Up the stairs, behind the cockpit. Don't talk to the Wattlebird."

The Dreth raised his eyebrows. "Who?"

"The pilot," the captain told him. "Don't talk to him."

He frowned but nodded. "There will be no talking." He glanced at Lars and addressed him as he'd heard some of the others do. "Boss?"

The team leader nodded. "I'll come with you." He fixed Frog with a steely glare. "Stay out of trouble while I'm gone. Don't do anything involving credits."

The nearest marines grinned, but he ignored them. "Let's go, Vishlog."

The warrior carried Stephanie where the captain had directed and found the crash couch behind the cockpit. He laid her on it gently and settled on the floor at the base of the bed.

"I will take the first watch," he told Lars and gave the pilot a hard look. "There will be silence."

Wattlebird shrugged and focused on flying. Whatever. He decided he'd be tired, too, if *he'd* just blown up a mountain. He didn't even complain when the two large cats came up from the hold and hopped onto the bed alongside her.

The Dreth did nothing to stop them, and feline-scented sheets or no, the pilot opted to let it go. After all, if a Dreth didn't want to tell the big beasts off, why would he?

CHAPTER NINETEEN

The rest of the team watched the volcano until the shuttle touched down in the *Washington Revere's* docking bay. As Vishlog struggled to his feet, Lars glanced across at him. "Do you want me to take her?"

The warrior shook his head.

They headed to their quarters and the pilot's reminder followed in their wake. "Three rounds, Johnny. You hear me?"

Johnny flipped his hand at the cockpit and nodded as he turned away.

"And none for those asshole marines," the Wattlebird added, making them all pause. The marines said nothing, but they about-faced as one and marched back onto the shuttle.

Johnny sighed. "Hold up, guys."

The team stopped to watch as the last marine disappeared. Several squawks and rattles issued over the intercom, and the sailors working in the hangar stopped.

"Marines," Johnny replied when one shot him an inquiring look, and the sailors went back to work.

A short while later, the marine captain and four of his squad reappeared and marched over to the team. "Navy Pilot Wattlebird is buying tonight."

He didn't explain what or why but simply stood and stared at them. When the team didn't move, he added, "You are dismissed. I believe the *Washington's* captain is expecting a report."

It was a poorly disguised order, but Lars and Johnny exchanged glances and decided they'd take it. They reached the briefing area beyond the hangar bay proper and stopped.

There, waiting for them, was a small cluster of men and women wearing the insignia of Naval Intelligence. Johnny looked at Lars as one of them approached.

With a hasty glance at Stephanie's sleeping form, the officer lowered his voice. "The captain says you've retrieved data from the rebel systems?"

Johnny gave him a curt nod and signaled for Frog to come forward. When none of the team members said anything, the officer tried again.

"Can we have it, please?"

Again, Johnny looked at Lars, and this time, the team leader nodded. "It's what we went for, and it'll save lives in the right hands. She'd want them to have it."

He ushered Vishlog past as Johnny and Frog unslung their packs and handed over the storage devices containing the data. They were about to leave when the intelligence officer laid a hand on Johnny's arm. "Is there anything you want to tell us about the trip?"

He shook his head. "Maybe later, when the boss is awake."

Frog caught the officer's glance. "What he said."

They'd reached the corridor and were on their way to their quarters when they met another officer. He hurried toward the hangar when he saw them but changed direction, and his gaze scanned them until he saw Stephanie.

Without stopping to greet any of the team, he stopped directly in front of Vishlog and pointed at her. "I need to speak to her."

He started to reach for her but the Dreth turned her out of his reach and looked at the team leader. "Would you mind holding her for me?"

Lars nodded, happy to do it, and took her carefully in his arms. Vishlog sniffed and turned toward the officer, the motion followed through with a jab directly to the face. The officer went down like a sack of potatoes and Lars choked on his own laugh in his effort not to wake Stephanie.

The warrior dusted his hands off and reclaimed her as he explained, "He might have woken her up."

Given how the officer had been moving and the fact he hadn't bothered to lower his voice when he'd seen she was asleep, Lars couldn't disagree. He merely followed when Vishlog stepped over the officer to continue up the corridor.

They turned the corner before their quarters to find a Naval security team waiting. Marcus pursed his lips and patted Vishlog's broad shoulder. "Uh oh. Don't worry, dude, get her inside. We'll take care of this."

He jogged ahead and signaled for the others to follow him. When they were ahead of Vishlog, he turned and moved backward as he spoke to them. "Let's form a chorus line, boys, exactly like we did when Lars celebrated ten and we didn't want the captain to see him wasted."

"Yeah, baby," Frog replied and pumped his fist.

Lars furrowed his brow. "I can't believe I don't remember that."

Johnny grinned. "With the amount of alcohol you'd drunk that night, we were surprised you even made it back to the barracks. Now, though, we'll line up and create a walk-through for Vishlog to walk down."

"Got it." Lars chuckled.

Marcus clapped. "Good. All right, Morgana's Team...of... fighting...bodyguards... Assemble!"

The guys walked up to the security team, then stood in front of them with their backs turned as they locked arms and blocked the corridor. One of the guards tapped Lars on the shoulder.

"Hey."

He shushed him. "Give us a minute. We need to get the Federation's witch to her quarters.

Frustration turned to anxiety. "Is she hurt?"

The team leader kept his arms rigid, aware of the subtle pressure to test the strength of the line. "Something like that."

They held the ship's security team at bay long enough for the Dreth to slip into their quarters and carry Stephanie through to her room. Once he had passed, Frog yanked the door closed behind him and the team leader stepped in to lean against it. The cats arranged themselves around his feet.

Bumblebee fixed the security chief with glittering eyes, lifted a forepaw, and extended his foreclaws to clean them one by one. The chief was unimpressed. "Not very subtle, is he?"

Lars glanced down but kept the chief in his periphery. "No, but he's a cat. Subtlety is not his strong suit."

"I take it you know why we're here."

Lars tilted his head at the door. "I have a fair idea."

"Will you hand him over?"

"Can we talk about it?"

The chief sighed. "I'm listening."

"Did you watch the feed?"

"Not yet."

"Well, when you do, you'll see the lieutenant intended to wake her, regardless of what we said. Not even your intelligence folk were that foolhardy—and you can check that on the feeds, too."

"Uh huh. And your point is?"

"If we'd said no, there'd have been an argument and she'd have woken anyway, and that would have been a very bad thing. Decking him was the fastest way to avoid that."

"You don't say." The chief's eyebrows raised but he didn't look convinced.

Lars remained propped against the door, and Zeekat moved to sit on the side the chief was on. Several of the security men shifted uneasily and their hands slid to their sidearms. Their superior signaled for them to stand down.

The team leader hurried to explain. "Have you watched the mission feed? I'm sure the pilot's transferred it by now and you've seen the reports on what she did for the *Meligorn Dreamer.*"

The chief looked thoughtful and Lars pressed his advantage. "She's not in a good mood right now, and she's worse when she's woken suddenly. You need to decide if you want a woman who can pull the magma of a small planetoid up to the surface to be rudely awakened by an idiot when you have this much power all around you."

He tilted his head and kept his body over the door handle, glad that Johnny and Marcus had come to lean on the wall on either side of him.

"Do us all a favor, Chief, and check the feeds. If you still want to talk to me about Vishlog's response, by all means, come and talk to me. It's not like we're going anywhere."

He left two men to guard the door. "You understand," he said crisply.

Lars gave him a tight-lipped smile and gestured to Avery and Marcus. "Keep them company." He met the chief's gaze. "I understand."

His expression displeased, the officer pursed his lips and nodded. "I'll be back."

The team leader maintained his smile while the rest of the security team left. "Marcus, Avery, no one enters or leaves unless I say so."

"Gotcha boss." They took up their posts on either side of the door and suppressed their grins as the two Navy security men settled in on the opposite side of the corridor.

Once the door had closed after the rest of the team. Marcus

glanced at Avery. "Lars is seriously killer-bad."

Avery turned and folded his arms over his chest. "Mhmm. Always has been, always will be."

The two snickered and settled in for their watch.

Vishlog set Stephanie on her bed and draped a blanket over her. When he was satisfied that she was comfortable, he left the room and closed her door carefully behind him.

A glance at the door to the common room showed it was shut. He eased the tension in his shoulders and stood at ease outside her room.

After a few minutes, Lars and all but two of the team entered. The team leader walked over, smirked, and put his hands in his pockets.

"I'm sorry I punched that officer," Vishlog said before Lars could say anything.

He waved it off. "He was being an asshole and tried to push it when she was asleep. If he'd woken her up like he planned to do, she might have fried him and she'd have been upset." He paused. "It's better if she's not upset. I'm not worried about that. If they come to take you away, go pleasantly—and take some popcorn for when she comes to get you out. I'm sure it will be entertaining."

Vishlog raised an eyebrow and thought about it, then they burst into muffled laughter.

In the High-Security Sector of the *Washington Revere*, the captain, the head of security, and the chief of intelligence stood in the main intelligence center, watching the mission at double speed. They stood quietly and tried to determine what their next move would be.

Captain Shale raised her hand. "Play it normal speed here."

They'd reached the point where Stephanie pulled the energy in the rebel control center. She drew so much that the translucent gleam became visible as mist-like sheets and grew even clearer as heat shimmered off the floor.

"Are her eyes black?" the captain asked, and the intelligence officer cleared his throat.

"Yes, ma'am. The files note this is a state Stephanie falls into when something called the Morgana is in control."

"Morgana is her surname."

"Yes, ma'am."

"So the name has a history."

"That is possible."

"Find it," the captain ordered.

"Yes, ma'am."

They fell silent as Frog and Johnny discovered the worm that destroyed the security system. All of them gave a small sigh of relief as the guys pulled their gear out of the system before it was infected.

"They didn't mention that when they handed the data over," the chief of intelligence muttered.

"They probably assumed they'd gotten clear in time and you didn't need to know," the security head told him.

"Even so—"

He was interrupted by the moment when Stephanie finished pulling in energy and dropped to her knees.

"I wouldn't touch her," the intelligence officer said.

"No, she's Stephanie, again. See?"

"Pause the feed," the captain ordered.

It stopped and the intelligence officer focused on her eyes.

The darkness was fading and some of the girl's natural blue shone through, albeit dulled by fatigue.

"She seems fairly out of it there," the captain pointed out.

The intelligence officer didn't comment but resumed the feed.

"Tiny legs," he snorted as Vishlog picked Stephanie up and the team began to race to the gunboat.

"It's a good thing you sent the marines," the head of security noted when the team reached the base doors.

"I like their trigger control," the captain added when Johnny smacked Lars's gun down. "Give them my compliments."

"Will do, ma'am,"

As the team scrambled into the gunboat, the intelligence officer switched the feed to the boat's external view of the magma working its way out of the mountain. They stared as it turned into a volcano and erupted, their eyes wide when they realized Lars hadn't been boasting.

"She really did create a volcano," the security chief breathed.

"And she really doesn't deal well when her men are hurt or threatened," the captain added, and reminded them of Stephanie's reaction when Brendan's ship had been clipped.

"Noted," he answered, and they watched the feed until the volcano had sunk back into the mountain.

The intelligence officer ended the feed, and the captain cleared her throat. "Boseman wanted to wake her up and get answers when the Dreth punched him?"

They'd watched the ship's feed of the incident, and it was obvious that this was what the lieutenant had intended.

The security chief nodded. "Yes, ma'am."

She gave him a stern look. "Tell Boseman to get his head outta his ass after they fix his jaw. Piss that witch off on *my* ship when she's just melted a mountain? The man is out of his mind."

When she really thought about it, her face darkened with anger. "I won't have him endangering my ship or my crew. Tell him the next time he pulls a stunt like that, he'll be in the brig pending trial."

And with that, she turned and stalked toward the door but paused as she reached it. "Tell everyone to let her wake up on her own."

Lars knocked on Stephanie's door the next morning.

"Come in," she called and unlocked it with a wave of her hand.

He stuck his head in and she smiled and gestured him closer. She sat in a lotus position, her legs crossed and palms upturned while she floated a foot above her bed.

Not quite sure what to make of it, he studied the air between her and the sheets and noticed the faint lines that suggested she was pulling energy. "Do you need any breakfast, or will this do it for you?"

She chuckled. "The energy doesn't fill my stomach. I'm starving. I feel like I could eat a mountain."

Lars raised a brow. "Hopefully not one that's on fire."

"No. I've had my fill of hot and spicy."

They both laughed and he motioned toward the common room. "I'll head down to the mess and bring it back. Normally, I'd say let's all go out, but I don't want to take Vishlog and run the risk of losing him to Security—and if he doesn't go, none of us do. I'd rather not test the Navy on this one."

She raised an eyebrow. "Oh?"

"He slugged an officer on the way in. The guy was going to wake you and looked set to argue, so Vishlog knocked him out."

"I slept through that?"

"You were pretty out of it. You wouldn't have slept through an argument, though, and I've seen you when you're woken. It's not pretty."

She smirked. "Worried about Morgana, huh?"

"She's nothing on you when you haven't had your first coffee."

Stephanie arched an eyebrow. "Speaking of which..."

Lars backed hastily away from her and raised his hands. "I'm going. I'm going."

"Hey, Lars..."

He stopped, his face wary. "Yes?"

"Tell Vishlog, thanks. The last thing I want is to blow up a spaceship because I got woken up wrong."

He grinned. "Coffee, right?"

"And stat!"

He pretended to flee, laughed, and snagged Avery and Brenden on the way out. To his surprise, the ship's security officers were no longer outside their door.

Her meditation over and Lars gone to find breakfast, Stephanie had time to think, and her thoughts immediately wandered to Todd. She wanted to know how he was doing and to see him laugh when she told him she'd blown up a mountain. He'd get a real kick out of that.

She dressed and stepped out of her room. To her surprise, the common room was empty, but she assumed that was okay. The team had been tired after their run through the rebel base.

At the common room's computer console, she ran a query search for Todd. When she couldn't find him, she frowned. She hadn't thought his mission had been that secret and he certainly wasn't.

It took a few moments for her to decide what she wanted to do next. She typed his name into the system once more and waited, but again, it drew a blank.

"Fine," she muttered and brought up a schematic that provided a basic floor plan for the deck she was on. Not all the spaces were marked, but there was enough that she could work out that what she was looking for wasn't on this deck.

"Hmmm. If I were a security section, where would I hide? Somewhere near Security? Probably not near the mess and maybe not near the forward deck…"

In the end, she wondered where Lars and her coffee were and if she could get back from the unlabeled area near the brig before he returned.

"This shouldn't take long," she decided and headed out the door, wishing she could take her HUD.

It would look funny and she didn't, but she took a moment to memorize where she needed to be as best she could before she left.

The guard outside the bulkhead leading to the unlabeled section of the schematic was a dead giveaway. When she made to touch the door panel and move past him, he put his hand out. "I'm sorry, ma'am, but you don't have permission to enter this section."

She grimaced. "Is there someone I can speak to? My name is Stephanie Morgana."

The guard cleared his throat and touched the comm in his ear. "Sir, there's a Stephanie Morgana outside. She'd like to speak to someone… Yes, sir."

He lowered his hand and gave her a nervous smile. "The lieutenant commander will be here in a moment."

Stephanie gave him a grateful smile. "Thank you."

There was an awkward silence, and she looked around at the bare corridor walls. She was tempted to lounge on them but wanted to make a good impression so she didn't.

While she waited, she decided to treat this as a business meeting. When the lieutenant commander arrived, she looked at him and glanced pointedly around at the corridor. "Is there somewhere private we could speak?"

"Right this way," he said and led her to a door set slightly back and to the right. On the map, it had been labeled as a meeting room. Now, she understood why.

The officer ushered her in and pulled the door closed behind them before he offered her a seat. "Lieutenant Commander Cunningham," he said by way of introduction. "It's nice to meet you, Ms. Morgana. How can I help?"

She took a deep breath and made sure to project a pleasant persona. "My friend, Todd, was injured in an operation at Sanmar's Rest."

"Yes, I am aware of that operation and its survivors."

Her ears pricked up at the plural, but she forced herself to focus on Todd. "I've tried to locate him in the system so I can contact him and see how he's doing, but I can't find him. Am I doing something wrong?"

Color touched his cheeks and he shook his head. "I don't think so, why?"

"Because I can't find him or any mention of the operation, and I don't know why. What happened out there?"

Cunningham's face reddened and he cleared his throat and leaned forward to put his elbows on the table. "I can't help you with what happened to Todd or how to get in touch with him, but I *can* assure you that he's okay."

Her face fell. "Can you tell me when I can talk to him?"

He shook his head. "I'm sorry."

"Thank you, then." She rose from her seat and took a step toward the door. He cleared his throat and she stopped.

"Can you tell me where your escort is?"

Stephanie frowned at him. "My escort?" At his nod, she replied. "They're fetching breakfast. Why?"

"Because none of you should roam the ship without one."

"I thought we were guests."

He blushed again, rose from his seat, and moved around the table to offer her his arm. "You are guests, and as such, you should be escorted so you don't run into any trouble."

Stephanie was about to say, "Like Vishlog," but she bit her tongue. It would probably be better if she didn't remind them of that incident. She still didn't like the idea of being followed around the ship, so she looked at his offered arm and patted him on the shoulder.

"Thank you, but I found my own way, here. I can find my own way back."

She went to open the door for herself, but he beat her to it. "I'm afraid I must insist."

A faint stirring of anger pushed through and she put her hands on her hips. "Don't you have better things to do?"

That stopped him, but he shrugged and looked at his watch. "Better than finding my own damn coffee for a change? And getting to do that in the company of a pretty lady? I don't think so."

Stupidly, she actually blushed at his blatant excuse-making and flattery and gave in. "Fine! You can take me back to my room, but *only* if we pick the coffee up on the way."

He smiled at that—a genuine smile—and offered her his arm once more. This time, she took it and kept her smile in place as they walked back to the team's quarters.

She didn't forget the coffee either, picked up enough for everyone, and insisted on carrying the tray herself. "You have escort duties," she told Cunningham when he went to pick it up, "and you really shouldn't have your hands full when you need to keep an eye on me."

"Now, now."

They reached the team's rooms in time to hear Lars shouting.

"What do you mean, she isn't here?"

Stephanie turned to Cunningham. "You'd better let me handle this."

He looked at her and very deliberately knocked on the door.

The team leader answered and jerked it open with a look of fury on his face. "Yes!"

His expression cleared when he saw her, then clouded when he saw who she was with. "What's she done this time?"

She interrupted him. "I brought coffee." She stepped forward, forcing Lars to step back, and blocked him with her body as she turned to the officer. "Thank you, Lieutenant Commander. I appreciate your help."

Before he could reply, she reached out and gently but firmly closed the door in his face. Lars stared at her.

"That was the head of their intelligence section. What did you do?"

"I tried to find out how to contact Todd. He told me I couldn't." She frowned. "He also said I shouldn't move around the ship unescorted."

"Too darn right you shouldn't."

"He said *none* of us should go unescorted."

The other guys in the room groaned.

"You know what that makes us, don't you?" Marcus demanded.

Stephanie shook her head. "No."

"Almost secured guests," Frog said brightly.

"As in prisoners?" She didn't like that idea.

"No, as in guests," Marcus told her. "Prisoners get locked in."

Frog came over and gave the tray a hopeful look. "Is that from the officer's mess?"

After breakfast and a morning going over their gear, Lars, Johnny, and Marcus headed out to get lunch. It was no surprise to find three bored-looking marines waiting for them.

"It's about time you guys decided to head for chow," Docherty told them.

"How'd your evening go?" Lars asked, and the marine laughed.

"Wattlebird will think of something to get us back."

The conversation cut off as the guys shut the door and Stephanie sighed. "Sorry, guys."

Frog waved his hand at her. "It's not your fault. We're all troublemakers here."

"I thought we were troubleshooters, Marcus."

"Yeah, well, when we can't find trouble to shoot, we go make some. It's easy."

"I only wish I could speak to Todd."

"Sorry. Can't help you there."

She sighed and began pulling energy in, making sure she'd recovered from creating a volcano. When she'd done that, she sat on the couch in the common room, a cat on either side of her, and flicked through the onboard entertainment.

There wasn't much. She'd barely settled on a re-run of an old movie classic when the others returned. Aside from the marines, they weren't alone.

"I'm Captain Shale. Do you mind if I join you?"

"Do we h—" Stephanie began, but Lars cleared his throat and she fixed a bright smile on her face. "No. Go ahead. Please, join us. I'm sure the boys brought enough for a guest."

The captain smiled. "If they didn't, I did," she said and stepped clear of the door so a steward could push a fully laden trolley through.

He set it in the middle of the room, saluted, and left. Frog lifted the cover and whistled. "This is sooo mu—"

Marcus smacked him on the back of the head.

"Thank you, Captain," she said, and the woman turned to the trolley and filled a plate.

"Let's talk while we eat."

Despite her words, there wasn't much conversation for the first few minutes after they'd all found a place to sit. When her plate was almost clear, Stephanie broke the silence. "So, what brings you here?"

The captain glanced at the door to make sure it was closed. "That intel you pulled. We've worked through enough of it to know there'll be another pirate attack, and this one looks major.

She leaned forward. "Do you know where?"

Captain Shale sighed. "Yes, but we can't get there in time."

Her disappointment must have shown on her face because the captain regarded her solemnly for a long moment before she continued. "But we *do* think we can get *you* there."

She jumped up immediately. "Great. When do we leave?"

The woman raised a hand to signal that she should sit again.

"We have two problems," she said, as she complied. "Firstly, the only ship we have that can make it there in time is an experimental one, and secondly, it's much faster than anything in the rest of the fleet."

"So?" She couldn't see a problem with either of these things.

The captain sighed. "So not even the fastest corvette could keep up with you, and the *Washington Revere* isn't that. You'd reach the attack coordinates in time, but you'd be without any back-up."

She paused to let that sink in. "Would you be willing to see if there is anything out there and if you can, protect their targets or track where they go if you're outgunned? R&D would have my hide if they lost their ship on a suicide mission."

Frog rolled his eyes. "Sure. Let's not worry about the contractors you send into the—" Lars cleared his throat and his teammate stopped, looked at him, and amended his planned finish. "The trouble. But *R&D*, well, we can't upset them."

The captain smiled and shrugged. "It is what it is," she told him, and her smile widened when he groaned.

Stephanie leaned back in her chair and rested her plate on her lap. She moved her gaze from one guy to the next and received a slight nod from each before she focused on the next.

When she reached Vishlog, he shrugged. "I go where you go, boss."

She turned her attention to Shale. "We'll do it, but you'll have to negotiate with Elizabeth Smith for the total charges for all of this, provided that we live—and I think she'll charge you if we die, too, so be prepared."

The captain nodded, her face serious. "I think the Navy can handle that."

Frog sputtered and Marcus elbowed him in the ribs. Stephanie didn't comment, and the rest of the team waited for the captain to continue.

Shale looked at her. "You'll go under the same conditions as before," she warned, and she grinned.

"I don't have a problem with that."

The woman pushed to her feet. "I'll need time to sweet-talk R&D into handing over their baby—and to convince them you don't need a passenger from their department. And I need a requisitions order for the equipment you need. The marines stationed outside will take you to Stores for that."

"Thank you," she said, her mind racing.

"Is there anything that comes to mind?" the captain asked as Bumblebee butted Stephanie's hand.

"Armor," she told her. "Especially for the cats." She glanced at Vishlog. "And our Dreth. What he has needs replacing."

For a moment, the warrior looked like he might protest, then he nodded. "Armor," he agreed.

Frog jumped in. "And guns."

Stephanie nodded and pointed at him. "Good call. We'll need guns—lots and lots of guns."

***

Eight hours later, in the ready room adjoining the shuttle bay, Stephanie pushed her cape off her shoulder. Elizabeth had negotiated a uniform upgrade and sent the programs for the replicators to copy.

Now, instead of the previous gray-blue, she wore pure black and she liked the change. She liked it on the team, too. "You guys look really good."

Lars smiled. His all-black outfit matched Stephanie's right down to the crest above the left pocket. "Yeah, but it's black."

She grinned. "Don't you know? Every witch wears black. It goes with our eyes when we get pissed off."

Around them, the guys checked each other's armor, and two of them examined Vishlog's. The Dreth stood patiently while Frog pulled a strap tight.

"Are you sure that's meant to be there, Vish?"

He nodded solemnly. "Yes. It is for the weapons' harness."

"Weapons' harness?" His teammate tugged on another strap. "I thought *this* was the weapons' harness!"

Vishlog laughed. "Yes, but *that* one is for the *other* weapons' harness."

Frog turned to Stephanie and Lars. "Moo-oom, I want two weapons' harnesses, too!"

The team leader looked at him, then at her, and tried for his best 'Dad' tone. "Look, Frog. I thought we agreed. You can have two harnesses like your brother when you're big enough to carry the same weapons he does."

As if on cue, Johnny and Avery picked up one of the Double Saber Gatling Guns and carried it to Vishlog. "When do you want this loaded up?"

Frog gaped at it and stamped his foot. "It's not fair!" He pretended to wail and managed a credible pout before he cracked up laughing and helped the others attached the huge weapon.

When they were done, the Dreth strode to the bathroom door and looked into the mirror. "I look good."

Johnny wolf-whistled and Frog cat-called, and he swatted at both of them before he looked at Stephanie. "How are the cats?"

"They're getting better," she replied and whistled.

Bumblebee and Zeekat stood and bounded to her. Their armored feet clattered across the floor, but the animals moved easily inside it. What they wore had been modified from old models of service K-Nine armor.

It had still taken an intensive three-hour training shift in the VR pods for them to be able to fight in it, but they'd learned, especially when Stephanie had stepped in. The two felines had been so busy trying to protect her from virtual monsters that they'd forgotten they were even *in* armor.

They hadn't even protested too strongly when they were settled into the real thing. Marcus eyed them dubiously. "How does that even work?" he wanted to know. "It's not like they can bite anything from there."

Stephanie laid her hand over the auditory sensors modeled into the set. "It uses a little virtual programming so the cats don't know it's the suit doing the biting but have the sensation of doing it themselves. It's the same for the claws."

Frog came to stand beside Marcus. "So, no teasing the kitties, huh?"

"Not while they're in this," she told him.

"Not if you like your nuts in one piece," Johnny added. He looked at Stephanie. "Honestly, those two fight dirty!"

As soon as they were ready, the team headed to the shuttle, where they found the rest of their requested kit. Their two pilots were already settled in and doing pre-flight checks. Wattlebird waved his hand to the side so they could see he knew they were aboard.

"How'd your night out go?" Frog called, and the wave turned into a one-fingered salute.

Snickering, they turned to the equipment crates.

"I thought we told them we could do our own piloting," Lars grumbled.

Wattlebird confirmed he was hooked into their comms. "Well,

you know how us Navy folk are. We simply don't trust a troop of mercenaries—"

"Consultants!" Stephanie snapped.

"Hooligans!" the team chorused in response.

She glared at them. "Not helping here."

The guys laughed and dug into the crates. Frog almost had a fit.

"Oh. Dear. Lord!" he breathed as he set the lid back. He reached into the crate and pulled something out, handling it with the reverence usually reserved for holy relics.

"What?"

"You asked for guns that shoot themselves and the Navy came through!"

"What do you mean?" Stephanie demanded, but he was busy plugging a programming stick into his HUD.

"Hey, Johnny, come over here. This is right up your alley. You, too, Vish. I've seen how you fly."

The team crowded around until Lars sent them to check the contents of the other crates.

Admiring whistles and exclamations of delight punctuated the next few minutes, and she simply stood back and watched them work through the gear like a swarm of kids let loose in the middle of a pile of presents.

They had examined the weapons and realized there were too many left over for it all to be meant for them when the marines arrived. She snickered as she gave them the heads up.

"It looks like you're sharing your toys, boys."

They didn't let her down and made their disappointment a loud chorus. The marine captain stepped inside. "Sorry to spoil your fun."

"Who says it's spoiled?" she asked him. "The more the merrier."

By the time they'd allocated the weapons, the pilots had closed the hatch and were warming the engines.

Avery watched as the marines showed them how to load the extra magazines into their harnesses, and then how to load even more. He shook his head. "I think there are more rounds here than was shot in all wars—ever."

Lars looked at him. "Come on. You're exaggerating. I…" He looked at bulging ammo pouches and well-stocked harnesses, then noticed the crates being secured in one corner by a pair of marines. "Okay, maybe not by much, but definitely a little."

As the experimental ship left the *Washington Revere*, Wattlebird's voice came over the intercom.

"Good afternoon, ladies and gentlemen. Thank you for choosing to fly Navy Experimental Airlines. This is your captain speaking."

One of the marines snorted but Wattlebird either didn't hear him or chose to ignore him.

"You will be happy to know they have given us not one, but *two* buttons. One of these is large and red and the other is green and also large, proving that size really does matter. For the Dreth among you, this should come as good news."

There was a round of good-natured chuckles and Vishlog grinned, but Wattlebird wasn't done.

"Before we push either of these suckers, we would like to remind you that this is a strictly non-smoking flight and that your tray tables should be secured in the upright position."

After a quick breath, he continued. "Also, make sure you're sitting in your assigned seats and that the harness and webbing are secured. We would hate to lose any of you mid-transition."

They exchanged nervous glances and doublechecked their harnesses.

Up front, Wattlebird cleared his throat. "Okay, we're about to hit the red button. The button that says go—or is that the green button? Hell, one of these buttons that will take your inside and make it your outside. We suggest you sit in the webbed chairs, buckle in, and kiss your sweet butts goodbye. We hit the red button in ten…nine…eight… Oh, screw it!"

The sound of his palm smacking the button echoed and the craft hurtled into space.

CHAPTER TWENTY

The pilot hadn't joked about their insides becoming their outsides. Groans echoed through the cabin as the universe twisted around them before it stopped abruptly. Everyone jolted forward. Stephanie looked at her team. "Is everyone good?"

They all nodded. Frog flung his harness off and jumped up to pump his fists. "That. Was. Awesome."

Marcus hauled him back into his seat as the ship accelerated again, albeit a little slower this time. The pilot spoke over the comms once more. "You guys might want to take a look-see." He opened a viewscreen on the bulkhead behind the cockpit.

In the distance ahead, they saw three small corvette class ships attacking a large, deep-space freighter.

"We should help," Brenden said.

Stephanie stared at the scene, then pointed. "Look over there. It's a big ass momma pirate ship. Take us there. They want to play. We will play. Take us right into one of their landing bays."

The pilot twisted and looked at her through the hatchway. His expression said she was crazy. "What if they don't have any landing bays?"

She smirked. "Make one."

"Gotcha." Wattlebird turned back to the front. "Hold onto your hats, folks. We've seen the long-haul. Now, let's see what this beauty can do in the short-and-fast department."

He left the viewscreen up and both teams stared, transfixed, as he opened the throttle and crossed the distance between them and the mothership in what felt like seconds.

The pilot swept the ship around under the leviathan's belly and waited while his co-pilot ran a scan.

"Portside and up. Twenty degrees to your left," she instructed in a soft contralto, and one of the marines gave a happy sigh.

The man next to him groaned. "Lesange is in love again."

"It's the voice," another added. "Every damn time. Give him a voice like that and it goes straight to his balls."

The co-pilot cleared her throat and they abruptly fell silent.

"Get ready to flip it in three...two...one... Now!" she ordered, and Wattlebird flipped the experimental and brought them squarely in line with a hangar door.

"She's magic," Lesange breathed.

No one answered him as the pilot opened fire on the hangar door and it vaporized.

"I want one," Frog muttered, and the marine captain snapped him a fierce glare.

"Get in line."

"Uh oh." One of the marines snickered. "The captain is in lust."

They fell silent as bodies floated past them. The hangar hadn't been empty. While the ships docked there were locked in place, the crewmen refueling or repairing them were not.

When the doors vanished, the hangar vented, and they were lost to space with its atmosphere. Wattlebird cruised through the opening until he saw an open landing pad and brought the ship down.

His voice spoke through their HUDS loud and clear. "Lock and load, ladies and gentlemen. This is where we leave you. Keep your suits sealed until you make it into the ship proper and thank you for flying Naval Experimental Air."

"Wait," Frog protested. "You're leaving us?"

He was unrepentant. "We can't leave the ship here. We have to drop you off and get out."

Stephanie shook her hands and small sparks cascaded off them. "Don't worry. We will take that one home." She pointed at the largest pirate ship attacking the freighter and smiled.

Vishlog's eyes grew wide and he leaned forward to peer out at the ship.

He glanced dubiously at Lars. "Is she serious?"

The team leader didn't answer. He and Stephanie were already waiting at the rear doors, the cats beside them.

On the command deck above them, the Dreth captain watched as his crew coordinated the three attacking ships. It was like watching a dance being choreographed on the fly—a beautiful and deadly dance.

The freighter was armed, but she hadn't brought an escort and they were close to one of the smaller ships being able to hard-dock with her. Once his men were inside, it would only be a short time before the ship fell.

"Tell me when you find it," he ordered as his smallest ship moved into position for docking.

The deep space scans had picked up a small blip. It might have been a ship, except it moved too fast and initial analysis couldn't identify it. As he spoke, his comms crackled and shrieked and one of the techs ripped his headset away from his ears.

The crackling was followed by a squeal before the viewscreen went fuzzy. He scowled and pressed a couple of keys on his console while the technician tried frantically to clear the image.

Before the man could resolve the picture, the screen went

black and a deep female laugh rippled through the speakers. "My name is Morgana. You are in my way. Prepare to be destroyed."

"What in Hrageth's holy balls was that?" the captain demanded and whirled to face his 2IC. "And where is that ship?"

A very feminine chuckle rolled out of the speakers and sent chills down his spine. "And *why* is this woman on my comms?" he demanded.

As he spoke, alarms squawked throughout the carrier and the lights flickered wildly overhead. One of the men working the system looked at him. "Uh…Landing Bay Twelve, sir. The ship is in Landing Bay Twelve."

What had started out as a lucrative day rapidly descended into chaos. When he hooked into the security feed for Bay Twelve, there was only silence and the darkness on the screen remained. They were about to flick to the corridor outside when a loud scream echoed across the room.

It was followed by voices shouting a warning. "We have cats! There are cats eating crewmen in Landing Bay Twelve. Does anybody read—*Ahhhh!*"

Everyone winced at the crunch that ended the scream. The growl that followed made their hair stand on end. The viewscreen fritzed and displayed pictures from over thirty cameras.

Landing Bay Twelve was empty save for the bodies of the dead, and those were floating into space. The airlock had cycled sometime during the glitch and now stood empty and closed. The corridor outside was littered with bodies.

The command crew searched the screen, looking for any sign of their invaders.

In one, they saw the figure of a goddess dressed in battle armor and bathed in light, a cape draped over her shoulders. She flung small glowing balls over a makeshift barricade of tables.

Everything they touched exploded—tables, chairs, heads…the wall leading to the next compartment…

Suddenly, one of the human pirates ran to a camera, his face contorted with terror "Please help us...they're not natural. They're demons—vicious—and there's no way to stop them!"

A growl interrupted him, and he was dragged from sight.

"Who turned the lights out?" a voice demanded from another screen. "It's so cold."

The moan that followed scraped through them and ignited a terror they could not name. The sound of blaster fire from another feed was almost welcome. It sounded so...normal.

Metal shrieked and their attention was caught as a large armored cat bounded across the screen. Solid rounds ricocheted off it as it cannoned into a team of pirates who tried to hold the corridor. Its forepaws wrapped around one of the adjacent pirates as its hind paws raked downwards.

Two pirates fell screaming and the third ran.

He didn't get very far.

On another screen, a trio of marines leap-frogged past each other as grenades decimated an internal corridor ahead of them. A third screen showed more marines and a civilian taking the armory apart.

A fourth screen showed a lone civilian, shorter than the rest and surrounded by a cloud of drones. He walked toward one of the auxiliary hubs and the drones eliminated the few crewmen who appeared to oppose him.

"Someone, stop him!" the captain shouted. A shudder ran through the ship, followed by the sound of an explosion. He looked at a technician.

"Landing Bay Four just vented to space, sir. There appears to be an angry Dreth screwing with the controls." He highlighted the appropriate visual feed, and Vishlog's black-clad form appeared, taking the relevant control room apart.

"Somebody stop him! For Hrageth's sake, don't let him—" Another convulsive shudder was followed by a dull boom.

"Landing Bays Eight through Ten just vented, sir."

"I know. I can see that. Will someone with *some* kind of competence kill these boarders?"

He stabbed at the control panel in front of him. "Damnation! I need to speak to *Targa's Wrath*. I want them back here to deal with this problem. Why. Won't. This. System. Work?"

One of the technicians worked his keyboard in a series of rapid-fire commands and the sweat beaded on his thick skin. "They're in our system too, sir."

"Well, get them the hell out of it."

The comms crackled again, and a female pirate's voice cried, "But I just got here. Stop it. Damn cats. I knew you were fucking evil. Captain, you better tell my family I died protecting them, not being *devoured by a huge pussy!*"

That broadcast ended in a shrill scream and another sickening crunch, and blaster fire issued from four other monitors. In a fifth, a swarm of drones hovered between a half-dozen pirates and a small man with a keyboard plugged into a mainframe.

The captain was almost beside himself. "Hrageth be damned. Get my fighters back here."

Stephanie's team and the marines raced through the ship and cleared the corridors, side corridors, and rooms as rapidly as they could. They broke off into small teams and left any room the cats chose strictly to the animals.

The felines showed no mercy, but they were never far from their mistress's side and constantly returned to check on her after they had cleared the enemy from the caves around her.

Stephanie kept her shields up and allowed her team to focus on killing pirates while she tried to determine the quickest route to the command deck. "My kingdom for a damned *map*," she yelled. "Where is the 'You are Here' arrow?"

None of them noticed when Frog took his flock of drones and

made a few educated guesses. Stephanie wanted a map? Well, he could find her one.

He left them to clear what they could and prayed he didn't find too many pirates in the corridors ahead. By the time the cats had cleared the crew quarters, he knelt beside one of the ship's auxiliary mainframes while the drones blocked the door.

The first thing he did was upload a worm to keep their security programs busy, and the next was to run several sub-routines at once. He left the docking bays alone. Vishlog had muttered something about creating confetti and fireworks before rumbling off along the flight line with Avery, Brenden, and Docherty in tow.

"Someone has to keep you boys out of trouble."

"Yeah. Good luck with that," Marcus had snorted as they'd left. It had been easy to slip away.

When he'd found the data Stephanie needed, he sent it to their HUDS. "I believe someone owes me a kingdom," he told them and gave himself remote access to the system before he started heading back.

The drones had created carnage outside, but he could now see where the team was and jogged along a path to intercept them. "I hope those assholes don't shoot me before they work out who I am," he muttered.

Ahead of him, Stephanie stopped to study the schematics he had sent. "And thank you, Froggie," she murmured as she identified where they needed to go.

"There," she snapped and marked the command center. "Find me and follow me in."

Muttered affirmatives issued over the comms and she took the lead through the maze of corridors and decks. At one point, she came to an abrupt halt and peered carefully around the corner. "Dammit, Frog, you couldn't have hooked me into the security feeds?" she grumbled.

He laughed. "Your wish is my command," he said, and she

stared at the display of the corridor beyond.

There were at least fifteen fully armed and armored Dreth pirates formed up across the hallway ahead. Their leader gave orders in Dreth.

Marcus whispered over the team's comms. "What are we waiting for?"

Stephanie raised a hand for silence and sent almost transparent pearls of magic up and out along the ceiling. "Work smarter, not harder."

Using the security feed for reference, she guided the tiny orbs until they were above the Dreth pirates, then directed a pearl onto each one. The moment it touched, it lit up like a beacon.

It also melted into a puddle that coated the surface it was on and then ignited. The Dreth screamed and fired blindly to shoot each other, the walls, the ceiling, and the floor. When the barrage stopped, she led them forward. They had only gone a few paces when a voice spoke over the intercom "I don't know what your tiny little squad has it in their mind to do, but you will not succeed and it would be a shame to kill you. You are all alone. Even your pilots have left you behind."

There was a pause before the voice continued, calm and reasonable despite the tension that trickled through it. "Don't make this hard on yourselves. We can use a team like you."

"Uh huh," Stephanie muttered, but the captain continued.

"We're trying to build a better universe."

The image of the burning ship flashed into her mind.

"A better world?" she snapped. "How? You're murdering—"

"No, no, no. We're *acquiring* what we need."

"What...bodies? Dead families? Other people's wealth? How is that what you need?"

"We don't kill families," he argued. "Never. They're too valuable in the world to come."

"Rubbish. I was there. You not only kill families, but you kill your own."

"We *target* only our enemies."

"You were going to blow up an entire *passenger liner*. I don't call that targeting. Your people were there to rob and steal."

"We need resources. We're working toward peace, something everyone needs. We need to be ready."

"We *are* ready!" she snarled as the energy flared around her body. Her voice dropped in pitch and those closest her took two steps away.

"Uh oh," Marcus muttered, and Lars summed it up in a single word. "Shit."

The marines with them snapped their blasters up and scanned the walls and the corridor for the enemy but saw no one. Stephanie picked up the pace, walking yet moving so fast they had to trot to keep up.

She pulled more energy as she went, dragged it from the walls of the ship, from the floors, and from space beyond. Finally, she stopped following the corridors and moved directly toward her target location, her magic blazing a path for them to follow.

* * *

In the command center, the captain glared at the screen as Stephanie's dark figure moved directly toward him. After a moment's hesitation, he contacted his fleet.

"*Targa's Wrath* and *Hrageth's Ascension*. *Targa's Wrath* and *Hrageth's Ascension*. Return home. Urgent assistance required. *Targa's Wrath. Hrageth's Ascension.* Your assistance is required. Return home."

He waited but neither of the other two ships acknowledged him.

"*Targa's Wrath and Hrageth's Ascension. Ebon Knight* has been boarded. You are recalled. Urgent assistance required."

This time, although neither responded, he saw the ships increase power and slowly alter their course toward him.

CHAPTER TWENTY-ONE

Brenden elbowed Avery, who elbowed Frog, who elbowed Vishlog, who was finally done with the games and turned to Lars and pointed at Stephanie. Her energy now shimmered over her skin and her hair moved wildly around her, breaking free from her braid. Her eyes had turned black and luminescent, and her teeth were clenched tightly.

They'd been focused on eradicating the pirates who appeared from beyond the next vaporized wall and hadn't watched her. Now, she had their full attention.

"Sonuva—" Lars muttered and ran forward. He ducked in front of her and tried to make eye contact. "Steph! Come on, Steph. You're still in there, right? You know we're on a ship, right?

She continued her advance, her face implacable under the HUD as she strode toward the command center. He jogged backward and hoped he didn't fall on his ass and get trampled.

He tried again. "Come on, Steph. Remember, if you let loose on a ship, you will blow us all to the end of the universe. Steph—Morgana! Listen to me."

Marcus came up and placed a hand on her skin. She snapped

her head toward him, her face angry. "Horrible things happen if we bust a hole in the skin, Steph."

The marines flanked them, fired at shadows that moved and fired in return, while the guys tried to get Morgana to see reason. The closer they got to the command center, the worse the incoming fire became. The shields she had thrown around them rippled and sparked under the impact of solid rounds and laser fire.

They crossed another room and she devastated another wall, this time taking the next one down with it.

"Horrible things, Steph," Lars repeated and tried to think of something to add to get her to listen. Unfortunately, she wasn't in control. Morgana was.

"Then horrible things might happen," she replied, her voice eerily calm despite the promise of vengeance within.

They crossed the two rooms. The first was some kind of gymnasium, but the second...none of them could work out *what* it was. Large steel balls were arrayed in neat shelves along one wall, and Stephanie-Morgana lifted them and floated a dozen of them through the air.

The steel balls ranged in size from soccer balls to medicine balls, and she spun them in a swirl of steel as she pushed ahead. The shields bulldozed a path through the debris in front of them.

Pirates emerged from the corridors around them and the steel balls spun through the front row to cut them down. Morgana walked on and the whirling balls moved methodically in a macabre dance of death around her.

She appeared to be deep in thought.

Shouts came from behind them and everyone pivoted as a large group of Dreth advanced in a rush. The enemy bellowed battle cries and raised their weapons to fire.

This, she noticed. She swayed to the side and brought both arms to the right and up and over her head to the other side.

The balls rocketed in a deadly wave to shred through the front ranks and swirl into the center of the massed pirates.

Carnage ensued, but Stephanie didn't stay to watch. She turned and continued toward the command center, wondering exactly what the Teachers of Meligorn would think now.

The magic she used was more than an illusion of power. It *was* power. She could feel it flowing in and around her and knew that without it, she and her teams would not have made it past the hangar bay.

She also knew that it was beyond magic to change the pirates. They believed they were fighting for a cause and for the benefit of all. If anything, that was an illusion. She dragged several pirates out from behind a broken wall and dropped them in the open.

Bumblebee and Zeekat raced forward and savaged two of them before they had even landed. Lars and Johnny killed another two. Stephanie-Morgana continued her progress and swept the balls through more pirates in a side corridor as she thought how beliefs could cause creatures to go against their natures but magic could not.

How exactly did that work? It was beyond her.

She vaporized the wall that concealed another dozen Dreth and let the team deal with them but dropped two more down for the cats. The bloodied mass of steel balls spun through a wall and into a Dreth who had pulled the pin on a grenade.

He fell and it exploded. The other pirates nearby died with him.

Stephanie resumed her musing as she drew closer to the dot on the map and seemed oblivious to her surroundings. Inside her mind, she journeyed much farther and contemplated the Mysteries as she pulled Dreth out from hiding for her teams and the cats to deal with or simply obliterated them with the balls.

Targa's Wrath and *Hrageth's Ascension* veered back toward the *Ebon Knight*. Resentful at being called back from the kill when their sister ship looked ready to dock, they didn't watch their long-range scans as closely as they should have.

They were so focused on trying to establish how the *Ebon Knight* had been boarded that they missed the small flotilla of Navy ships that appeared in the system. By the time the scans had sounded the alert and drawn their attention to the enemy presence, the first salvo of missiles was on its way. Both the *Targa* and the *Ascension* tried to take evasive action and failed.

Their sister ship hid in the shadow of the freighter's signal. When *Targa* and *Ascension* exploded, she ran.

On the *Ebon Knight's* command deck, the captain lifted the protective cover from a non-descript black button on his console. He hesitated momentarily, licked his lips and swallowed hard, then pressed it.

"I apologize for having to bother you, but I believe we will need you to make an appearance. There is a witch on my ship."

CHAPTER TWENTY-TWO

The Navy had sent its fastest ships—two corvettes and two frigates. In mass, they equaled the *Targa* and the *Ascension,* but in firepower, they were somewhat better. Their crews moved with quiet confidence in the control room as the small flotilla headed into battle.

"Missiles away."

"Fire again."

"I don't think they've seen us."

"They can't be watching their scans." Lieutenant Bailey monitored the missiles' flight and the targets' behavior. He saw when the two pirate vessels realized they were under fire. "They've noticed us now."

"Not fast enough."

"Give them another dose to be sure."

"Gunnery will be upset."

"Good. It's time they did some buying."

They watched as their missiles converged on *Targa's Wrath* and she vanished from their screens. A second wave of missiles reached *Hrageth's Ascension* and it followed the other into oblivion. Bailey straightened and the crew chief looked at him.

"What about the mother ship, sir?"

"Leave it. The Witch has boarded it and we are under strict instructions *not* to blow her up."

"Aye aye, sir."

On the *Ebon Knight*, Stephanie had almost reached the command center. She dropped the steel balls and hurled several balls of fire at the Dreth instead. One after another, they fell victim to a magical firestorm.

Something pulled at the energy around her as if someone had walked across the web-like strands that connected her to the universe. She paused and blocked incoming fire with the shields as she closed her eyes and listened with every part of her body.

It took her a couple of heartbeats to understand what her magical self heard and where it came from but when she did, she pivoted toward it.

"Get behind me," she commanded. "Stay behind me," she added when they obeyed.

Bumblebee noticed a Dreth creep closer and started forward, only to have her bop him lightly on top of his armored head. It brought him up short.

"Listen!"

Both cats looked at her, then at the pirates moving on their flanks. She glared at them.

"Listen!"

They caught the growl in her voice and lowered their heads to slink behind her with rumbles of protest. Agitated, they kept glancing toward the approaching Dreth, but Brenden laid his hand on Bumblebee's shoulder and leaned on the cat to let him know he was there, and Marcus did the same for Zee.

In front of them, Stephanie began drawing more energy to herself in much the same way she had in the rebels' mountain base. Sheets of it hazed around her, vanished in waves inside her, and passed through her armor as though it was no barrier at all.

The small strands of hair that had escaped during their fight through the ship drifted up to form a halo around her head. Bumblebee looked at her and hissed, then took a step away from her.

Marcus glanced at Zeekat and saw the feline staring fixedly past her. Before he could say anything, the marines snapped their blasters to their shoulders and aimed them unerringly in the same direction.

The marine captain's voice rumbled low through their comms. "Hold fire. Wait for the witch's signal."

"What the hell is that?" Brendan asked and kept one hand on Bumblebee as he raised his blaster with the other.

Lars reached toward Steph but thought better of it, although he remained ready to grab her and drag her to safety. Marcus wanted to ask him where he thought that was but couldn't say a word.

The being that approached them was at least as big as Vishlog and just as well-built. He wore armor unlike anything they'd ever seen—seamless and gleaming but moving with him as he walked.

His helmet, however, was another matter. It looked nothing like a modern helmet but rather like it had been taken from the pages of Earth history and blended seamlessly with the space armor he wore. It had a smooth, rounded top and a slender piece of metal reached down over where the bridge of a human's nose would be.

Two eye holes were carved out of it and two large pieces of metal curved to cover nonexistent cheeks. Marcus thought he should be able to see the bottom of the creature's nose and some of its lips and chin.

Hell. He should have been able to see its eyes, too, but he couldn't.

There was nothing but darkness beneath the helmet, a featureless well of black.

The helmet turned until it seemed the entity beneath looked directly at Stephanie. She returned its gaze without flinching, even when it raised one long, dark arm and pointed at her.

"Interesting. I think I will keep you as a prize, young one."

Every blaster readied and every trigger finger started to squeeze, but she snapped her fingers and their muscles froze so not a single shot was fired.

"You…" she said, and her mind raced as she tried to understand what she saw. A creature of nothing. Something magical enough for her own magic to alert her to his presence when her other senses hadn't seen him coming.

She studied him, trying to sense his power and noting a complete absence of any kind of energy she knew. Pure darkness and a sense of nothing? She knew this.

Stephanie pointed at him. "You are Nihilism. The opposite of Energy. You are the vacuum."

The entity cocked his head. "You have some knowledge. Not enough, but more than you should. My people will consume as we always do. We will reduce the casualties of the coming war. Join us. Save those you love from the horrors. Your honor and wisdom will be rewarded."

Instinctively, she shivered. Inside, she spun the gMU she had gathered tighter and tighter to make it as concentrated as she could. She only had one opportunity, and she couldn't let him know what she was doing.

Sweat dripped down her forehead and Nihilism laughed, his deep tones mocking. "I can feel you. Your energy cannot beat mine, and mine—"

A small explosion detonated beside him and shields of midnight appeared around him as he took a hasty step away from it. The team glanced toward the sound but saw only wall.

The alien did, too. "That was unwise."

As he spoke, a curling tendril of magic lashed out. Stephanie made a slashing movement with her hand and cut through the black. The tendril fell to the deck and vanished into hissing vapor.

His next attack used her idea of fireballs but took it to the next level.

He threw orbs of blackness, the aura of cold that emanated from them so intense it burned the air around it. She dodged those but between each orb, he added darts of black lightning and several of these penetrated her defenses.

As the battle intensified, her magic released her protectors and they moved clear. Brendan and Marcus dragged the cats aside and the two teams, contractors and marines, crouched low. They pressed against the walls, unwilling to leave but not able to intervene.

The lightning made her muscles convulse and her teeth chattered violently every time a bolt struck home. As the onslaught continued, she found each one more difficult to avoid than the last and each counterattack harder to make.

Her shields pulsed and weakened under the relentless barrage of dark magic. She felt her power waning and fatigue dragged at her spirit and mind.

Nihilism's power was heavy, and it cut deep inside her mind and soul. The alien laughed, and she raised her head and gasped with pain.

Still, she faced him squarely and spoke. "You see, the problem isn't me trying to overcome your magic. The problem is me rearranging this ship's interior without being able to see what I'm doing."

Her hand began to pulse with a blend of purple energy streaked with silver and blue streaks. She took a deep breath and whispered, "I sure hope this works."

She curled her hand into a fist, flung her arm toward the wall beside him, and launched energy to spiral into it. It drilled into the center of the wall and spread, sending traceries of magic across the entire surface.

Nihilism's helmet turned as though the alien watched the effect. He seemed to study what she'd done before he turned to face her again. "Pathetic."

Stephanie held one hand up and her lips curled into a satisfied smirk. "Wait for it."

Bumblebee made an uncertain mew, and she snapped a glance toward him. "I've got you, kitty."

She clapped and flattened twin shields of magic over the teams and the cat to pin them against the walls and hold them there. A loud pop was rapidly followed by the sound of tearing metal.

The wall blasted open and Nihilism was dragged clear of the deck and ripped through the gap. His body careened out of the ship and into the depths of space.

Anchored to the deck by tendrils of magic, she whipped her hand up and directed a long pulse of energy toward the hole to cover it with a shield of magic as she drew more power to help her drag the ship's hull back into place.

It was hard since she still couldn't see what she was doing. This time, though, she could almost remember what it had been like before she'd undone it. That helped. It wasn't perfect, but it was enough.

It took her a little time, but when she was done, she rubbed her hands together and turned to the others. "Did anyone notice where he went? I'm not really sure whether he can live out in space or not."

Releasing the shields that held her teams, she told them, "There is one last place we need to take before we can head home."

The marker for the command center pulsed in their HUDs, and they raced toward it. Most of the pirates had fled during her battle with Nihilism.

Some had been lost when she'd rearranged the outer hull and others when she'd put it back together again. The cats and teams dispatched any who'd been foolish enough to remain.

They attacked the bridge fast and hard. Stephanie vaporized the Bridge entrance to allow the marines and her team through.

Neither gave the pirates any quarter. The instant they had one in their sights, they fired and cleared the command center with brutal efficiency, but left the captain for her.

Her fists blazed with energy as she stared at the captain, who stood with his hand poised over the self-destruct button. He raised his gun to his temple and smiled at them. "You will get nothing from me. You will go up with the ship, as will I."

He pounded his hand on the switch as he pulled the trigger and his brains erupted all over wall behind him.

The team tensed and waited for the explosion, but nothing happened. As the captain dropped lifeless to the floor, his hand slid off the button and revealed the magical shield that had protected it.

He'd caught the shield fair and square, but the button had not been pressed. She gave them a looked laced with tiredness and battle fatigue. "We've lost too many people. We need that information."

Frog rejoined them. He'd slipped from the hiding place he'd found while he'd waited and now hurried up to the communications console. "Let's make this simple."

After a few quick adjustments, he pointed to Stephanie and Lars. "You two need to do this. I have to answer a transmission from a Navy corvette going by the name *Coyote Stallone*."

"Say what?" Marcus began, but the marine captain approached. "I can help you there. I've transited on the *Coyote* a few times."

He looked at the two exhausted teams and glanced at Stephanie. "If I could suggest something..."

She waved for him to continue.

"If the *Coyote* is on its way in, they could do the mop-up here."

She followed the path of his gaze and saw how tired the two teams were from hours of fighting. "Done."

Her decision made, she stood beside Lars as he put the call out to the pirates left on the *Ebon Knight*. "Your captain is dead and your ally has deserted you. You will stand down or the cats will start to hunt."

Stephanie glanced to where the two cats lay stretched on the floor and thought it was a good idea they'd stayed out of camera pick-up range. Ending the transmission, Lars followed her gaze and managed a tired smile.

"They'll never know."

CHAPTER TWENTY-THREE

The broadcasters on Earth were ecstatic.

"This is Amelia Howard and welcome to tonight's Federation News Broadcast," the anchor said and smiled at the camera. "Heading the list tonight is the news of a successful fight against the Dreth pirates. This has been the Navy's third win since the *Ebon Knight's* capture three weeks ago."

She glanced at her notes and refocused on the camera. "At this time, it is not known if the special tactics team and advanced Naval ship involved in the *Knight's* capture were also used in this foray as well."

The camera panned out to show the co-anchor, a male Meligornian with a wide smile, his vibrant silver hair cut short and slicked back. "That is great news, Amelia. On the political front, we've also heard rumors of secret talks between the three worlds."

"That's exciting, Jalel. Tell me, does anyone know what *those* might be about?"

"Well, Amelia, some experts are saying the three are discussing where to go next now that the pirates are on the defensive, but there are those on the fringe who hint at the possibility that there is *another* alien species headed our way."

"Another alien species? Wow. I'm not sure how I feel about that," the woman replied and didn't quite hide the fakeness in her reply. "In other news, one of the universities has been given a substantial endowment to start working with more of those making up the top two percent of students who can't afford training after high school in NorAm."

"Is that really true, Amelia?"

"Jalel, it is absolutely true. There has been some serious speculation on the virtual capitol hill with almost everyone taking credit for the increase from the politicians who say government oversight is responsible to several business groups who claim they thought it was time they stepped in."

She smirked slightly. "And then there are those universities who say how much they accomplish on their own. Whichever way you look at it, there are many folks who say how much they support those who can't afford a higher education."

"That sure would be nice, wouldn't it?" he agreed and once again displayed his perfect smile. "And speaking of those who can't afford a higher education, did you know our witch has a new boyfriend?"

Amelia's lips formed a perfect 'O' of shocked surprise. "Jalel! Say it isn't so! Because that'll break quite a few hearts if it is. Do we know who it is?"

He smirked as though he had a secret to share. "Well, Amelia, there was Piotr Brandt, lead singer of Eis Bjorne."

She put her hand on her hip. "Jalel! It's not nice to tease. You know that was his publicist."

Jalel gave a hearty laugh. "This is true, and I am sad to say we've heard a lot of potential names but no one has stepped forward to confirm them. It seems that agents are up to their usual tricks and claim a relationship simply to push their brand name stars ahead."

Amelia gasped. "How underhanded."

"I know, but never fear. The Federation News folk are working hard to crack the reality of that tough little nut before anyone else does. When that happens, you'll hear it first, here."

She gave him a happy smile. "Well, there's nothing to say the new boyfriend isn't in fact a new *girl*friend, Jalel."

The anchor raised his eyebrows and his purple-hued eyes sparkled. "Amelia, are you sure?"

"Of course not, but so far, there have been three women to make that claim and, you know...where there's smoke..."

"We could always ask her," he suggested. "After all, she's just returned to Earth, and it's possible we'll get to speak to her ourselves. We could ask her then."

Amelia clapped and bounced like an excited child. "Finger's crossed, Jalel. We would love to hear what she has to say."

"That's right, we would." He chuckled. "We will cut to break but stay tuned. When we get back, we'll talk about the budget committee's blatant attack on the Gov-Sub standard of living investments, get the weather for the next five days, make a beautiful Meligornian quiche-styled dish with famous Mage Hannah, royal chef and now Earth television star. We'll be back right after this."

Far from the nosey news cameras, the recruiters gathered at their normal conference room table. This time, none of them seemed too excited about the Federation report. Instead, they waited for the command captain to enter and take his place.

He moved immediately to the business at hand. "Okay, let's go over a couple of things really fast. I know that the fourth species of being has been twisted into a rumor, but I can assure you that it exists. The new species is known to work with traitors from all three worlds in an attempt to subvert the defense of the planets. The danger is real, people."

One of the petty officers raised his hand. "We also need to start preparing more potential recruits. So, we will work with BURT and begin implementing more tests and games for those who like to rent immersion pods. It will be an option to begin their training in the Navy."

"We can gamify it," one of the recruiters said with a smile. "We could make it an honor to pass all the tests necessary to go through full training."

"Wait," another said and shook his head. "So, they will pay to go through our boot camp?"

The whole table went silent and then broke into a lively discussion of how to implement the suggestion. It was definitely something they wanted to happen. Another petty officer rubbed her face and tried not to yawn. "Maybe we could send them a shirt as a prize if they can manage it?"

"I second that one," one of them said.

"Me too," the captain replied. "Good work."

She beamed with pride and the commanding officer took a deep breath and flipped his notes open. "So, that was a lot simpler to resolve than I expected. Let's move on to the second item of the evening. University recruitment. How do we go about it?"

"We'll make it a competition like we're doing with the immersion pods," one of the team said.

"But won't that be obvious?"

"Not if we attach a little funding to it as part of a grand prize," another officer replied, and they groaned. He raised his hands. "Wait, hear me out."

"Go ahead." The captain's tone said it had better be good.

"The universities all compete," he continued. "They have huge competitions for music, for dance, for writing, for the sciences, and for programming. Basically, for everything. We make ours a leadership focus and attach a fast-tracking through officer's training to it as an option for successful candidates."

The others stared at him as if he'd grown an extra head.

"Think about it. We need candidates for the hack teams, analysts, and administrative officers, but the best students are snatched away by big business, so we attach a touch of personal prestige to it, then institutional prestige and a cash incentive...and then there's the entry fee..."

That got their interest and they hashed it out so that the only expenditure for the prize money would be the loss of two entry fees, while they would gain the ability to identify and incentivize potential recruits in the officer ranks.

"That's a good start. I'll take that with the immersion pod scheme and see what the brass says. Which brings us to our final discussion. The recruitment or draft status of Stephanie Morgana."

The petty officer sighed. "Well, it has become very hard to coordinate. She is now a full citizen on Earth, Meligorn, and Dreth, which complicates things."

The captain scowled. "Right, but we have all three planets in the Navy. What's the big deal?"

She shrugged. "It seems that neither the Meligornians nor the Dreth want her in the Navy, so it would be an intergalactic disaster if we succeeded in drafting her and then pissed off both our allies in one move. So, drafting Morgana is DOA."

He was still hopeful. "Maybe there is some way we can negotiate with her and her group. Don't write it off yet."

The whole team choked down the urge to laugh. Finally, one of the POs spoke very tentatively. "Sir, do you know how much the last negotiation cost us?"

CHAPTER TWENTY-FOUR

A young man with tousled brown hair stood in the white room and his eyes danced wildly around as he stared at the outfit he wanted to select. It floated higher, then lower again but when he tried to grab it with his hands, it slipped through his fingers.

Finally, he found the instruction plaque that told him to simply touch the garment and it would dress him. It was his first time in a pod, and he felt like an idiot. Maybe there was a reason people like him didn't get the chance.

BURT came over the speakers. "Welcome Marshall James Agrippa to your test for the Government Required Opportunity. To be tested for a placement and possible financial assistance in a prep school, you must be tested physically and mentally."

James, like clockwork, asked the same question Stephanie had asked during her first session. "How do you physically test me if I am lying down?"

He chuckled. "The system capabilities are beyond in the moment testing. Through your blood, circulation, heart rhythm, and approximately six hundred and eighty-nine other factors, the system can see what your physical health score will be."

"Oh," he said and scuffed his virtual shoe on the ground. "Cool."

BURT made the human sound of clearing his throat. "Now, where was I… Oh, yes. For this government-required opportunity to be tested for a placement and possible financial assistance in a prep school, you must be checked both physically as well as mentally."

The young man didn't respond but the AI knew he was nervous. He could read it in his body language and through his rapid heart rate. "It is noted that you attended the New York Federation Board of Schools, public sector. You excelled, came in first in your class for logical and legal debate, and four out of the six other major Primary areas of study, including three of the six Prime Learning Objectives as spelled out in Federation Educational Decree 18.32. This makes you a prime candidate for excelling during this testing today. And luckily for you, I will be your testing agent."

The world around him faded to black and BURT continued as he processed the program. "While you will be tested per the requirements of the Federation Educational Board, there are two new tests which are included and do not affect your main score in any way. You may, in fact, choose to bypass these tests and leave early."

"No," James answered quickly and narrowed his eyes at the pinprick of light in front of him. "I'm curious. I'll take them."

Todd sat up in his hospital bed. He swiped his hand across the virtual magazine tablet he'd nicked from the waiting room.

He was reading a three-year-old issue of Federation Weekly that talked about the major bombing that had leveled the rest of the Arch in St. Louis.

"You would think, after switching from paper, they'd be able to keep up with the issues." He sighed and set the tablet down.

The messaging system beeped, and a virtual screen flickered from the end of his bed. "You have a new message."

"Show message." Todd sighed again.

It was a letter from the Navy and his command. He was finally being discharged from the hospital. The letter stated that he had been "acceptably healed," whatever the hell that meant.

He waved his hand in front of the screen and acknowledged receipt with his palm print before sending it. Less than two minutes, later his door opened, and his nurse entered.

She brought his belongings and held a tablet out so he could sign several documents for release.

Todd turned and swung his legs over the side of the bed. As she flipped through, he put his palm print on the panel or thumb-printed each page. "I thought I'd be here forever."

She chuckled. "I don't know about forever, but none of us expected you to leave so soon. Even the doctor was surprised by how fast you healed. But one shouldn't look gifts in the eye, right?"

He smiled, nodded, and thanked her for everything as she left him to dress. Even though there was barely any sign of injury on the outside, he still experienced pain.

That aside, he looked forward to leaving the monotony of what felt like his medical incarceration. He took his time getting dressed, then sat on the chair to lace his boots. That done, he used his tablet to check his Federation Navy documents to see where and to whom he should report next.

As he read them through, he realized that he was being given two weeks' leave so he could visit his family. Given that he was on the third-line space station somewhere near Mercury, he assumed he was too far out to be able to do that.

Not to mention the fact that he really didn't have anything to go back for. While his parents would be glad to see him, his friends would be busy working or elsewhere, and that included the person he wanted to see most.

Apart from that, there was the expense. With his recruit-level income, it would be a stretch to book anything.

He decided to look anyway and searched the web for prices and schedules, but nothing fit. Thoughtfully, he bit his lip and cleared the page.

Of course, he might be able to call his parents instead. He looked at his call list. It didn't take him long to realize that even though the calls he'd made were expensive, he'd been given some call time by the Navy.

Sitting in the hospital wouldn't get him out of the hospital and regardless of whether he went anywhere or not, he couldn't stay in the ward. Todd grabbed his bag and wandered out and over to the Navy side of the station.

On leave and with nowhere to go meant he had to check into Naval Lodging. The girl at the front was young and sweet and smiled at him almost immediately.

"I need to check into lodging," he told her and handed her his military ID.

She nodded and scanned the ID into the system. As she did so, she looked at him in surprise. "You do know you have a two-week leave, right? Why aren't you going home? Nowhere to go?"

He shrugged. "It's more about the budget than anything else, to be honest. We're far out here, and everything is three times as expensive. I've only just gotten out of the hospital today, so I haven't been able to really put any thought into it."

She looked at his name and then his service team and looked at him with wide eyes. "You were in the first attack at that colony, right?"

He nodded and didn't say anything about it. She covered her mouth and squealed. "Oh, my gosh, I can't believe you're in here right now. You know you're kind of famous, right? Your face was on one of the Federation Historical photos of the event and the press ran with it. The Navy pulled you out of the public system and the hospital kept all visitors away, saying you needed full and focused healing."

Todd was taken back. "That's pretty cool."

The girl pulled out a separate computer, a thin laptop, and typed into it quickly. "Give me two seconds and I'll see if I can't help you out."

She scanned the info in front of her and nodded with a smile. "Few people actually have enough credits to go anywhere when they're here, but you have to know how to work the system. You choose the ships going to where you want to go. Hey, here is one and it leaves in… Wow. It leaves in an hour and a half. It'll be preparing to seal up anytime now."

Her wink as she picked up the phone was encouraging. "Yes, Hi. I wondered if you needed any shipboard help for someone on limited duty?"

The guy on the other end scanned his notes. "Yeah, actually, I might be short a beginning engineer in the engines area. Do you have anyone?"

Todd had heard the conversation and gave her two thumbs-up. The guy must have looked at a clock. "Oh, and they need to be ready to leave, *now*."

She put her hand over the receiver and whispered, "Go, now. The ship is the *Norma Gene 56974*, bay ninety-eight, fourth floor."

He bowed to her, mouthed a quick "thank you," and heaved his duffel over his shoulder as he hurried out. She lifted the phone back to her ear and smiled. "He's on his way to you right now."

There was a slight pause on the other end. "Has he gone?"
She smirked. "Yeah."

"How are you, sis?" the guy asked. "It must be someone special if you're pulling the family card on me to get them heading to Earth."

She gave a breathy sigh. "He was one of the guys from Sanmar's and just got out of the hospital."

"Damn, that means he's one of the three," her brother replied in awe.

"Three what?" she asked.

Her brother thought for a moment before he responded. "There are three guys who were in the hospital from that Operation. One of them was visited by Morgana before she went back to the base and *destroyed it.* Rumor is, she knew one of the three personally and didn't appreciate him getting hurt like that."

"Wow, that's intense," she replied. "I guess when you're friends with Morgana, she doesn't forget you."

"I guess not." He laughed.

"Well, he was kind of cute, but I'm not sure about cute enough. Perhaps it was one of the others. Who knows?"

He cleared his throat. "Look, I'm really sorry, but I've got to go. We're sealing up as soon as he gets here. I hope he ran."

She laughed. "Well, he *did* move kinda fast. I'll let you go. Stay safe out there."

"Always, sis. Always," he promised and ended the call.

Vishlog growled at his tablet, his fingers too big for the buttons. It beeped at him to signal a new message and drove him nuts. He finally managed to shut the notification up and was able to bring it up to discover it was a personal message from Jaleck. He stood and looked around the ONE R&D building, unsure of where he could and couldn't go.

Elizabeth walked through the main area and noticed him standing there, looking like a lost tourist. "Are you all right?"

"Oh good, it's you," he replied.

She chuckled. "That's a better reaction than most people give me."

The Dreth stepped a little closer to her. "Do you have a private place where I can receive a chewing out?"

The woman flinched and nodded. She pointed across the hallway to a conference room. "And good luck, buddy."

She pressed her lips together and shook her head in sympathy as he walked dejectedly into the room and closed the door behind him.

Once inside the room, he sighed. The tablet beeped again and reminded him that the message was on hold and waiting. He growled and entered his credentials to see it, set the tablet on the table, and activated it to display the hologram.

The picture flickered and revealed the inside of the ambassador's office. The door opened and she walked in, paused, and took a deep breath. "Hello, Vishlog. I have heard from a third party that the Dreth have attached one of their best to support the witch Morgana and that this soldier has given exemplary service and is a credit to his people."

She allowed herself a brief smile—a compliment in and of itself—and then continued. "Because of this, I have been given permission to offer you the opportunity to move to Stephanie's employ. I was honored to receive this suggestion and am honored to grant you my permission, but also to deliver you my personal appreciation for delivering service above and beyond the normal expectations of any Dreth warrior."

His jaw dropped as she explained the attachments she'd forwarded, that she was not dismissing him, and that he had the right to refuse the honor if he so chose.

Finally, she clapped and smiled. "We are so very proud of you and all that you have achieved in our name. We are proud to name you Dreth."

With that, the ambassador took a step back and sketched a rainbow with her hands. "Your life gives us hope and honor," she intoned.

Jaleck then did something that Vishlog had never expected to see. She bowed, put her foot back, and lowered her head and held this for a full thirty heartbeats. It was a Bow of Great Respect, rarely given and not something he'd ever expected to receive.

When she straightened, she fixed the screen with a serious stare. "Anytime you wish to talk and I can move my schedule, the time is yours, Vishlog. It is good to see you have found someone you can respect."

She signed off and he sat there and stared at the screen for a very long moment. When he finally stood, he took a long deep breath in, his back a little straighter than before.

He couldn't believe it. After all the years, he had found a home with the witch of the Federation and her protection team—as crazy as they were. He had found someone he could believe in and follow. He had the honor and respect of working for Stephanie Morgana.

In that moment, he knew he would never question his purpose again.

CHAPTER TWENTY-FIVE

Stephanie sat across from Elizabeth with Burt coming through on audio. "First of all, it's really nice to be back."

"It's nice to have all your shenanigans back," her mentor replied with a smile.

"We definitely missed you," Burt added.

She stretched her arms out in front of her, her fingers interlocked. "So, while we were working out in the great beyond, I learned so much about what we need to work on as a team. The scenarios changed from pirate capture, to bombs, and battling pirates on ships. It was chaotic and we definitely need to practice so that we can move through fights like that with almost cat-like reflexes."

Both of the felines looked at her and almost immediately put their heads back down. Ms. E gave them a cautious glance, still not sure about them. They snored lightly and she relaxed a little. "Don't forget the whole lava thing and creating volcanoes."

"Yeah." She shook her head. "That was...interesting, to say the least. I would also like to have an understanding of basic operations, both in the Federation Navy and outside it. And we probably need to know more about how marines work because I think we'll see more of *those* guys in the future, too."

She took a breath, obviously ticking things off in her head. "I almost forgot. We need training on flight simulators for different ships. I really need to get with either the programmer or the AI so they can implement that into the team training."

"Right," BURT replied, not ready to explain to her that he was essentially both. "We can arrange that, or I can handle it for you. Start putting notes in the system with specifics so that I can compile them. I'll need specific examples for the programmer, too, if you can manage that."

"I can do that," she replied. "Now that I am home, though, I really want to dive back into my ideas on helping to fix the environment."

She paused and half-expected either of them to steer her back to more operational topics. When they didn't, she went on. "From the simulations, we know it's possible, but not within a lifetime or even ten lifetimes. I played with the idea of creating a kind of spray or gas created from the energy to pump or dump on places. But I feel like it would simply return to the core. There's no guarantee it would stop and clean things up. It needs direction."

"That it does," BURT replied, glad she had realized that. "What else?"

"A water treatment facility," she said slowly. "Something that uses the energy to cleanse. And then, my last idea was to create some kind of machine that ran off magical energy."

They both paused. Elizabeth put her hand on Stephanie's arm. "You believe you can create technology here on Earth to run off eMU to clean the environment?"

Stephanie shrugged and scratched Bumblebee when he rubbed his horned head along her thigh. He rested his chin on her knee. "I'm not totally sure on any of it. I suppose we would need to patent it to ONE R&D and research and develop it. But yes, I do think I could create that."

Her mentor liked the sound of that. "What about things like air quality and recycling?"

She snorted. "Recycling, that's great. In the 80s to the 2060s, recycling was all the rage, but the trash was collected and never sent anywhere for processing, so the whole thing broke down."

"But you should be able to handle what's here with magic? Right?" Ms. E. asked.

"Actually, now that you mention it, I think I might." She tapped her pen against her lips. "And if not, my magic would do one hell of a job sorting that stuff out. I could actually reuse things, even if I couldn't recycle them."

Elizabeth chuckled. "The edge of the universe is your limit, kid. But, as a word to the wise, I would not share those ideas with anyone, especially not the Navy right now. Not unless you want to be leashed inside a lab until you die."

"Yeah, that is not really on top of *any* of my lists, except maybe the one of Things to Avoid at All Costs."

She laughed. "I'd like to know why, though. Imagine a way to run magical effects without a wizard? That's like creating guns again when knights had all of that armor and then poof, instant equalization. The Navy would want it and so would everyone else. Until we know the R&D, I don't want to let this idea out of here."

"Agreed," the other woman replied with a grin. "You also need to know that I negotiated the consulting fees for you and your team's efforts. I also got the acquisition order for the ship you captured, as well as 2.2 billion credits."

Her grin turned serious. "The Navy thought I might balk and walk away if they simply denied it, so I explained that I had more than enough money to use for the new mercenary company— Morgana, Incorporated."

She watched Stephanie's expression range from surprise to

horror to disbelief but didn't let her interrupt. "I said I'd give you a week to get a crew there…and they decided to negotiate in good faith."

Stephanie shook her head. "I'm sorry, did you just say 2.2 *billion?*"

"Yes." Elizabeth smirked. "The ship is worth close to ten billion credits, so it was a steal for them. We only need about half a billion to outfit a ship you need, maybe seven hundred and fifty million or so. Each of your team members will receive a cool twenty million credits deposited directly into their account and you will be stupid rich."

She laughed at the look on the girl's face. "So, you have a choice. You can continue to risk your life to save the Federation, or you can retire and hire shirtless men to wave palm fronds in your general direction."

When she started to laugh, Ms. E. had to wait for her to calm down before she could continue with the discussion. "Have you any idea which way you want to go? If it's the rugged good-looking males with no shirts, we don't have to purchase the ship."

Stephanie smirked. "Not that half-naked men waving large leaves doesn't have a certain allure, but I think my help is needed in this war. It's what Morganas do."

"Good," Burt said. "Because the ship was ordered last week and you have a lot of training to do."

BOOKS BY MICHAEL ANDERLE

Sign up for the LMBPN email list to be notified of new releases and special deals!

https://lmbpn.com/email/

For a complete list of books by Michael Anderle, please visit:

www.lmbpn.com/ma-books/